Readers love the Bad in Baltimore series by K.A. MITCHELL

Bad Company

"…an entertaining, emotional, sometimes funny, oftentimes sensual story with two likable MCs…."

—Love Bytes

Bad Boyfriend

"I really really loved this book. It was sexy, fun, quirky, heartwarming and everything amazing."

—Gay Book Reviews

Bad Attitude

"I really loved this book, it's an interesting look of opposites attracting and finding out that they're not that different after all."

—Diverse Reader

Bad Influence

"Great job, KAM, you brought Silver to life for me and I'm very happy to have known him."

—Rainbow Book Reviews

Bad Behavior

"…this was a phenomenal story. I was sucked in right from the start and I couldn't put it down."

—The Blogger Girls

By K.A. Mitchell

BAD IN BALTIMORE
Bad Company
Bad Boyfriend
Bad Attitude
Bad Influence
Bad Behavior
Bad Habit

READY OR KNOT
Put a Ring on It
Risk Everything on It
Take a Chance on It

Published by Dreamspinner Press
www.dreamspinnerpress.com

BAD
HABIT

K.A.
MITCHELL

Published by

DREAMSPINNER PRESS

5032 Capital Circle SW, Suite 2, PMB# 279, Tallahassee, FL 32305-7886 USA
www.dreamspinnerpress.com

Bad Habit
© 2018 K.A. Mitchell.

Cover Art
© 2018 Kanaxa.
Cover content is for illustrative purposes only and any person depicted on the cover is a model.

Trade Paperback ISBN: 978-1-63533-746-4
Digital ISBN: 978-1-63533-747-1
Mass Market Paperback ISBN: 978-1-64108-078-1
Library of Congress Control Number: 2018906771
Trade Paperback published November 2018
v. 1.0

Printed in the United States of America
∞
This paper meets the requirements of
ANSI/NISO Z39.48-1992 (Permanence of Paper).

For Andy, who kept asking for their story.

Acknowledgments

THANKS ALWAYS to Erin, fic midwife extraordinaire, Jenna, and B.F.S. Thanks to the guys at Collar City Guitars for answering all my weird questions. Thanks to Erika for an excellent macro edit.

Chapter One

THE NEW kid, Liam, was a fucking punk. Everyone knew not to touch Scott's stuff.

Scott ran his tongue on the inside of his fat lip. He'd won anyway. Hit the motherfucker in his eye, mouth, and gut before Derrick pulled them apart. Scott shot a look over at the chair three spots away where Liam sat. Fuckface smiled back at him.

Scott rolled his eyes and went back to staring at the door to the conference room. Some social worker was supposed to show up and counsel them on resolving their issues. Scott had been through the drill before. He thought things were pretty simple. Don't touch me or my stuff and there won't be any fucking issues to resolve.

But Scott had done a few stints in the hole, which was what everyone at St. Bennie's called the lockdown rooms over the gym. A mattress and a bucket to piss in and food when someone got around to bringing it. He'd play the game with the social worker. Anything beat what had happened to him when he first got here, being held down for a shot of Haldol in his ass to turn him into a zombie for forty-eight hours.

"Hey," the Liam-ratfucker said.

Scott stared at the wood grain of the door. Part of it looked like a freaky skeleton with a big alien head.

"Let's just settle this now," Liam-can't-buy-a-clue went on.

Scott dragged his feet in from his sprawl to get ready. If he had to go to the hole, so be it. Rep was all he had. "You wanna go again, bitch?"

But Liam didn't make any moves toward him. "No. I mean, I'm sorry I touched your box of whatever."

There wasn't much in the old shoebox. Two fading pictures, a Batman valentine his older sister had given him, and a *Rugrats* washcloth—though where he'd gotten that, he couldn't remember.

"You put it in the fucking trash."

"I said sorry, okay? I didn't know it was important."

That was a problem. As soon as people knew something mattered to you, they could hurt you with it. Scott shrugged. "Just don't touch any of my shit, and it won't be a problem."

"Okay."

Scott stared at Liam. He wasn't acting scared of another beatdown, didn't sound sarcastic. He sounded nice, and not even fake nice like a new social worker. Liam had been at St. Bennie's for a month and people liked him. Reason enough for Scott to hate him. Not that he needed a reason.

The social worker finally showed up. Shit. It was that bitch Kristin who hated Scott. His and Liam's hall staff Derrick was with her.

She started in on him before she even opened the conference room door. "I've told you before, Scott, violent behavior is not going to help you get out of here. A foster family is not—"

"It was my fault, Miss Kristin," Liam-can't-keep-his-mouth-shut cut in. The number-one rule of survival here was *Don't volunteer information.*

That stopped her midbitch, though. "Liam? Derrick, let me see the incident report."

"Put it in your mailbox an hour ago." Derrick leaned against the wall behind Scott.

"Well, can you at least tell me what it said?" Bitch Kristin sighed like Derrick should have been able to whip the paper out of his ass.

"Eight twenty, Scott came into the common room, hauled Liam off the couch by his left arm, and punched him in the mouth. Liam swung back, striking Scott in the face. I initiated a restraint on Scott. Gerry restrained Liam."

Derrick was big, solid muscle. If he took you down, you didn't get back up. Gerry was big too, all of it in his gut. Scott wondered if that was the first time Liam had been restrained and how he liked three hundred pounds pressing into his back.

"So it was unprovoked." Bitch Kristin was happy about that.

"I did provoke him." Liam must have wanted to spend a couple days in the hole. "I threw his belongings in the trash."

Belongings? Who the fuck said that kind of shit?

Kristin deflated. "Why would you do that to your roommate, Liam?"

"Someone dared me to."

"Who?"

Liam was smart enough to shut his mouth then. Henry, Scott bet, or Curtis. They'd both been laughing next to Liam on the couch.

Liam turned toward Scott. "I'm sorry, Scott. I promise not to touch your stuff again." Liam stuck his hand out.

Scott felt the adults' eyes burning into him but concentrated on Liam's. They were a mud-mix of brown and yellow-green, one swollen from where Scott had punched him, but the other looked friendly.

What the fuck. Guy like Liam would probably be out of here in a couple months. Scott flexed his sore knuckles and slapped at Liam's hand in a brief shake.

They'd missed the main lunch, but Derrick took them down to the cafeteria so they could make sandwiches before going to class.

"Jesus, that Kristin has it in for you." Liam reached in front of Scott to grab a giant scoop of institutional peanut butter from the can. "Whadja do?" He licked the knife and stuck it back in, barely missing Scott's belly.

He curved his spine out to avoid the touch, but it still made the hair on his arms stand up.

"Got born, I guess. Plus I'm unplaceable."

Liam dropped a dab of jelly on his mountain of peanut butter and folded the bread over, then repeated the process on the other half.

Scott had never seen anyone make a sandwich like that, but it looked like a good way to get some extra food.

"My mom will probably get clean in a couple of months, and she'll petition to get me back." Liam folded his second slice. "At least this place is better than the one I got sent to in Florida."

They hadn't said more than ten words to each other since Liam had been shoved into Scott's room a month ago, just when he'd been hoping they'd given up on sticking him with a roommate.

"What's so better?" Scott said, slapping margarine on a slice of bread.

"Smaller roaches." Liam laughed.

But Scott remembered there was more of an issue to resolve. They grabbed juice cups and the least soft apples from the bin before they sat at a table and ate slowly to kill more time.

"Who dared you?" Scott muttered low enough that Derrick couldn't hear.

Liam wiped his face on the back of his hand and shook his head. He moved his eyes toward where Derrick was leaning on the counter, peeling an orange. "Later."

"Yeah, whatever." Scott could find out himself. He didn't need Liam and his fake niceness.

"No. Really. Promise." Liam tried a big smile, then winced.

Fuck it. Scott wasn't apologizing for hitting him. Ratfucker had it coming.

In their room that night after showers, they had about twenty minutes before bed check. Scott shot a quick look to make sure nothing had been disturbed in front of his new hiding place, hauled up his boxers under his towel, then tossed it away before getting in Liam's face. "Who the fuck dared you to mess with my shit?"

"No one."

"I swear to God—"

"No one. I did it on my own."

Scott was so surprised, he sat down on the bottom bunk. Should have known better than to believe Liam was anything but another asshole trying to fuck with Scott.

"I wanted you to talk to me."

"You'll be talking to my fist again in a minute." Scott jumped back up.

"You never talk to me, but I've seen you shoot me looks. When you think I don't notice."

Scott froze. Liam couldn't mean it like that. No one could know that. Not ever. Scott had that safely locked away. Safer than the shoebox, safe as it could be, deep inside. Even he only let himself think about it late at night, staring at the ceiling and hating it even when it made him so fucking hard he ached. Liam had been the first one with a face. Before it had just been pieces. The curve of some guy's ass. The cut of a hip. Width of a shoulder. Mouths. Dicks.

"In your dreams, queerbait." Safest thing was to throw it back on him.

Liam rolled his eyes. "Yeah. I am."

Scott's mouth went dry. This little fa… he could just say it?

Liam put a hand on Scott's chest.

Hot. Shivery. Terrifying.

Scott's muscles locked down under those sensations, which was how Liam managed to shove him back onto the bunk, so hard Scott bounced against the bolted furniture and thin mattress.

It was why he still couldn't say a word when Liam knelt in front of him.

Barry, the night staff, yelled for everyone to get in their rooms.

Liam winked his unswollen eye. "Fifteen before bed check. Wanna fight some more or want me to blow you?"

TEN MONTHS later Scott stared hard at the filthy ceiling through dry eyes as Liam wiped some snot on his shoulder.

"I'll write you. And remember the email address I told you to get so I can find you when you get out." He pressed quick short kisses along Scott's collarbone.

"Yeah. I got it."

"I love you." Liam's tears made their kiss salty. But that wasn't the reason Scott couldn't make himself kiss back. Or say what Liam wanted to hear.

"Uh-huh."

"Scott."

"What?"

"Can't you, like, even agree that this sucks?"

Scott's lips cracked as he opened them. "It sucks."

But he'd known this would happen. Hadn't hoped for one fucking second that things would stay like this. Happy was for people too stupid to know better. And Scott sure as shit knew better.

But it would have been nice to get more than ten months of this. Of Liam. It wasn't only the blow jobs and quiet, frantic grinding that Scott kind of liked even better than when Liam sucked him. It wasn't just having a body to hold, the idea of having contact that wasn't meant to hurt but to make him feel better.

Together they were more. No one dared start shit with them because it meant taking both of them on. Scott might be good at landing a punch, but Liam was sneaky and mean. He could twist staff around his finger, and no shit ever stuck to him. The other assholes could call them fairies and cocksuckers, but when Liam laughed at them, Scott didn't care as much either.

He swallowed. "I'll miss you."

Liam lifted his head from Scott's chest. "Holy fuck. Did it actually hurt you to say that?"

"Yes. Like someone punched my nuts. Kiss 'em and make 'em better."

Liam shoved at his shoulder. "Say it first."

Scott sighed. "When we get out of here…," he forced out in a monotone.

Liam took the next line. "We'll get a place."

"And you'll go to college."

"And you'll be a fireman."

"You'll go to med school."

"And become a doctor and buy you your own Batmobile."

Scott had to laugh. Liam always jacked up the game till it was stupid.

"And while I'm driving in my Batmobile, you can give me road head, Robin. Better get your practice in now or I'll never let you in the Batcave."

Chapter Two

Now

MAYBE THE first weekend in August was a great time to stand out on an open field with hundreds of shining steel heat reflectors. In Antarctica. At the car show at the state fairgrounds in Timonium, Maryland, way too fucking far from anyplace to catch a decent breeze, it was hot as fuck.

Which was exactly what Scott said to Jamie as they both studied the '65 Ford Galaxie Jamie had his eye on.

"And how hot is fuck, ya think?" Jamie said.

Scott leaned over the engine as he inspected the connections on the plugs. "Don't know about you but for me, depends on how tight his ass is." He kept his voice low enough only Jamie could hear.

They'd waited until the owner had gone to lunch, not wanting to show too much interest, but some things didn't mix with the car-show crowd. Openly gay guys talking about ass fucking was high up on that list.

Jamie snorted a laugh and lifted his head out from under the hood. "Ain't that the truth." He wiped his face on the sleeve of his T-shirt. "At least this is a dry heat."

"Yeah, only about ninety percent humidity today." Scott squinted around the popped hood at the glare on the windshield where the For Sale sign was. "So what's he want for it?"

"Seventeen fifty."

Scott whistled. Christ, what he could do with a spare grand, let alone almost two. Not have to sell his Mustang for rent money for starters.

Jamie pointed out the features. "The interior's okay, so's the frame, and it's one hell of a shiny paint job." They had both admired the two-toned red-and-white style. Nothing like classic Fords.

Scott straightened from his lean into the engine. "Engine's clean enough to eat off. You been under her?"

Jamie nodded. "Exhaust needs an overhaul. I'm not giving him more than twelve hundred if I decide to take it. Wanted a second opinion."

Scott dropped his overshirt on the dusty pebbled ground and scooted under the frame. Damn. The seller obviously thought no one would bother getting a look from underneath. Good thing Jamie had sent him a text.

With the light from his phone, Scott scanned the transmission housing. "Fucking bastard."

"What?" Jamie squatted.

Scott wiggled out, and Jamie gave him a hand up.

"Sorry, man. You were right on the exhaust. Probably seizes up like a virgin. But there's an oil leak between the engine block and the transmission. Slow enough that you wouldn't know from starting it up, but I'm betting the main seal is going."

"Son of a bitch." Jamie sat and ducked under.

Scott passed him the phone for light.

"Right at the transmission bell housing."

As Jamie muttered under the car, Scott bent back over the engine to check the manifolds.

"What do you want the Galaxie for?" Scott said to the beam of light flashing up through the engine. "Thought the truck was fine now."

Jamie had been working—mostly adding features—on a '68 F-100 for almost as long as Scott had known him. Back in May, Scott had spent most of his free time helping Jamie take out the door motors and fixing it up after it rolled into the bay. Jamie hadn't wanted to talk about how, but since there was another guy involved, Scott bet a friends-with-benefits situation had gotten complicated.

"The Galaxie's not for me." Jamie's voice drifted back up. "What a fucking bitch."

"You see it?"

"Yeah." Jamie wriggled back out and sat there. "What did you want with Galvez this morning? You looking to sell your Shelby?"

It choked him to admit it. "Maybe."

"Ha. Warned you Mustangs were pussy magnets. Unless that's what's making your dick hard these days."

Scott made a disgusted sound in the back of his throat. "No."

Jamie patted the red- and white-walled tires. "Damn shame." He looked up at Scott. "You know, if I find another one and you put in some work with me, you can drive it sometimes. I mean, check that sweet interior. You can actually fuck a guy in it. Unlike your bitch Mustang." He pushed to his feet. "Even with room for your pathetic hair, punk." Jamie jabbed at Scott's shoulder.

"Fuck you." Scott didn't take the bait and touch the short tips of the inch-high mohawk he had glued up this morning.

Jamie had been ragging on him for almost ten years now, ever since he'd busted Scott for possession of stolen property when he was seventeen. Despite being a cop, Jamie wasn't a complete asshole. They got together to work on their cars often enough, though lately Scott couldn't do any work that wasn't bringing in cash.

Jamie sat back down like he'd been shoved. "Shit. It's the whole fucking circus. Sorry about this, Scott. Maybe they didn't see me." He rocked his shoulders back and forth as he tried to disappear under the car.

"Huh?" Scott looked over his shoulder. From Jamie's sudden panic, he expected bill collectors, process servers, zombie hordes. There wasn't anything out of place in the crowd of sunburned and sweaty people flooding the field at the East and Beast Car Show.

As Scott watched, a big guy built like the Rock but with long hair and a beard caught Scott's gaze and stared back, then nodded. Scott glanced to either side of him to see who the guy was nodding at. He sure as hell didn't know anyone who looked like he was starring in an action film franchise. Then he realized the guy was nodding at someone with him.

"Are they coming this way?" Jamie called from under the car.

The big guy was weaving through the people in their direction, along with whoever he'd nodded at. Maybe Jamie's overcompensation for being short had led him to pick a fight with the big man.

Scott studied the group. "If you mean a pro wrestler, two pretty preppy types, a Mr. Studly Salt-and-Pepper, and some goth kid with a camera, yeah, they are."

"Fuck," Jamie spat.

The goth kid in black jeans, black T-shirt, and a spiked leather cuff got to the Galaxie first. He tossed his black hair off his face and kicked Jamie's ankle with a black-sneakered toe. "Why'd you ditch us, asshole?"

"Because I hoped you'd fucking take a hint." Jamie hauled himself out, movements slow and sullen. "Uh, not you, though," he said to one of the preppy guys in an apologetic tone Scott had never heard Jamie use before.

However fun it might be to watch Jamie get harassed by this circus, it was more drama than Scott needed. People were starting to stare.

He bent down and grabbed his phone out of Jamie's hand. "Gotta run. I'll keep an eye out for that induction hood you wanted. Catch you around."

The goth kid took Scott in with an assessing stare. "Nice sleeve." The kid nodded at the ink on Scott's left arm.

Each one of the designs meant something special, but they flowed together into one. He was used to people commenting on it, though every time, he flashed back to getting that first small tattoo. Everything else he'd added had been to distract him from that symbol.

"Thanks." Scott nodded back.

That precious fucking moment went on exactly a half second too long, so instead of being ten steps away, Scott was standing right next to the pale, sweaty preppy dude when he wobbled. Scott tried to steady him, but he was dropping too fast. Mr. WWE got involved, lunging across the space. His bulk drove Scott a step back, and he fell backward over someone's cooler. Next thing he knew, all three of them were going down. Scott landed ass first on the puddle made by the overturned cooler. The prep and WWE knocked out one of the poles from a shade canopy, and it collapsed on them.

There were splashes of applause; then people crowded around the entertainment, offering help, but mostly taking pictures with their phones.

WWE growled as he threw off the canvas canopy. "Damn it, David. I told you to drink the water, not carry it around. He's okay." The force of his assertion—along with his size—moved some of the onlookers back.

Scott studied Preppy David. He wasn't passed out, but he was pasty and shaking.

"He's not used to lifting anything but a drink outside air-conditioning," Jamie said from behind Scott.

Scott extracted himself from the mess, jeans cold, wet, and muddied.

"I'm fine," Preppy David said. "It's just fucking hot." He gestured at the destruction around him. "We should probably try to put this tent back up."

Preppy David tried to move, but there was a reason Scott had named the other guy WWE in his head. His grip on David meant he wasn't going anywhere.

"You are getting out of the heat and getting some fluids into you." WWE had what Scott knew all too well as a cop voice.

Hell, two of 'em. Now would be a good time to retreat.

A John Deere Gator pulled off onto the grassy edge where they stood, and people with first aid bags jumped out. Definitely time to go.

He took a step toward escape and ended up face-to-face with one of the first aid workers.

No.

Face-to-face with Liam.

The hair that always used to flop onto his forehead was shorter now, his jaw clean of familiar scruff, but it was Liam. Six years since Scott had last seen that face, since he'd woken up to a five-word note instead of the man who'd been sharing his bed. His life.

Rage flashed bright and hot.

Scott punched Liam right in his clean-shaven face. His knuckles made a satisfyingly solid connection to the side of Liam's nose as Scott followed through, driving from his shoulder.

Liam sprawled backward. The shock of anger fizzed out, leaving Scott with a flat hum in his head. He reached for Liam, maybe to shake an answer out of him, maybe to apologize and help him up. Scott would never know what he'd planned because his arms were barred behind his back and someone was shoving him, forcing him away from the chaos on the ground.

"I'm a cop. I got him." Jamie snarled the words along with some revolting moisture into Scott's ear. Jamie had to be talking to someone else, though, because Scott already knew what Jamie's job was.

A guy in a ball cap and flag T-shirt slammed his fists into Scott in a boxer's quick uppercut and gut jab. His body tried to curl in to protect itself, but Jamie still had his arms. Blood flooded Scott's mouth from a split lip, breath trapped in a spasming diaphragm. That hurt, was going to hurt a lot more in a few minutes, but in that instant there was too much adrenaline in his system to feel much.

Jamie spun Scott away from the free swinger. "Police, asshole. Back off. I got this. You want an assault charge too?"

Without waiting for a response, Jamie marched Scott down the grassy center aisle between cars. A snapped-out "Baltimore County Police" cleared the way through startled faces. Scott stumbled along, his brain absurdly focused on how Jamie, a good five inches shorter, could completely control Scott with that grip on his arms.

At a point where a lone maple interrupted the line of cars, Jamie shoved Scott forward, releasing him to battle tree roots and momentum for balance. He caught himself, palms smacking into the rough bark.

He pushed away to get the tree at his back, not sure where the next attack might come from.

"What the fuck is wrong with you, asshole?" Jamie's face was as red as his hair. Scott was surprised fire wasn't shooting from Jamie's nostrils along with his heavy breath. Jamie had no way of knowing this was the third time Liam had dropped in on Scott's life, like the whole thing was some kind of fucking game. *Hey, look, me again. Surprise.*

Okay, Scott's random punch in the face of an apparent stranger deserved an explanation. Though he couldn't help thinking Jamie should have grabbed the guy who'd punched Scott instead. He brought his thumb to his lip, ran his tongue over his teeth to see if they were all there. As always, he caught on the one Liam had chipped. That had been an accident. He remembered Liam laughing in triumph, then the horror on his face. *Shit, I'm so sorry, Scott.*

Where to start with the explanation? Back at St. Bennie's? Or a couple years later, Liam coming out of nowhere, walking up and tapping Scott on the shoulder as he looked up into the undercarriage of a Grand Am at a Sears Auto Care Center in Towson. Scott had almost punched him that time too, though just in self-defense from someone being up in his space. A week later Liam had talked Scott into getting that apartment together.

Or the big kick in the guts? When he'd woken up to that fucking note after the best two years of Scott's life. What the fuck did any of this matter to Jamie anyway?

Scott settled on "It's complicated."

"Complicated?" In two steps Jamie had Scott pinned up against the bark of the tree. "You punched a paraplegic, probably a vet, in the face for no goddamned reason. Now you give me *complicated*?" Jamie shoved him harder and stepped away. "If I hadn't hauled you out of there, they'd be mopping up your remains for a week."

Scott latched on to a single word in the spew from Jamie's lips. *Paraplegic.* But that was crazy. Liam wasn't in a wheelchair. He'd stepped out of the cart. He'd walked. "He wasn't a paraplegic."

"Quadripl—" Jamie waved both arms. "What the fuck ever. Guy has a metal leg."

Scott didn't know how it happened, but he was on his ass staring up at Jamie. None of this was real. Some fucked-up version of the night terrors he hadn't had since he ran away from St. Bennie's.

No. Unlike in a night terror, he could move. *Focus, McDermott.* A text from Jamie asking him to come check out that '65 Galaxie, so Scott met him and—

How did that end with him sitting in the grass thinking about Liam missing a leg?

What did you do, Liam, you dumb impulsive fuck? Shit. What did I do?

Scott scrambled off the ground. He had to find Liam. Find out what happened.

"No way." Jamie shoved him back down. "I'm telling you, people back there wanted to gut you. I thought about it myself. Poor guy goes to war and gets his leg blown off and you take a punch at him for…." Jamie squinted at him. "You gonna finish that sentence for me sometime?"

"No. Gonna arrest me?"

Jamie shrugged. Scott reached for the cigs in his pocket, then realized the denim shirt was back on the ground next to the Galaxie.

He glanced up at Jamie. "Got a cigarette?"

Jamie's hand moved reflexively to his chest, then dropped to his side. "I quit."

"Fuck this." Scott shoved his hands into his hair, fucking up his 'hawk.

Jamie leaned over him. "You make a habit of punching handicapped people?"

"No." Scott bit off the rest of his response. *No, asshole.* He had a feeling he wasn't talking to the Jamie who shot the shit when they worked on cars together, but Officer Donnigan and his damned badge.

"So why's he special?"

Scott looked away.

"Don't give me more of that 'it's complicated' crap, McDermott."

Scott ripped up some grass, less painful than ripping out his hair. "He had both legs last time I saw him. Honest to God, Jamie, I didn't see that—" He swallowed. "I didn't even notice. Fuck, how could I not notice?" His guts clenched and spasmed, bile coming up sharp to burn the back of his throat, his sinuses.

Liam. Torn apart somewhere on the other side of the world. Blood pouring onto pale dusty ground. How could Scott not have known about it somehow, not have felt it?

Jamie sighed and shoved his hands in the front pockets of his jeans. Did he carry a spare set of cuffs? He knew Jamie's job these days was more about cleaning up after drunk assholes in the harbor than chasing down teenagers who had only been trying to earn some cash, but he wondered if he was going to get to hear Jamie tell him *You're under arrest.* Again.

"So, I'm guessing you've seen more of this guy than just his two good legs?" Jamie arched his brows.

"Yeah."

Every hard inch. But it wasn't just that. Once, Scott had known everything about Liam. How he laughed. How he rubbed his left eyebrow with his thumb when he was thinking, the way his jaw jutted out just before he came. Every taste and touch and smell and sound.

Scott had thought he'd known the rest of Liam too. Who he was. What he thought. What he wanted. Until he disappeared like he'd never existed. Like *they* had never existed.

"Jesus fucking Christ." Jamie blew air noisily through his lips. "The fuck I need another round of some gay soap opera. What happened to just getting your dick sucked?"

"This from the guy whose truck I just helped clean up because it went off a pier after a fight with his—"

"Finish that and I swear to God I'll arrest you right now." Jamie took a deeper breath, steadier. "Okay. Here's what we're going to do. I'm going to go back and check on the fallout, find out if he's pressing charges."

Liam wouldn't press charges. If it hadn't been a sucker punch, he'd have come back swinging before Scott could shake out his hand. But Scott didn't really know this Liam. And he definitely didn't know the Liam who'd been to war, had come back without—Scott had to see Liam.

Jamie grabbed Scott's T-shirt. "Oh no. You are not coming with me. You are going right home, where you will eat, sleep, shower, and shit with your phone next to you so if I call you, you better pick up."

"Fine."

"That does not mean go home *after* you go looking for the ex you just punched in the face, you got it?"

"I got it."

"Anything on your record I should know about?"

That trip to the tank after the bar fight didn't count since he hadn't been charged. "Shouldn't be."

"Why the fuck do I keep ending up in the middle of all this shit?"

Maybe because you're an asshole wasn't going to help Scott out much. And it was only half true. Jamie could act like a total asshole, but he actually did give a crap. Had when Scott had been seventeen, did now.

Scott shrugged. "You know what they say. Look for the common denominator."

"And for those of us who failed algebra?"

"Maybe you're a shit magnet."

"Eat me. You stay the fuck out of this, McDermott. Stay far, far away. Go home, you got me?"

"Absolutely," Scott lied.

Chapter Three

AIR-CONDITIONING WRAPPED a chill around Liam and Kishori as they steered the gurney into the fairgrounds' first aid building.

Their patient, still pasty and shaking, let out a dramatic sigh. "Oh, excellent. Five minutes in here and I'll be good as new." David call-me-Beach Beauchamp hadn't wanted to get on the gurney, but a look from one of his friends had cut his argument off midsentence. Good thing, because Beauchamp wouldn't have made it ten steps before collapsing again.

"Walsh," their supervisor snapped at Liam from behind the dispatch desk.

"With a patient." Liam wrapped the arm cuff around Beauchamp's upper arm while Kishori pulled out an IV kit.

Gillespie came out to stand behind Kishori's shoulder, towering over her. "Prakash here can handle him."

Liam stared at Gillespie in shock. The guy was a micromanager, but mostly about paperwork.

"She might not even bleed on him."

At Gillespie's words, Liam became aware of the copper filling his mouth, the drip of blood from his nose. Everything he'd forced out of mind to concentrate on his job slammed back into his consciousness.

Scott.

Just as angry as he'd been the first time Liam had seen him.

And twice as fucking hot.

Liam stopped himself from bringing his hand to his face. "I'm fine."

"I'm sure you are, but you're not working on a patient until you clean up." There was no arguing with the glare behind Gillespie's glasses.

Kishori gave him an I-got-this look with her brows. "I'm sure Mr. Beauchamp won't complain."

"Not about being left in your lovely hands, ma'am." Beauchamp's voice was thin, but the drawl was clear.

"Walsh." Gillespie jerked his thumb toward the bathroom.

Liam barely had time to take off his gloves and turn on the tap before Gillespie shouldered through the door.

"What the hell happened out there? Victim clip you?"

"No."

Liam soaped up his hands and then let himself examine the damage in the mirror. It was pretty gory. His nose was still bleeding. Fat drops, bright with fresh oxygen, rolled over his mouth and chin to join the spreading stain on his light blue uniform shirt. It throbbed and stung, pain forcing itself into notice now that the hyperfocus on his patient was gone. He soaked some paper towels and wiped off the blood.

"Walkies lit up with chatter about a fight breaking out. That you?" Gillespie passed Liam some gauze.

"Don't know. I was focused on the victim." Liam felt his nose, no popping or shifting, just pain that radiated into his eye sockets. The right nostril had stopped bleeding already. He rolled the gauze and stuffed it up the left. "Anyone else come in with injuries?"

"No. Apparently there was a cop on the scene." Gillespie folded his arms. "So get your statement ready."

Liam wiped his face off again, then washed his hands and spoke to the mirror. "When the victim fainted, he took out one of those pop-up canopies. Maybe I got whacked with a pole. There were a lot of people crowding around."

Gillespie still blocked the door. "I know you've got stuff to prove"—he glanced down at Liam's prosthesis—"but that doesn't mean you gotta put up with crazy bastards taking a swing because they got issues."

Issues. Interesting way to put it. He and Scott were a long way past issues. Or proving themselves. Had Scott seen Liam's prosthetic? It shouldn't be possible but sometimes Liam forgot about it himself, until he tried to take a step. "I'm sure it was some kind of accident."

As they walked back down the hall, Gillespie's walkie spat out a call about someone's foot getting run over in front of the Miller Building. "Copy. On our way."

Liam reached for fresh gloves. "I can ride—"

"You can stay here and not run into any more poles, clear? I'll call Saunders and have her meet me." Gillespie went out the back.

As the door closed behind him, a rush like the opening gates at the track hit the front door.

"Beach?"

Before Liam had time to answer, the crowd pushed into the treatment bay.

Was Scott friends with the victim? Was he there now?

Liam charged in behind, but none of them had dark brown hair, darker eyes, and a ready snarl on full lips. He caught a glimpse of their patient, who now reclined on the bed like a Roman emperor, the similarity reinforced by the way his friends hovered like attendants.

Kishori's voice was clipped but polite. "If you insist on declining intravenous fluids, you need to sign this refusal form."

One of the new arrivals, the man built like a pro linebacker, intercepted the clipboard before Kishori could hand it to the patient.

Liam took as deep a breath as he could through one nostril and started on crowd control. He slipped in between two of the five men—did they travel in a group in case of random volleyball games?—and turned to face them. Being blood-spattered had usually given him some authority as an Army medic. Maybe it would have an effect on these guys. "I know you're concerned about your friend, but you need to give us a little room to work." He bit back a grimace at the nasal whine in his voice.

A short redhead in a tight blue T-shirt rolled his eyes and started helping. "The man's right. Let's hit the waiting room. Want to show me where that is?" The redhead pinned Liam with a stare. There were only three welded-to-the-wall plastic chairs near the desk, but there was a lobby in the administration offices that shared the building.

Liam led them to the staff-only door. "Through here. I'll come tell you when he's finished." A look over his shoulder showed that the big guy was still hovering around the patient.

When Liam went back to urge him out, he found the redhead still at his elbow. "Officer Donnigan. Baltimore County Police." He flipped open a badge and then put it away in his back pocket. "I want to talk to you about your bloody nose."

"It'll have to wait until after I see to my patient."

The policeman gave a nod. "I'll wait."

Kishori was swabbing Beauchamp's arm for the IV, the big guy looming behind her. Her braid had slipped out of its bun and hung over her shoulder. "Make a fist for me, please." She looked up as they came back. "Officer Donnigan, would you please ask Mr. Fonoti to step aside for a moment."

The policeman choked off a sound that sounded like a laugh. "Sure thing. Mr. Fonoti?" He smirked as the big man stepped out and followed him toward the desk.

Beauchamp gritted his teeth as the needle slid in. "I really don't mind him staying, ma'am. After all, he got me to take your advice on sticking that needle in me."

Kishori leaned over. "Mr. Beauchamp—"

"Call me Beach, please."

"—do you feel safe at home?" she finished.

He blinked, blue eyes wide behind long lashes. "Safe?"

"Yes. Does anyone hurt you or make you feel that they will?"

"Uh… not—" Beauchamp stammered, looking down. "No. Ah, to tell you the truth, I'm safer than I've ever been." His cheeks had a hint of a flush.

Liam had already picked out at least three of the guys as gay. Now some other stuff fell into place. He glanced down at a leather cuff on Beauchamp's wrist, its mate clutched in his fingers. Kishori must have had him take it off for the IV. Liam didn't get all that leather and bondage stuff, but there was no reason to make Beauchamp sweat about it. Beauchamp saw the direction of Liam's gaze and made an appeal with blinked eyes.

Liam nodded. "I'll tell the officer your friend can come back in, then."

Beauchamp sighed with relief. "Thank you."

Liam found himself alone with the cop when Beauchamp's boyfriend rushed past them to get back to his bedside.

"You going to tell me about your bloody nose now?"

Liam shrugged. "There was a crowd. It happens. No big deal."

The cop grunted in disbelief. "Maybe. But a lot of witnesses might say someone aimed right at you."

Liam met the guy's gaze and gave him the nothing-to-hide half smile that had worked on social workers and judges and lieutenants. Though it probably was less effective with the bloodstains. "I didn't see anything like that."

"Anything like what?"

"Whatever hit me."

The cop scrubbed at his face. "You two are peas in a pod."

Liam's skin prickled with awareness. Donnigan meant Scott. Did he know Scott?

The kickstart to Liam's circulatory system made his nose throb with pain. "Us two?"

"Something you want to add?"

"No, Officer."

"So you don't know what hit you. You interested in finding out?"

"No."

"'I don't know what hit me' is your official statement?"

Liam hadn't done multiple rounds with the social welfare system and not learned a few things. "Do I need a lawyer?"

"Fuck no. Psychiatrist, maybe." The cop turned and slammed through the door to the administration side of the building.

LIAM BRACED a hand against the dash as Kishori parked the Gator back in its slot behind their building. They'd delivered a rehydrated David Beauchamp and stern boyfriend to Gate 4. Over the stink of exhaust from the Gator, Liam's one working nostril delivered a dose of cigarette smoke. The hair on his arms stood up. There was no reason it had to be Scott—probably half the people at the car show smoked. But Liam knew he was here.

He went inside with Kishori but grabbed his afternoon energy drink from the fridge and waved it at her. "Taking five outside if you need me."

Liam tapped the top of the can and pulled the tab as he stepped out. Cigarette smoke hung in the hot air. Scott sat on top of the broken picnic table out back, Doc Martens on the seat, muddy jeans ripped at the knees, puffing away like he waited for Liam there every day.

Oily doubt twisted Liam's stomach, self-consciousness robbing him of the coordination he'd spent five thousand hours of physical therapy to regain. He should have worn jeans. Except it was the third ninety-plus day in a row, and he'd never given a shit if people saw his prosthesis before.

None of those people had been Scott.

Liam forced himself to take a long drink from his can of Brooks Blast before making his stiff, halting way across the baked-dry grass and powdery dirt.

As Liam reached the picnic table, Scott leaned back and took a long inhale, then blew the smoke off to his left.

He pointed the cigarette at the can in Liam's hand. "Don't you know those things will kill you?"

Laughter and tears fought for space in Liam's throat. Jesus. Scott. Liam had missed him. Missed *them* in a thousand different ways.

He couldn't say that out loud, though. Not when he'd been the one to leave. Though he'd left *for* Scott. Because of what Liam had forced Scott to be. Liam tried to push something through his dry mouth, a word, a sound even, anything to let Scott know why.

I'm sorry. I was scared. I was stupid. Damn, you look good.

The only sound he could make was "Scott."

Scott made a disgusted sound in his throat and put the cigarette back to his lips. This time the exhaled stream came right at Liam's face.

"So." Scott rested his arms on his knees. "You've been keeping busy, huh? Still gonna save the world?"

"Scott." Liam wanted to tell him everything. How losing his leg had been his own fucking fault. That he fucking knew better now. Some things you couldn't fix. But God, how he wanted to fix this now.

"You said that, yeah." Scott tapped his cigarette out lightly, brushed away the end, and tucked it in the pack. "I just came to say sorry for punching you."

"Sorry? You admit you know the word?"

Scott's lips thinned. "Yeah, well, I didn't know about"—he pointed at Liam's prosthesis—"all that."

He'd missed this too. The rush and challenge of sparring with Scott.

"So you're only sorry about hitting me because I'm down a leg? Fuck you."

Scott's mouth twisted, offering a glimpse of his gap-toothed smile.

Liam pulled the gauze out of his nose. He wasn't having this conversation honking like a goose. "Besides, not like it was the first time." He put the gauze and the can on one of the cracked wood planks.

Scott nodded, then pushed off the table and stood in front of Liam.

"Wasn't fair. You didn't see it coming." Shaking out his arms, Scott lifted his chin. "You get a free shot."

Liam stared at him.

"One-time offer, here." Scott made a *c'mon* motion with his hand. "Try not to break any teeth this time."

"I'm not going to hit you."

"Why not? I owe you one."

Jesus, Liam owed him so much fucking more. He'd been afraid of doing even a tentative online search for Scott after rehab, terrified of what could have happened. But he was here. Alive. Safe.

"I don't want to hit you."

"No?" Scott dipped his chin and arched a scarred, pierced brow in the infuriating superior expression Liam knew better than his own reflection.

Liam moved, though he'd swear it wasn't a conscious decision any more than the contraction of his heart that kept his blood moving. He grabbed Scott's shirt and kissed him.

Motor oil, menthol smoke, and cinnamon gum. Scott. The instant their mouths touched, the familiar jolt pulled Liam closer, reminded him how he'd never been able to get close enough.

Scott shoved a hand between them and pushed Liam away. He staggered, then caught his balance with a hand on the table. They stood glaring at each other, Scott breathing hard in the heavy air. Scott took another step back. "What the fuck was that?"

"Me taking my free shot. Didn't see it coming?"

"Crazy ratfucker." Shaking his head, Scott sank onto the bench.

Liam sat next to him and scooped up the can to take another drink, remembering when he'd asked Scott about his favorite insult.

"It's like saying the guy has a small dick, right? Because how small would your dick need to be to fuck a rat?"

Now Scott pulled out his lighter and flipped it through his fingers, despite the swelling on his knuckles. "The fuck happened to you?"

Liam had seen him do that same trick with a knife, knew the fluid fingers had dozens of white nicks from the learning curve. He watched the shining barrel flash in the sun. There were so many ways to answer him. Starting with why he'd run. Why he'd needed to run to something that would keep him from coming right back.

He deliberately stretched out his right leg, the ankle joint pointing his fake foot toward the sky. Watching it always gave him the sensation of floating, disconnected from his body. His leg, but not a part of him. After two years he was used to it, except for all the times when he wasn't.

"I joined the circus." He turned to see Scott's expression. "Lion taming isn't as easy as they make it look."

Scott snorted a laugh; then the lighter made the pass across his fingers again. "Yeah. Guess it's none of my business."

"Army. Afghanistan. Twenty-eight months ago. I don't like to talk about it." But not for the reasons most people thought. Explaining that what had happened was his own fucking fault didn't make him—or them—feel any better. Didn't make him less maimed. Or Ross any less dead.

Scott flicked the lighter on. "Shit."

"Yeah."

"But you're—I mean, they'll pay for school now that you—" Scott exhaled in a rush. "Doctors only need a good set of hands."

"There are programs, if I decide I want to go back."

"Decide?"

Liam finished off his Blast, trying and failing to ignore the stare that burned into the side of his head. Maybe being a doctor was all he'd ever talked about back then. But he'd earned a little time to think about it. Right?

He stuffed the wad of gauze in the empty can and crumpled it against the bench. "How many cars do you have now, Batman?"

"Just one. Might be selling it, though."

"Time for an upgrade?"

"There is no upgrading a '68 Mustang GT Fastback."

Liam gasped. "Why the hell would you sell a car you claimed was a blow job you can drive?"

Scott swung a foot, kicking the bench. Vibrations ran up into Liam's socket.

"Beats selling blow jobs."

"Huh?" Liam lifted his foot off the bench.

Scott pocketed his lighter. "To make rent."

Shit must really be bad if Scott was planning to sell his dream car.

"I don't have a lot, but I banked most of my service pay."

Scott leaped off the table. "Don't. Jesus, Liam. Just don't."

"You put me through two years of school. Kind of the least I can do."

Scott shook his head. "You don't owe me shit." A laugh that was mostly disgust made his lips curl. "Except maybe a why."

Fear. Guilt. It started a fresh tumble of what Liam always thought of as guilt worms wriggling in his stomach. The nights he'd felt Scott's heart jittering under a palm pressed to his chest, even in exhausted sleep. Finding a prescription bottle full of dexies with a stranger's name on it. Scott trying to kill himself or ending up an addict like Mom because he was working two full-time jobs to pay the bills and keep Liam in school.

"I had to."

"Yeah. Read the note." Scott relit his cigarette. "Forget I asked."

Admitting Liam had made a terrible mistake then—about all his mistakes—wasn't going to fix anything now. Wasn't going to slow the writhing bundle of worms making him nauseous.

"Is that why you came looking for me, to ask that?" Liam picked up the crushed can.

"Point to you, genius. Guess college wasn't a complete waste."

"I'm sorry."

"Don't be. At least it gave me a chance to say this to your face: bye, Liam. Have a nice life." Scott walked away.

Chapter Four

As soon as Scott rounded the corner of the administration building, he savagely punched the air in triumph. That was the first time ever he'd gotten the last word with Liam. His satisfaction barely lasted another five steps because no doubt about it. That had been the last, last word between them. Delivering the sneered goodbye he'd been hanging on to for years left him hollowed out. He hadn't realized he'd stopped walking until some fucknugget crashed into him from behind.

"Asshole," the guy muttered.

Ignoring the protest of sore knuckles, Scott tightened his fist and spun around. "What was that?"

The guy looked like a Viking, a hulking blond a half foot taller, but he lifted his hands palms out. "Hey, man. Just watch where you're walking."

"You ran into me." Scott's phone buzzed against his hip. A split-second hope that it was Liam distracted Scott enough that the blond ratfucker slipped away.

Not that it *could* be Liam. How would he have Scott's number?

And no way was Scott disappointed at that.

He dragged the phone from his pocket.

Jamie—acting as Officer Fucking Donnigan, probably. Just what Scott needed.

"What?" he grunted.

"You're fucking welcome," Jamie snapped back.

"For what?"

"For starters, me keeping you from spending your weekend in holding, ya ungrateful bastard."

Some small-dicked Chevy driver cruised past with his idle set to overcompensatingly loud.

"Wanna tell me where the fuck you are?" Jamie sounded more like a cop than ever. "'Cause I distinctly remember telling you to head straight home and stay out of trouble."

"I'm driving there right now."

"And I'm six foot fucking four. You want your shirt back, meet me at Gate 4."

Shit. Scott did want his shirt back. The denim was worn paper-thin, down to thread in spots, but it was soft as rabbit fur on his skin. Besides, his cigarettes were in it. The almost-empty pack he'd lifted from an unattended table on the way to talk to Liam was down to half a butt.

Though most of the foot traffic at Gate 4 was headed out for the day, there was a mile-long line of sweaty adults and whining kids at an ice cream stand and a small herd crowding the table of a huge distributor of parts for vintage cars.

No sign of Jamie, though despite his red hair, he was short enough to get lost in the crowd. One of the preppy guys from before was there, though. Not the one who had passed out. This guy's clothes, light-colored shorts and a button-down shirt, were already enough to make him stand out from the T-shirt-and-jeans crowd, but something else about him set him apart even more. He had a face like a magazine model, all cheekbones and perfect wavy hair, but it wasn't even that. There was a pocket of quiet around him, radiating from the stillness of his body. Scott had seen the same from kids in placement, the ones who survived by being invisible.

But as Scott got closer to him, he could tell the man wasn't scared or nervous at all. He studied everything around him, taking in the glued tips of Scott's hair with same detached amusement as he did the leather-and-studs-wearing baby in a stroller. When the guy turned his full focus on Scott, the look felt itchy, reminding Scott of the way shrinks always tried to probe his guts with their questions.

Scott knew how to deal with that fuckery: turn it on them. He closed the distance between them. "Hey. I'm Scott. You must be Jamie's—"

"I'm Gavin." He stuck out his hand.

Scott wanted to let the offer hang there until the guy felt stupid, but he found himself responding, bruised knuckles and all. At least Gavin didn't feel the need to prove something with a crushing grip. It was just a normal squeeze and pressure from a dry palm that made Scott conscious of how filthy his own hand probably was. He stopped himself from biting on his thumbnail.

This quiet stand-and-watch guy was Jamie's boyfriend? It was enough of a shock to think of anyone putting up with the prickly bastard, let alone someone like this. The sex must be out of this fucking world. Scott couldn't imagine they didn't drive each other crazy once their dicks were soft.

"So, where you know Jamie from?"

"Socially." Gavin's faint smile said he knew what the question really meant. "We met while swimming."

A loud snort of laughter in Scott's ear had him turning to see that Jamie had decided to actually show up.

"Here." He shoved the threadbare shirt at Scott.

Scott immediately grabbed for the half pack he'd had in the chest pocket and came up empty.

"Don't worry," Jamie said. "They didn't fall out. I chucked 'em."

"I suppose it's no good saying you owe me eight bucks."

Jamie made like he was pretending to think. "Uh—no."

"Christ. Ex-smokers and their fucking self-righteous bullshit."

"I'm not entirely sure the self-righteous bullshit is a result of him having quit smoking. I see it as more of a fixed character trait," Gavin said.

"Nobody asked you, Montgomery." Jamie's familiar snarl was all bark, though the goofy half smile on his face as he said it left Scott stunned. The expression darkened as he turned on Scott. "And you. You are one lucky son of a bitch."

"Really? Where's my winning Powerball ticket?"

"You must have dropped it when you punched your ex in the face. Settle for being lucky he's not pressing charges."

Scott squared his shoulders. "What did he say?"

"For fuck's sake. Do I look like a sixth-grade girl?"

Scott thought about pointing out that yeah, there was a lot of sixth-grade puppy love in the look Jamie had given Gavin, but that wouldn't get Scott the information he wanted.

Jamie shook his head. "He said he must have got hit with one of the canopy poles. Your name didn't come up."

Scott gave in and bit at his dirty thumbnail. That didn't mean anything. It wouldn't be the first time Liam had lied to cover Scott's ass.

"So I guess that leaves you free to go kiss and make up or whatever." Jamie made exaggerated kissy noises.

"Yeah, thanks." Scott glanced at Gavin before stuffing as much of the shirt as would fit in a front jeans pocket. To Jamie, Scott said, "And thanks to your boyfriend for thinking to grab my shirt."

Jamie's heavy brows lowered to intensify his glare. "What makes you think my boyf—Gavin was the one to pick it up?"

"'Cause he seems like a nice, thoughtful guy."

"And I'm not?"

Scott smirked.

"Maybe I'll drag you to the tank anyway."

"Sure you will. And spend the rest of your Saturday off doing paperwork."

Jamie sighed. "Jesus, McDermott, maybe you wanna learn to back down."

"And maybe something"—Scott flicked his eyes to Gavin—"has turned you mellow. I'll text if I spot another Galaxie."

MUCH AS Scott hated to admit it, Jamie was right. Scott should leave. He had his shirt back. He needed smokes and to figure out how close he was to being evicted and if he should take the thirty-two grand that Galvez guy had offered him for the Mustang. He absolutely shouldn't be headed back through the fairgrounds toward the administration building. Toward Liam.

But Scott couldn't just leave. Couldn't do to Liam what Liam had done to him.

Scott couldn't just disappear into smoke.

Thanks for not having me arrested. That was all he was going to say. The words sounded casual enough in his head.

Then it would be up to Liam. If he wanted to talk or explain, Scott would listen. And Scott wouldn't be the one who'd walked away.

He heard Liam's voice before he rounded the building corner to the back.

"…busy today. Got more paperwork to fill out."

"I can *see* you were busy," a high, soft masculine voice answered.

As Scott rounded the corner, he saw the man reach for Liam's bruised face.

The guy was bigger than his voice made him sound, tall, with a deep chest, but Scott zeroed in on the light brown hand on Liam's face. Tall or not, Scott could take the ratfucker. Him and his hand that was now cupping Liam's face. It was only those long black braids that made the man look bigger than he was. *Get your fucking hand off Liam's face.*

Liam flicked one of those braids over the guy's broad shoulder. "Tell you about it later."

"I'll come in and wait for you." The handsy bastard turned to look at Scott. "Can I help you?"

"Scott?"

Fuck. Now Liam had seen him. Liam jerked away from Braids.

The guy grabbed Liam's shoulder as he stumbled but kept staring at Scott. "Scott? *The* Scott?" He looked down at Liam. "I guess 'busy' is one word for it."

Liam had his balance now, but Braids didn't let him go. "Uh." Liam's throat bobbed. Then he smiled, his old fool-the-social-workers smile. Did Braids know how fake that smile was? Did he know Liam could use that smile to sell shoes to a snake? "Scott. This is Deon. He's—" Liam used the pause to give the smile another boost. His teeth were still bright and perfectly even. "—my physical therapist."

Deon wrapped his arm around Liam's shoulders. "I *was* his physical therapist. Now I'm his boyfriend."

Like he hadn't been making that obvious from the second Scott rolled around the corner. "Right." Scott looked at Liam. "Well, I only"—he swallowed the *came back here*, no point in giving Deon extra information—"wanted to say thanks." He jerked his chin at Liam's face and the building behind him. Liam would know what he meant. *Thanks for covering my ass with the cop.*

He backed off a step and got a hand on the corner of the building. It was cheap aluminum, baked to a shimmer in the sun, and it sizzled the skin off his fingers and palm. He kept his hand there, focused on the pain he could control. A pain he could use to push down the tearing in his gut that told him to punch that smile off Liam's face.

Scott kept his path close to the building as he made his escape back the way he had come.

"Nice to finally meet you." Deon's words followed him.

It took everything Scott had to keep walking, to not turn and find out how many punches would put that big guy down. Scott settled for the satisfaction of picturing how that would look, nose smashed and those stupid braids spread out on the dusty patches of earth.

"Scott, wait." Liam's words should have made Scott take longer strides, but the lurch in the steps that came after him wouldn't let him.

Six years of distance between them, and he still felt that impossible pull anchored somewhere under his ribs. Same old ache. But not the same Liam. Not that short hair, the clean jaw, or some motherfucker in braids with an arm around him. And not that metal leg.

"Scott." Liam had cleared the corner now.

Scott shouldn't turn back. Because if Deon and his braids were there with Liam, Scott was definitely spending the rest of the weekend in jail.

"It's just me," Liam said, like he still could guess what Scott was thinking.

Usually with Liam, Scott didn't feel that itch behind his shoulder blades, the need to protect his back. But right then he wanted to press it into the melting aluminum as though that would offer him any protection from the kind of damage Liam could inflict.

Liam shook his head. Not in a *no*; it was the motion he'd always used to shift the wave of hair off his face. Except there wasn't any need for it now. Scott's fingers twitched remembering the feel of the thick silky strands, dragging Liam up for a kiss with the taste of his own dick on Liam's tongue. *C'mon. Want to fuck.*

"I looked for you. I mean, after I got out." Liam's voice was low.

Out of the Army? Out of the hospital? How fucking hard had he looked?

"What for?"

"Same reason you came back here."

"Doubt it. Like I said, just wanted to say thanks for not having me arrested."

Liam smiled. His real one was crooked, and it made his muddy eyes as light and clear as good whiskey. And just as dangerous to Scott's sense of self-preservation. "Yeah, right." The smile faded. "You haven't changed."

"You have." But that wasn't exactly it. Liam was the same. The space between them wasn't.

"Ask me." Liam threw it at Scott like a challenge. "Go ahead. I can see it on your face."

Why did you leave? What really happened to you? Are you actually in love with that man-bear in braids? What came out was "What the fuck was up with that kiss?" He barely stopped himself from licking his lips. He couldn't remember the last time he'd kissed anybody he'd hooked up with. He'd been turning his face away from that kind of vulnerability for years. If dicks got sucked right, no one complained.

"I had to."

"Right. And I'm the one with impulse control issues." He'd read his own therapy reports, the whole long list of what everyone thought was wrong with him. Why no family even took him as a foster kid for long. Oppositional-defiant disorder, attachment disorder, poor impulse control, conduct disorder, intermittent explosive disorder, irritable mood disorder. As if irritable mood disorder didn't apply to every fucking shrink or therapist who'd sat across the table from him with that constipated expression, lips shriveled like a cat's asshole.

"God, I missed you." Liam took another step toward him, eyes showing more hints of gold in the bright sunlight. Even with a foot of space still between them, Scott's skin buzzed with awareness, the memories etched into his nerves.

Bastard could work the knife right down to bone. "Yeah? I can tell." Scott's control shattered. Must be that old intermittent explosive disorder again. He shoved Liam back a step. "How fucking hard did you look? I've never left."

He walked away while Liam stumbled for balance against the building. Guilt—*he's only got one leg, you dick*—gnawed fresh holes in Scott's chest.

"Scott, wait." At least Liam was smart enough to not touch him. "I meant it. I still—we've been through so much together, can't we—"

Scott stopped but didn't look back. "What, be friends? No. We can't." *I can't.*

He started walking again while he still could.

Chapter Five

DEON STOOD next to the picnic table, in the same place Scott had stood when Liam kissed him. Liam had barely taken a few steps back around the corner before Deon started spilling apologies.

"I was a dick, I know, sorry." Deon put his hands up. "Running into the former love of your life turned me into a possessive little bitch."

"I don't know." Liam forced himself to smile. His nose throbbed like hell. He bet he'd have two black eyes. Scott had never been one to pull his punches. Not even with Liam. To Deon he said, "Kind of alpha dog of you."

"Woof." Deon laughed. "But, Li"—Deon started to put an arm around Liam, but must have read his rigid posture and let the arm drop— "are you okay? And what the hell happened to your face?" He shot a look in the direction Scott had taken.

Liam couldn't blame Deon for the suspicion. For one, he was right, and for two, Scott had always vibrated belligerence—especially around people he didn't know. Liam wasn't thrilled at Scott's version of hello, but Deon wouldn't understand any better than that cop had.

"It was a circus. Guy took out one of those canopies when he passed out from heat exhaustion. His boyfriend—"

"Gay day at the car show?"

"Just like Disney World. Seriously, they were in a pack like a bunch of lesbians."

Deon had minored in sociology. That should give him something to chew on.

Liam squeezed Deon's arm. "Anyway, just let me finish up the paperwork and I'll be ready to go."

"Not so fast, Superman. How does any of that add up to your face looking like you took a softball to the nose?"

Shit. So much for Deon wandering off with the sociology distraction.

"Too many bodies in a small space plus loose canopy poles equals a whack to the face." The best lie was an almost truth.

Deon cupped the back of Liam's neck and scrutinized the damage. "Looks pretty bad for a random shot from unanchored aluminum. Someone must have got you with an elbow."

Liam upped the distraction level. "Wasn't my favorite part. Check this: Kishori did a domestic abuse eval on the guy."

"What?"

"Gets better. I mean, her instincts are right. The boyfriend is hulking around like a bodyguard, but then I see the leather cuffs on the patient, and they aren't for decoration. Not with those D-rings."

"Fifty Shades of Gay."

"Yup. A little on the freaky end for me, like the guy wasn't allowed to blink unless his Daddy told him to, but definitely into it, not abuse."

"How are you going to write that one up?"

"Carefully."

Deon wrinkled his nose as he followed Liam into the cool air of the first aid station. "Who was smoking?"

"Uh—Scott."

"Oh."

Any hope of pushing Scott's appearance to the back of Deon's mind had vanished with that whiff of mentholated tobacco. At least Deon wouldn't chase him into the office demanding an explanation. Confrontation was Scott's style. Deon would wait.

The waiting lasted until Deon's Honda had turned out of the lot and they were stuck in traffic in front of the shopping plaza. "It must have been weird, seeing him. After all this time."

That neutral, pleasant tone pissed Liam off more than an accusation would have.

"Are you asking if I knew he'd be there?"

"No." Still patient. Calm. "This isn't about me. I'm asking if you're okay."

Because Deon knew Liam wasn't. Which stupidly drove him to deny it. "Why wouldn't I be?"

The light changed. Deon's hands tightened and then relaxed on the steering wheel as they moved forward. From one heartbeat to the next, exhaustion slammed Liam flat. He wanted this conversation, this whole fucking day, to be over.

"Yes, Scott was important to me. We went through a lot together." Like having to go with Scott when they found his sister's body, thinking he'd never be as terrified again as he was that night when Scott fell apart, the shell of angry protection dissolving in agonized sobs. And then finding himself twice as scared when he found the pills. Fear and love and belonging in a messy tangle Liam didn't think he could ever sort out enough to explain.

"I still care about him. But I haven't seen him since we broke up six years ago. And I'm pretty sure he doesn't ever want to see me again. 'Specially after the way I ghosted him."

Deon nodded and put on his blinker, gliding into the left-turn lane.

"You think the back way will be worth it?" Liam stared at the brake lights ranging ahead of them.

Deon's apartment in Towson was a straight shot down York Road, less than ten minutes away once they got through the traffic. Fucking MVA was holding Liam's license hostage until he either got a car refitted with left-foot driving pedals or took a rehab course. Not being able to drive left him feeling as helpless as if he were in a chair again.

"Not really." Deon brought them onto a tree-lined road. "Thought you'd rather just go home, but if I'm wrong—"

"No. I'm—no. I think I need to crash." His mom would be at an NA meeting. His stepdad and stepbrothers were at some sports thing. Liam could pass out in his room and not have to answer any questions about his face.

Fuck Deon for being right. Fuck him for being so goddamned understanding. Fuck him for being a wonderful, considerate boyfriend. Fuck it all.

"Sunday dinner tomorrow?" Deon asked as he stopped in front of the three-bedroom ranch Mom had moved into after marrying Greg.

"Yeah. I'll be out by five." Liam took off his seat belt, then pushed off on his good leg to lean over and give Deon a quick kiss. "You're really kind of awesome, you know that."

"I try."

LIAM TOOK the bowl of potatoes off the counter and carried it into the dining room.

Deon winced. "Damn, Li, now that I see it in the light, it *is* bad."

Liam put the potatoes down in front of his stepbrothers and reached for his nose. Purple-red spread from the bridge of his nose under each eye, worse on the right side where more knuckles had landed. He'd had a headache all day, and the hot, heavy rain that had been falling since early afternoon hadn't made it any better. At least that made the car-show crowd leave early. Not that it did much good when Liam was stuck without a ride.

"Are you sure it's not broken?" Deon asked.

Liam's mom came out with the chicken. After sliding it onto the table, she rested a hand on his shoulder. "I'm sure if it was, Liam would know."

"Nothing they can do if it doesn't need to be set." He sounded like an adenoidal fourteen-year-old. And felt about that mature. His leg hurt too. Hot needles jabbed bone-deep from his hip to his no-longer-there toes. He resisted the urge to shrug his mom's hand away.

He patted it and moved stiffly around the dining table to his seat next to Deon.

"Bad PLP?" Deon murmured.

Liam managed a curt nod.

"It's the weather," Deon said, which Liam knew already, thanks.

"What is?" Mom eased the potato bowl away from Kevin, Liam's eleven-year-old stepbrother, and passed it to Deon.

Deon scooped out two good-sized potatoes. "Phantom limb pain. It can be triggered by barometric pressure changes."

That pulled nine-year-old Justin's attention away from where he was drowning his despised spinach in gravy. "Cool. So you have, like, a ghost leg?"

"If I kicked your foot, could you feel it right now?" Kevin peered at Liam from across the table.

"No one is kicking anyone," their father said firmly.

His prosthesis was the only source of conversation Liam had with his stepbrothers. As repulsively fascinating as they found both the leg and the stump of his thigh, they still grumbled about being shoved together in one bedroom in order to give Liam his own space when he'd moved in ten months ago. "I'd feel it in my stump like always, from the socket," he told Kevin. "This is just my brain getting the signals screwed up somehow."

"Or a ghost leg," Justin put in.

Liam had to admit a ghost leg was a lot more interesting than confused axons in his peripheral nervous system. "Or it's a ghost leg," he agreed. Though what haunted him from the accident wasn't twenty pounds of bone and muscle. It was Ross. On fire.

"Dork." Kevin rolled his eyes at his brother.

Though they left Liam out of it, Kevin and Justin started a foot-kicking battle under the table.

"I hope today was less stressful for you." Greg took the platter of chicken Liam passed him.

"It was, thanks."

Four years ago, Mom and Greg's wedding had felt like most other Mom-triggered random events in Liam's life. He'd been on active duty, had seventy-two-hour leave for the service. But unlike most things involving his mother, this marriage—and her sobriety—had stuck. Having a stepfather still felt strange.

"No blasts from the past today?" Deon said, and if Liam's leg wasn't killing him, he'd have kicked Deon. Hard.

Mom was quick to jump on that. "What kind of blast are we talking about?"

Liam swallowed some dry chicken. "He means Scott." No point in trying to deny it. Deon was obviously going to drag it out. "And no, he didn't come back today," Liam added for Deon's benefit.

"Scott?" Mom repeated. "Scott McDermott?"

Kevin and Justin had no idea who Scott was, but even they could sense the tension and abandoned their contest over who could flick a bread crumb the farthest in case this was more entertaining.

This had never been Liam's life: cozy family dinners on Sundays. He'd never asked for it. All he'd ever wanted was for his mom to get help and stay clean. *But I have so much to make up for, baby.*

"How is he?" His mom's voice was as neutral as she could manage.

She and Scott had never had a high opinion of each other. Mom had actually used the words *juvenile delinquent* more than once. Scott couldn't see past his own mommy issues. Whenever they'd been in the same room, Liam had felt like a meaty bone between two hungry dogs.

How was Scott?

He'd been Scott. Snarled like Scott. Kissed like Scott. The whole dizzy pull of him had taken less than thirty seconds to turn Liam inside out again. Which was exactly the reason why they couldn't ever work. At least Liam had learned his lesson now. Knew he couldn't save everyone. And if he forgot why for even a second, he just needed to look at where his right leg used to be.

To his mom he said, "He's the same. Still piss"—he glanced at his stepbrothers—"angry."

"Of course he is. He will be until he accepts that it's making his life unmanageable."

Liam recognized the phrasing from one of the twelve steps and bit the side of his tongue. He was glad to have his mom back, but he wished everything wasn't always about her steps.

"Can I be excused?" Kevin asked.

"Do you want to be excused from dessert?" Greg glanced at the spinach hiding under a thigh bone.

"No." Kevin slumped back in his chair.

"How was practice?" Liam said to stave off any whining.

"Wet." Kevin shoved his plate a few inches.

Justin appreciated the change in subject, though. "If you got a special foot attachment, I bet you could do really far kicks, like, and go to the NFL."

"I don't know if it would work like that."

"I saw some guy online running on these spring blades. Why couldn't you get something like that for kicking?"

Liam opened his mouth, but he didn't have an answer. He almost wished he was still listening to his mom on what was wrong with Scott.

Deon jumped to Liam's rescue with an explanation about joints, pounds of pressure, and force, which would probably bore Justin off the topic.

God, Liam's head—his face—hurt. He almost pinched his nose, then realized what a stupid idea that would be.

"You can be excused and still get dessert." Greg's voice was low under the onslaught of questions from Justin.

Liam managed a smile. "I can help clean up."

"Kevin is perfectly capable of loading a dishwasher." That earned Greg an eye roll from his son. "But if you feel up to it, I need a hand in the garage."

When Deon started clearing the table, Liam followed Greg into the attached garage. Other than Greg's seven-year-old red Ford Fusion, Liam couldn't see anything Greg might need a hand with. Liam could change the oil and air filter, but he wasn't Scott, who could see through an engine to know when one spark plug was dirty. Liam imagined Scott there with them now. *At least your mom had enough sense not to marry some asshole who drives Chevys.*

Greg went around to the back and lifted the trunk. "I put these in here for traction in the winter and keep forgetting to take them out." Greg laughed. "I know it's August, but I might as well get them out now. Save on gas."

Liam looked in at two bags of cat litter. Really? This was what Greg needed help with? With a shrug, Liam bent to grab the closest bag, but Greg put a hand on Liam's arm.

"You know I played basketball in college."

Liam shot Greg a confused look. Not that the fact was hard to believe, considering he was well over six feet tall, but it seemed like a strange time to bring it up.

"Caught a lot of elbows to the face. Some accidental, some not. That"—Greg pointed to Liam's nose—"is from a not-accidental punch."

Liam brought his fingertips up to his forehead as if that could hide the evidence.

"You can tell me to mind my own business, but I noticed you slept here last night."

Greg was keeping track of his sex life now? Liam knew he should jump in with a complaint or an explanation, but he had no idea what Greg was getting at.

"And your mom drove you to work this morning."

Oh. Then the rest of the dots connected. Poor Deon. Liam remembered Kishori questioning their patient while his Top hovered. Had everyone Liam knew been dragged to some kind of sensitivity training last week?

"Deon didn't hit me." Liam had no idea how anyone could think Deon would hurt another person. He even swerved to avoid hitting an already dead squirrel. "He wouldn't. Ever." Liam's anxiety ratcheted up. Deon was stuck in there doing dishes with Mom. "My mother doesn't think that?"

"No. I didn't say anything to her. I don't know anything about how two men, ah, who are together, might handle a domestic disagreement, but—"

"I swear, sir." Liam pointed to his nose. "This happened in the confusion when I was trying to get to a patient."

The sound Greg made suggested he needed more convincing.

Liam used a scrap of truth to bolster the lie. "There was a crowd. If someone did take a deliberate swing at me, I didn't see who it was." Fractionally true. He hadn't known for sure who had hit him until after. Until he was hunched over in shock and pain, knowing he wasn't imagining things, that the guy who looked like Scott actually was Scott.

After a long stare, Greg gave Liam a nod. They both hoisted a bag of litter onto a shoulder.

"I'm driving the boys back to their mother's. Want to come along for the ride?" Greg asked as they lowered their bags onto a shelf.

Did Greg have plans for more one-on-one questions, or was he offering Liam an escape from Deon? Not that Liam needed one. Or wanted one. Deon was steady and supportive and definitely nothing like Scott. Not that there was a reason to compare them.

Liam shook his head and winced at the extra stab of pain.

Greg frowned. "I hope that's not going to ruin things for your big debut."

Liam hadn't even considered what effect his swollen nose might have on his voice. Backward Gaze might only be the house band for Schim's Tavern, but they wouldn't want their new lead singer making honking noises through Reeve's lyrics.

In rehab, one of the shrinks had made Liam sit down and make a list. Not bucket list stuff, not exactly, but stuff he'd never done and had always wanted to. Things to try, once he finished PT. Liam had sweated it until someone walked by humming some old Johnny Cash song. With a jolt, he'd slipped back to Ross guiding Liam's fingers into place on guitar strings, thwacking his knuckles when he screwed up a chord. In a flash, he'd scribbled *Join a rock band,* though the likelihood of it had ranked up there with spontaneously regrowing a leg like he was part starfish. At least until Deon found the list and held him to it.

Two auditions later, Liam was surprised to get a call back from Reeve and Backward Gaze. From the first practice, everything about singing had felt so perfect and so wrongly self-indulgent that Liam would have kept the opportunity a secret. Except he still needed a goddamned ride everywhere.

"They're—we're kind of grunge, so the look should be fine," he told Greg with a half smile. "But don't tell them I said that."

A shared secret would make Greg forget his questions faster.

Greg arched his brows as Liam leaned in to say, "According to the industry, grunge is dead. Totally last century."

Since Greg had probably spent his twenties banging his head to Soundgarden and Alice in Chains, he laughed, exactly like Liam had meant him to.

Needing to lie down with an ice pack was the reason Liam gave Deon for why he wasn't coming over tonight. Though Deon didn't argue, the length and intensity of his stare had a lot in common with the one Greg had given Liam. Next up was getting Mom to leave him alone, but finally he shucked off her offers of help with his leg and his ice pack and was alone in his room.

Liam opened his phone to the probably illegal, certainly unethical picture he'd snapped of David Beauchamp's treatment form. He enlarged it so the phone number scrawled at the top was legible. After shutting the door, he moved to the window and had shoved it up before remembering his days of sneaking out, even from the ground floor, were over. Assuming he and his droid leg could make it out and over the bush, he'd never get back in that way.

Not that he really needed to sneak out. He wasn't doing anything wrong. This was just about making sure Scott was okay, restoring the balance. He'd put Liam through two years at Towson; it was only fair Liam help him now. He remembered Scott brushing off the idea of selling his dream car with *"Beats selling blow jobs."* Liam would do this and then he'd be able to let it go.

He typed in the number and pressed Call. The drawled *hello* meant he had the right guy, but he said, "David Beauchamp?"

"May I ask who's callin'?"

"This is Liam Walsh, the EMT who treated David at the fairgrounds yesterday."

"Ah. Hello, EMT Walsh. What can I do for you?"

"I'm following up on your care. How are you feeling?"

"Much better, thank you. I must say I've never heard of follow-up from a first responder. Is this some new insurance regulation?"

"No, not at all. Just a routine check-in. Did you decide to seek follow-up care with a physician?" Liam scrambled for a way to steer the conversation to the cop who'd asked Liam if he was pressing charges. The cop had been one of the group to come to the first aid station with Beauchamp's boyfriend. *"You two are peas in a pod."* The cop knew Scott, would know where to find him.

"I didn't find it necessary. As I believe you were aware at the time, I have someone who enjoys keeping a close watch on me."

Most people—people with nothing to hide—were glad to answer even peculiar questions if they perceived the person asking had some kind of authority. Liam had relied on that and an encouraging smile to smooth his way more than once.

Filling his voice with that smile, Liam said, "Now, one of the men who came in with you identified himself as law enforcement. I—"

"EMT Walsh?"

When Liam paused, David Beauchamp went on, "I consider myself somewhat gifted in the fine art of bullshit. Therefore, I have a finely calibrated sense of when someone else is engaged in shovelin' it. What exactly did you call me for?"

After a long breath, Liam gave him the truth. "I have to find somebody."

Chapter Six

SCOTT LET the outer door of his apartment building bang shut behind him.

Fuck this day. Fuck this week. *Fuck my whole fucking life.*

He stomped up the stairs to find his down-the-hall neighbor Mrs. Freeman struggling with her groceries on the second landing of the four-story walk-up.

"Hang on, Mrs. Freeman. Let me get some of those."

She paused and leaned on the banister before facing him. "Scott?" She squinted. Even though it was 11:00 a.m., the stairwell was dark with shadows since the light bulbs were out—again.

"Yes, ma'am." Scott picked up a few of the bags and gently pried the rest off Mrs. Freeman's arm. She was eighty if she was a day, far too old to have to haul all this upstairs, let alone on the bus. "I would have driven you after work if you asked."

"You're a sweet boy, but it was such a nice day." Her wide-brimmed plastic straw hat bumped into his chin.

It was hot as hell out, and the old lady was still bundled up in a sweater. He held himself to her achingly slow pace up to the next landing.

She looked down at her wrist and then peered at him again. "What are you doing home in the middle of the day?"

Scott gritted his teeth. He was the best goddamned mechanic Dressler had. The ratfucker should have stood by him. Scott was doing the customer a favor warning him that his dickhead teenaged son was grinding the hell out of the clutch on his Miata. Instead Dressler had fucking fired him.

After a few seconds of silence, Mrs. Freeman gave him a sympathetic look. "Oh, hon. Not again?"

So maybe it was the third time in two years his perfectly logical response to idiot customers fucking up perfectly fine engines had cost him a job. Fuck 'em all. Scott would open his own damned garage.

"You come over later. I'll make you that noodle casserole you like."

He didn't exactly like it, but he'd praised the first one she'd made for him to thank him for driving her to the store. Now he was stuck with it. But given the fact that until he got his last check from Dressler, he had a grand total of sixty-seven dollars to keep him fed, gassed, and in cigarettes while he looked for another job, noodle casserole sounded perfect.

"Thanks, Mrs. Freeman. Let me get the door for you too."

They reached the top landing.

"Oh, sweet Lord Jesus, I'm sorry, hon."

Scott followed her gaze to the bright yellow note taped to his door. He dragged Mrs. Freeman's groceries with him as he read.

Three-day notice to terminate tenancy... rent outstanding in the amount of two-thousand eight hundred dollars.

He leaned against the shittily plastered wall and let his head *thunk* back against it. Guess Galvez was going to get the Mustang after all.

"C'mon in, hon," Mrs. Freeman called from her open door. "No point in fretting on an empty stomach."

GALVEZ'S SHOP was a wet dream—minus the mouth on Scott's dick. Three bays, one with a lift where his Mustang was sitting, and gleaming racks of parts and tools. Scott walked next to Galvez as he shone a flashlight up into the Mustang's belly.

Scott pointed out what was original and what he'd replaced. He and Jamie had overhauled the exhaust last fall and smoothed out the dings in the body from that motherfucking hailstorm.

"Thirty-two, like I promised." Galvez had coppery-brown skin and a distracting pair of bristling black eyebrows.

Thirty grand would pay off his back rent and the rest of his debts, but it wouldn't be a drop of what he'd need to open his own place.

"What are you going to do with her?"

Galvez's brows joined up across his nose like a fuzzy caterpillar. "Her?"

"The car."

"Ah. Brighter paint, new rims, then send it California and sell it to some studio guy for fifty."

The fuck. Scott could do that himself. Screw the rent. For fifty he might actually be able to find a place to start his own garage.

Scott put a hand up on the Mustang's solid axle. She'd been the best thing about his life since Liam left him. She could take him farther than back rent.

"I'll think about it," Scott told Galvez.

The caterpillar looked like it was about to jump off Galvez's face. "Last spot on the trailer. Deal might not be there later."

"I'll take my chances."

Scott always had.

THREE DAYS later, Scott was hoping he had enough chances left to just catch a few hours of sleep. The lights in the parking lot almost blinded his tired eyes. Towson Campus Security had just swept this lot five minutes ago, so maybe he could sneak in and pass out for a while.

He and the Mustang were running on fumes. He'd dropped his last twenty getting her to a quarter of a tank and himself enough cigarettes to stay sane. He'd have stolen one or the other, except the Mustang got noticed. He had the anticamera cover on his plate, but there just weren't many dark blue '68 Shelbys out there.

He should have just used his cash to start out for somewhere else. He had nothing to keep him here. No apartment. No friends. Sure as fuck no family.

And here he was crawling around Towson as if, what, Liam was going to come jogging up with that smile he only gave Scott? The one that made his heart kick and his insides defrost because for once in his life Scott mattered.

That was gone. Liam wasn't jogging anywhere these days, and he was saving his smiles for fucking Deon.

Scott rolled down the windows to catch what breeze there was on a humid August night and crawled into the back seat. Not that he could really stretch out back there, but it beat getting the pattern on the leather bucket in front etched any deeper into his ass.

He'd just smoke half a cigarette now, half in the morning. If he stayed ahead of security, he could probably manage another shower in the athletic building. He'd gotten familiar enough with the campus when Liam was going here.

Scott ended up smoking the whole damned thing, dragging every last rush of cool thick smoke into his lungs and holding on. When he hit the filter, he flicked the butt into the night sky and watched his exhalation follow it.

Sharp raps on the hood jerked him awake into a blistering morning. He sat up, scrubbing at his face, lie ready to go.

"Hey, I'm just waiting for my girlfriend to get out of class."

"At seven thirty in the morning? Try another one, McDermott."

At the familiar snarl, Scott shaded his eyes against the glare. "Jamie?"

"What the hell are you doing? Three fucking calls in the last twenty-four about a suspicious guy in a '68 blue Shelby Mustang. University security thinks you're about to take out the place with an AR-15." Jamie wore some kind of uniform, but it wasn't the standard blue.

"Thought you were out playing bumper boats in the harbor."

"Clocked off. Then that description came through the radio."

"Wanna search my car?"

Jamie stuck his head in and jerked back. "Fuck no. Smells like ass and ashtray. What the hell—"

It was too late to hide the bag Scott's dirty shorts were sticking out of or the bag of Slim Jims Scott had been living on.

"Are you living in your fucking car?"

"What the fuck is it to you?"

"Right now you're trespassing and damned lucky I'm the one who woke your ass up. How long have you—"

"Since none of your goddamned business." Scott needed to piss. He'd have thought he'd sweated out every last drop of fluid overnight, but he couldn't be that lucky. He needed coffee and a cigarette. More, he needed to take the Mustang back to Galvez and see if he could still get that thirty-two grand for it.

He climbed out. Jamie could watch him pee in a bush if he got off on it.

Jamie shoved him back against the car. "Get in. Let's go."

"Where?"

"The Little Home for Fucked-Up Queers."

"Can I piss first?"

"No. And if I look back and you aren't following me, I will fucking arrest you."

Chapter Seven

JAMIE PARKED his F-100 in front of the driveway of a two-story redbrick house with white shutters that looked pretty much like all the other redbrick houses on the street. If it was the Home for Fucked-up Queers Jamie labeled it as, there wasn't so much as a little rainbow flag out front. Scott tucked the Mustang behind a middle-aged minivan and walked just slowly enough that, by the time he stood by Jamie on the front steps, the cop's red hair was bristling off his head in frustration. A ten-year-old Buick with new tires squatted in the driveway.

"You're friends with someone who drives a Buick?" Scott muttered.

Jamie snorted. "Different tastes. Thank God I don't have to drive it." He leaned over to peer in a front window, then glanced down at his phone.

"Maybe they're closed today."

Jamie turned to glare at Scott, then raised a fist to knock and almost punched the guy who opened the door.

As Scott took in the sight of the bare, muscled chest above a pair of boxers, he decided he wouldn't be the one throwing the first punch if it came to that. He recognized Salt-and-Pepper Studly from the day at the car show. Right now there was a glint of something hard behind the sleepy blue eyes. Scott had the urge to raise his hand before asking if he could use the bathroom.

The guy studied Scott back, his eyes narrowed. Scott had seen that judgment too many times not to know what it was. He thought about a *what-the-fuck's-your-problem* challenge, but he was too damned tired. He shook his head and stepped backward off the stoop.

Jamie latched on to Scott's shoulder. "Quinn, this is Scott. Been living in his car."

Like it was this guy's business where Scott tried to catch some sleep? He should have just stayed in the apartment and waited for the sheriff.

Someone slipped up behind Quinn. Should have known it'd be that goth kid from the car show, this time in a neon-green silk bathrobe untied over black briefs. The kid shoved the hair off his face. "Meet us in the backyard. I don't want to—you?" He stared at Scott. "The guy who punched the EMT? What the fuck, Jamie?"

Jamie held up the hand that wasn't gripping Scott's shoulder. "It was his ex, who, I guess, had it coming. Anyway, the ex didn't press charges."

"So?" the kid said.

"Who here would be glad to punch my ex in the nose?" Quinn asked in a rumbling voice.

"Fine," the kid huffed. "Just go around back."

Jamie released his grip on Scott's shoulder. "Now, Eli, hasn't Daddy trained you to pick up your toys? I'm sure you guys could figure out how to turn it into a kinky game."

Eli batted long, thick lashes at Jamie. "Jealous of our playtime?"

Jamie's cheeks flushed dark under his freckles.

Whatever the hell these guys got up to was none of Scott's business. And he planned to keep it that way. He started to ease back off the porch.

Jamie grabbed his arm again.

"You're freaking out your guest," Eli said. "And I'd rather not wake up Silver and Marco."

Scott looked from Quinn to Eli. "You guys got kids?"

Jamie coughed a laugh next to him.

"Moving day is next Friday." Eli's smile was faked sweetness. "Gavin tells me you and your truck will be free then."

"Shit."

Jamie's bitching was going to have to wait. Scott seriously needed to piss.

"Uh." He resisted the urge to raise his hand. "Can I use a bathroom or you want me to water your bushes out back?"

Eli rolled his eyes so high they disappeared under his hair. "Down the hall, behind the stairs. Then come out through the back door in the kitchen. And be quiet unless you want a horny eighteen-year-old grinding on your lap."

Kidneys no longer on fire, Scott headed for the back door. As Scott cut through the kitchen, he found Quinn, now in a T-shirt, scrambling eggs and frying bacon, but right then, Scott only had a hard-on for the coffee dripping slow and dark. He took a big whiff of the fragrant steam.

Quinn put a mug down on the counter in front of Scott. "Here. Need sugar?"

Scott shook his head as he snatched up the ten-cup jug and filled the mug. Add in a little nicotine, he'd be ready to face whatever Jamie had dragged him into.

Quinn pulled down some plates and three more mugs and shoved them into Scott's hands. "Make yourself useful and take these outside."

Scott's stomach was gurgling from the smell of the food, so he bit back the *Do I look like a waiter?* and accepted the stack.

"So you running a hostel here or what?"

"Something like that."

"I'm guessing this Silver and Marco, they didn't have anyplace else to go?" Scott indicated the upstairs with a jerk of his head.

At Quinn's nod, Scott said, "Why get involved?"

Quinn's mouth twisted in half a smile. "Why not?"

Scott balanced all four mugs, including his full one, on the stack of plates as he took them out to place on the patio table. Now maybe he could get to actually enjoy the coffee. He wrapped his hand around his mug.

Eli snatched it. "For me? Thanks, hon. How about some forks?"

Scott wasn't sure why he let the kid pluck the mug out of his hand. He shook his head as he went back into the kitchen.

Quinn already had forks and napkins waiting. "Take this and the coffee. I'll be right out with the food."

"You do this a lot?"

Quinn gave a soft snort of laughter. "It's been a busy summer."

After bringing the rest of the crap to the table, Scott poured himself another coffee and walked toward the back edge of the yard, where thorny-vined roses climbed an eight-foot wooden privacy fence. He lit his second-to-last cigarette and fought the urge to test the barrier by jumping to grab the stockade-point tips. He couldn't do that and hang on to his coffee, and running wouldn't fill his stomach.

Even this early, the sun had burned off the dew, but it was going to steam with humidity later. Quinn's was comfortable thanks to the central air unit humming away at one corner of the house. Not that Scott was staying—assuming anyone asked him. He'd had enough of people who claimed to be helping. There was always a catch.

"Put it out and come eat," Eli called.

Scott tapped the end gently against a fence post and tucked the remaining half away for later.

From the first mouthful, he was fucked. He ate like a starving dog, unable to hide it, doing everything but burying his face in the plate. When he thought he'd puke if he shoveled in another slice of buttered toast, he finally faced their stares.

"Thanks. Good breakfast."

Eli smirked at him. "Glad you liked it. So now that you've got something in your stomach, what's your sob story?"

Scott glared at Jamie, then shrugged. "Don't have one. Thanks for the food, but—"

"But bullshit." Eli cut him off. "I get it. You're a total badass. You don't need anyone. Now that we're clear on that, explain why Jamie found you living in your car."

Scott tightened his jaw and stared at his empty plate.

Eli sighed. "Silver, Marco, and I were all thrown out by our families for being queer."

"Yeah, well, my mom left before I even knew what my dick was for, let alone how I wanted to use it," Scott found himself saying.

"Okay." Eli leaned back in his chair and sucked down some coffee. "But that wasn't this week. Jamie said you work as a mechanic."

"Yeah. I did. All the good it did me." What the fuck. They wanted to hear it, fine. "About four years ago, some lawyer guy tracks me down. He says he's bringing a lawsuit about this placement for kids I was at until I ran away at sixteen. The lawyer says he's got a couple other dudes that were there to join in."

"Suing for what?" Quinn said.

"Abuse, neglect, living conditions."

"Sexual abuse?" Eli leaned forward.

"Nah. Improper restraints. Mostly it was about these punishment lockdown rooms. So anyway, it was me and five other guys who had been at St. Bennie's. The lawyer said we'd be getting millions."

Scott's mocking laugh at how stupid he'd been burned his throat, and he tossed off the last of his lukewarm second cup.

"Whatever. I got thirty grand."

"And you bought the Mustang." Jamie sounded like he'd just lined up all the pieces.

"Yup. Of course, the next time someone tracked me down, it was the fucking IRS. How the fuck did I know I had to pay taxes on it? Bastards garnish half my paychecks with the penalties and shit. Last time I switched jobs, I got behind in rent and I just couldn't catch up. Course, being fired didn't help." Scott shrugged. "So then I got evicted and didn't want to wait for the sheriff."

Jamie leaned his arms on the table. "When was that? What did the notice say?"

"That I owed more'n I make in two months when I do have a job. So I left. It wasn't that great of an apartment."

"Why the fuck didn't you call me?" Jamie demanded. "I'd have told you to stay put. Evictions aren't that easy."

"So he can just go back?" Eli said.

Jamie shook his head. "Not once he abandoned the place. They'll have changed the locks, sold anything he left behind."

"Just a half-dead coffee maker and a chair I grabbed off a curb. Had a Murphy bed." The Mustang was all Scott had that mattered anyway.

"You find another job yet?" The way Jamie was looking at Scott turned his full stomach sour.

Like Jamie wasn't the kind to mouth off to some asshole. Of course, he had a badge to back him up. "Been looking." Scott shoved another piece of toast in his mouth.

"Why were you fired?"

"Difference of opinion," Scott said through his mouthful.

"Yeah, I bet." Jamie snorted.

Eli drummed fingers tipped with black-painted nails on the table. "So what we need is a cash-only job, preferably with minimal human contact, and a bed until you can get caught up."

"I'm not crawling back to that shitty apartment."

"So don't," Eli snapped back.

"What do you care?" Because Scott knew damned well there was always an angle.

"You got some better plan?"

Scott didn't so he shut his mouth, but sooner or later they'd want something.

"The shelter?" Quinn suggested.

Eli rolled his eyes. Again. "He's gotta be almost thirty."

"I'm twenty-seven."

"See?" Eli said as Jamie talked over him. "Shelter isn't close to being cleared for habitation. Shit-ton of interior work to do still."

"What do you think of modeling?" Eli turned to Scott.

Here it was. "And all I have to do is take my clothes off?"

"Well, just your shirt." Eli studied Scott's tattoo sleeve. "One of my online friends is a writer. Wants a tattooed cover model for his next book." He flashed a grin. "Elijah married a senator's kid or something. He can afford us both." Eli tapped his chin. "Six hundred for an hour or so sound good?"

"Just my shirt off?"

Eli leaned close to whisper in his ear. "Hon, you and I both know why I'm not interested in getting in your pants." He paused and then, on a barely audible breath, he whispered, "Bottom boy."

Scott wished he could hide the heat in his face as Jamie and Quinn stared at him, though he was sure they couldn't have heard.

Jamie pushed his chair back with a scrape of iron on stone. "If you've got this under control, I'm—"

"Going to bring Scott home?" Eli finished with a bright smile.

"What?"

"We don't have any more room and you're always at Gavin's. Scott can stay at your place."

"I am not always at Gavin's."

A thin jingle was the only warning before a little flop-eared brown-and-white dog raced around the corner of the house and vaulted onto Jamie's lap. It began licking his jaw.

The sight of Jamie with some scrap of fluffy overbred dog on his lap made Scott laugh. A second later, Gavin followed the path the dog had taken but stopped before landing in Jamie's lap.

"Got your text." He put a hand on Jamie's shoulder. "Annabelle and I missed you joining us this morning."

Eli grinned across the table. "Gavin, has anyone ever told you you have exquisite timing?"

"Do NOT smoke in my fucking house." Jamie led the way into the hall.

"Yeah, I heard it the first thirty times. Like you still don't have tobacco stains on your ceiling."

"I'm getting around to repainting it. Fucking stucco."

When Eli had delivered his announcement about where Scott should stay, Jamie had pointed out that Walmart was usually pretty good about letting people sleep in their cars in their lots. But two seconds later, he'd caved with a sigh. The pressure might have come from Quinn's arched brows or the way Gavin's thumb rubbed the side of Jamie's neck, but Scott suspected the deciding factor was the steady stare from Eli, who apparently had everyone's balls in his pocket.

"For how long?" Scott had wanted to know after Jamie gave in.

"Till you find someplace else," Eli had said before anyone else could get a word in. "Given the company, I'll bet you want to get on that." He'd winked at Scott.

"Fuck you, brat." But Jamie's response had sounded like he was only going through the motions.

Now Jamie shoved some towels in Scott's hands and said, "And for fuck's sake, shower before you sit on anything. I gotta work again tonight so I'm going to crash. Whatever you do, do it quiet." He stopped in the doorway to his bedroom. "What garages have you tried?"

"Jerry's and the Best Care Auto in Overlea."

Jamie frowned and drummed his fingers on the doorframe. "Try Two Bros in Catonsville. How pissed was Dressler?"

Scott thought of the dark red face under thin wisps of hair, spit flying out with his words. "Kind of foamed at the mouth."

Jamie shook his head. "You know how I was saying to pick your battles? Might be a good time to learn." Jamie punched Scott's shoulder and disappeared behind the bedroom door.

Two Bros wasn't hiring. They told him to try A-plus Air and Radiators, but *they* said the summer had been slow and they'd had to let people go. Scott smoked three cigarettes as he took the long way around the city back to Jamie's place in Dundalk, hating himself for driving outside the loop just so he could cut through Timonium. Like suddenly knowing Liam was there made it home again.

Scott had made two folded halves of a peanut butter sandwich—Liam style—before realizing it. He didn't smash up Jamie's plate, just took the sandwich outside and took two bites before starting to feed the rest to some bold squirrels and sparrows while sitting on Jamie's back steps and smoking. He'd have helped himself to some scotch too, but Jamie didn't have anything stronger than light beer.

Not that Scott needed a drink. He'd lived just fine for years with the hole Liam leaving had made, let it scab over, buried the thought of it, moved the fuck on. Ten minutes spread over two conversations shouldn't have changed that. Sure as shit shouldn't have made him feel fucking worse. Liam was old news.

After one last bite for himself, Scott threw the last hunk of sandwich to the skinniest squirrel lurking at the edge of the driveway, who snatched it and ran up the cement wall of Jamie's garage and over the roof with three bigger bastards in hot pursuit. *Hope you get to laugh in their faces, dude.*

Next morning, Scott lay on an air mattress staring at the yellow ceiling through early light when Jamie banged on the door to the guest room, cop style.

"Better not be jerking off on my sheets."

"The fuck do you want? Thought you had today off. Go spend it trading places with your rich boyfriend's other lapdog."

Jamie slammed the door open. "The Queer Angels Miracle Network came through. You got a job." He waved his phone at Scott as he struggled free of the squishy vinyl.

"What kind?"

"Barback. Some place called Schim's Tavern, up in Charles Village. Near Johns Hopkins."

Now on his feet, Scott grabbed for the phone, but Jamie jerked it away.

"Checked it out. Kind of a dive. Some noise complaints when they have live music." Jamie's phone buzzed and he swiped at it. "Go up today after two. Ask for Chai. And don't give her any shit about her name." He frowned. "Tell her the Rooster sent you and don't argue with her." He looked at Scott. "If they're dealing out of there, I don't want to fucking know. Watch your ass."

That might have been good enough for Jamie, but Scott hadn't stayed alive this long just taking other people's words for things. While Jamie was in the shower, Scott snuck into Jamie's room and scooped up the phone from where it was charging on his nightstand. The code was easy enough to crack. Since the phone looked new, Scott put in the date Jamie's dad had died. Dates had always stuck in Scott's head. January 10, last time he saw his mom. October 22, night they called him about his sister.

September 14, the day Liam left him.

Scott was a little disappointed that Jamie's boyfriend was just listed under "Gavin" and not something Scott could mock him for like "Sugarlips." Gavin's texts were the most recent. Scott scrolled up.

If you think the place is okay, here's the rest of the message from Beach. See you in a bit.

The next was a copied image of a text from "Beach."

Apparently this is a covert op. The contact is Chai. Don't make fun of her name. The code is "Rooster sent me." Also, don't disagree with anything she says. You have to tell me how this all turns out. For my memoirs, of course. Love to Sergeant Boyfriend.

Scott put the phone back on the nightstand and slipped back out of Jamie's room. Whoever Beach was, he sounded like a dick, but Gavin didn't seem like a guy who would fuck someone over without good reason, and if Scott had ever met anyone more anti-practical-joke than Jamie, it was news to Scott.

What the hell. It wasn't like he had anything better to do than feed the squirrels.

Chapter Eight

SCHIM'S TAVERN was in an old building on the corner of two side streets. Glass windows in front gave it a look like one of those old corner markets. Before picking a spot for the Mustang, Scott cruised the block. A 7-Eleven on North Howard, some row houses, an abandoned one-story warehouse of some kind. Schim's bricks had been painted blue at some point, but the sun had blistered and faded them on one side. The bar shared an alley with a tire store and a wall with a barber shop that led to more row houses.

There were two bikes, Triumphs, in a spot near the front. Scott took the next spot down, then admired the custom paint on one of the Triumphs' tanks. There was enough wear on both to say they were ridden, not just for show. Scott scanned the signs in the windows and doors for any indication it was an MC hangout. Most of the stickers and posters advertised beer and upcoming bands, but the door had a row of service stickers. One big US veteran eagle sticker next to a POW-MIA emblem, then ones for Korea, Vietnam, Iraq, and Afghanistan.

Everything didn't have to remind him of Liam, but the fucking universe was giving it a damned good shot.

The AC unit sticking out over the front door pissed down his neck, so he stopped pussying around, yanked on the handle, and stepped inside. His eyes took a while to adjust from the bright sun to the dark inside. A long wooden bar with about twenty different taps stretched to his right, the flags on the ceiling matching the stickers on the door. A woman with her hands braced on the lacquered wood peered at him. She had springy orangish curls and pale brown skin covered in freckles. Her eyes looked friendly, but her voice was suspicious. "Can I help you?"

"Yeah. I'm looking for Chai. Here about the barback job."

She came around the end of the bar and studied him. They were alone in the bar except for a guy running a broom across a stage in back.

"How'd you hear about the job?"

Scott felt like an idiot but said, "Uh, the Rooster sent me."

She nodded. "Okay. Here's your interview. Swap out the Doggie Style. My brother Reeve'll show you where to put the empty. Reeve."

The guy on the stage turned and stepped down, moving through a beam of sunlight. There were twice as many freckles across his cheeks as on his sister's. He wore his hair in long dreads, parts dark brown, parts dyed blond and red, all of it pulled back in a ponytail. His eyes, damn. Scott didn't spend a lot of time checking out a dude's face if he wanted to hook up. But Reeve's eyes were stupidly pretty, big and dark with thick lashes that looked like they brushed his high cheekbones. Jesus. Scott wanted to snarl to hide the warmth in his cheeks.

"Barback? Thank Cthulhu. I almost broke my hand this weekend." Reeve's grin made his eyes even prettier.

"Maybe," his sister warned. "He's changing out a keg. Make yourself useful."

Reeve led the way to a hallway and then a door. "It's only eight stairs. I'll help you drag it if you want."

Scott knew a test when one got shoved in his face. "I can handle it."

The cellar was cool, with a cement floor, and not surprisingly smelled like a brewery. There were kegs stacked two high along one wall and liquor cases along the other. A dolly leaned against a keg. The Flying Dog Doggie Style keg was on the bottom row, but Scott hadn't been expecting anything easy.

It wasn't that bad to lift, and he had a momentary thought of hoisting it up the stairs without the dolly, but two steps toward the dolly took care of that stupid idea. He strapped it down with the bungee cords and dragged it up, one step at a time, then wheeled it behind the bar. He'd never set a tap, but looking at the hookup, he figured it out and got them swapped. When he straightened, Chai slapped an application form on the bar in front of him.

He looked down at it, and at the space for his social security number so the fucking IRS could keep peeling away half the eleven dollars an hour he'd be making.

Chai put her hand over the application. "Few house rules you need to know first." She pointed at two pictures behind the bar. "That's my grandfather, Pop Schim."

The one framed pic looked like every Army graduation picture Scott had seen. Another one showed a much older guy working the taps, his right arm a prosthesis that ended in a hook. And all at once Scott got it: "Rooster," like the Alice in Chains song about Vietnam. He wasn't stupid enough to say that out loud.

"If someone toasts him, we all stop and toast him."

Scott nodded.

"Two, no disrespecting other vets. Everybody keeps their politics out of the fucking bar."

"Got it."

"Which is not to say we don't sometimes need help with some stupid motherfucker who needs to get tossed."

"I'm good with that."

Chai gave him a steady look, then snorted a laugh. "Yeah. I bet. Don't do it unless you're asked." She took her hand off the application and handed him a pen.

He stared down at the lines and boxes, tapping the pen. He needed a job, right? What the hell difference did it make if he was never going to get out from under that fucking tax bill?

Chai's hand covered the application again. "Problem?"

"Nah."

"Where'd you serve?" Chai asked.

Scott could give two shits about what people thought was honorable or right. He'd never been able to afford that kind of bullshit. But this wasn't something he could lie about.

"I didn't."

"Fine. You don't have to talk about it."

She pulled the application away.

Well, so much for that.

But Chai didn't throw him out. "Sometimes we get volunteers. We reimburse them for their expenses in cash."

"Like what kind of cash?"

"You got a place to stay?"

Scott shrugged.

Chai folded her arms. "I got a cot in a storeroom. We could use the nighttime security. You give me 3:00 p.m. till closing. You get the spot to crash and seventy bucks a night. But you drink our stock and you're out. Deal?"

It wasn't minimum wage, but without the garnishment, he'd get to keep everything he made, maybe enough save up enough to get an apartment again.

"Um"—he dragged a hand through the flop of hair he hadn't bothered to glue up—"I drive my old neighbor to the store on Mondays."

"Lucky you. We're closed Mondays."

Swear to God, if one more person tried to tell him how fucking lucky he was….

"You got a name?" Chai stuck out her hand.

"Scott."

"Reeve'll show you the cot. Don't park in the back on Tuesdays. Deliveries. And hey, Scott." She poked the pocket of his shirt where his cigarettes were. "You fall asleep smoking and set this place on fire, you better hope you die in it. It'll be a whole lot less painful than what I'll do to you if you live."

The room was narrow, little more than double the width of the ancient Army cot against the wall. There was an industrial sink at the back, shelves stuffed with paper goods and glassware along the other wall.

Reeve shut the door and leaned against it.

Scott arched the brow that had the scar from some asshole's ring his first time in holding.

Under the freckles, Reeve's cheeks flushed. Yeah, the guy had sexy eyes and full soft lips, but Scott could honestly say he wasn't in the mood.

Reeve looked away. "Uh, yeah, I'm not gay, more like flexible, you know, but—"

Scott put a palm on the door near Reeve's shoulder and leaned. Heat licked across his balls from the way Reeve looked up at him. Not that Scott would do anything about it. He needed this job. "The kind of flexible where I suck your dick now but then we don't ever talk about it?"

"No," Reeve blurted, then swallowed and licked his lips. He probably wasn't even twenty, and prettier than Scott's usual taste, but there was something about the guy that made it hard not to pay attention. "I'm not saying that," Reeve said. "I—saw you looking at me and I wanted—just I've got other stuff going on right now, so not that I don't, but not right now."

Scott had to bite the inside of his cheek to keep from laughing. He pushed away from the wall. "That's good. Because I'm afraid your sister would run up on me if I touched you."

"Run up on you? Dude, where'd you grow up?"

Scott shrugged. "Hell."

"Oh, local? Me too." Reeve offered a fist to bump.

Scott shook his head and bumped back.

THE THIRD morning at Schim's, Scott woke up with a leg slung over the side of the cot and his face smushed against a wall. A not completely unpleasant buzz ran along his jaw. As his brain started firing on all cylinders, he worked out what was causing it. Deep throbbing bass. Not from the street but through the walls.

The stage at the back of the bar. Bands. Right.

Oh shit. What time was it?

He lunged for his phone and the cot flipped, sending him crashing onto the industrial cement floor. It hurt like fuck, but he'd rather damage himself than crush his cigarettes or even his cheapass prepay phone.

The bass stopped.

Christ, it was only 11:00 a.m.

Scott hadn't managed to drop off before the too-damned-chirpy sparrows nesting under the eaves had woken up to bitch at each other over whose turn it was to feed the kids. He got himself and the cot upright. The music started again. Not just bass this time. Full melody, tickling his memory, but again it cut off just before Scott could name it.

Some rock band practicing or tuning. Based on names like Purple Suck and Rage Mist littering the posters and stickers he'd seen in the back hall and men's room, he'd figured the bands that played at Schim's were either metal or punk.

As he moved to the sink to wash the sweat and stink off him best he could with a bar towel, more tuning and feedback echoed through the pipes. By the time Scott went into the men's room to piss, they'd moved on to playing a few bars.

"We need it dirtier for Mac's pickup." Reeve's voice. He had a weird nasal hum Scott could recognize even on the speakers. More strummed bars. "Yeah. Let's try that."

Scott was curious, but he also really wanted to go out to smoke. If he stuck his head into the bar, he could see himself getting roped into being a roadie. They'd probably be setting up for a while.

The band crashed into the opening of an old Puddle of Mudd song. Just the first six notes sparked an explosion of memory. Hell, how many times had he and Liam fucked to that song?

Even more reason to go outside. Except if he didn't listen to the rest of the song, it was like letting the memories win. Maybe the band would fuck it up. Maybe Reeve would sing it in that nasally voice and Scott would be free of it. Fuck if he was going to suffer the damned earworm all day.

The voice that rumbled in on the first verse made the hair stand up all over Scott's arms and neck. Gaining strength, the singer crooned, and Scott swore his 'hawk would lift on its own.

He rounded the corner into the bar.

Liam, lips close enough to suck off the damned microphone, dipped to a smoky, throaty whisper before slamming into the chorus.

Liam tore into the melody, sang the words he'd breathed into Scott's ear, as deep into him as Liam's dick had ever been in his ass. The past swallowed Scott up so completely he could feel it in his stomach. The shuddery tension, the fight in him finally surrendering under Liam's body holding him down, giving him a safe place to let go and come apart because Liam would always be there to look out for him.

Now Liam was up there in front of Scott, hands working the neck and strings of the guitar cradled against him as he issued the same sexy promise in the lyrics, then let the pain of loss scream through.

Scott had spent six years killing and burying every stupid soft thing Liam had dragged out. Hope and love and belonging. Goddamn the bastard for showing up everywhere in Scott's life like they were still sharing it.

"Fuck you." Scott whispered it, because he didn't even want to give Liam the knowledge that Scott gave a shit, that it mattered if Liam could stand up there and sing that song in some cover band, share those feelings between them with random drunk people swaying along with the music.

But the words fell into the lull between the chorus and the second verse, and Liam turned and stared right at Scott.

So he said it again and left.

Chapter Nine

LIAM JOLTED toward the edge of the stage as Scott disappeared. He wanted to jump down and run after him. Amp lines and his leg held him back. By the time Reeve, Dev, and Mac lurched to a stop, Liam was carefully settling the Epiphone Casino that Reeve had loaned him in its stand on the stage.

"Exactly what the fuck is he doing here?" Deon shoved away from the table where he'd been sitting.

"Some fucking closed rehearsal, man," Dev muttered from behind his kit.

Reeve looked from Liam to Deon. "He works here." Reeve slipped the strap of his bass off his neck. "Didn't you—"

"Can we take five, please?" Liam would explain things to Deon. He didn't need to hear it from Reeve.

"Yeah, whatever. I need to get right." Mac jerked free of her Gibson.

"Yeah, yeah. I just want to get through at least one set before we all take off, all right?"

As Liam stepped down from the stage, Dev started complaining. "Reeve, seriously, man, I'm not sure this is going to work out."

But Dev's issues were going to have to wait until Liam got the rest of this sorted out.

Deon wasn't waiting this time. "So your ex just happens to work here?"

"Can we wait so Reeve doesn't end up writing a song about this?" Liam tried humor, but from the look on Deon's face, that wasn't going to fly. "C'mon." He sighed and led Deon through the side door to the alley.

Deon shook Liam's arm away as soon as they were outside. "What the fuck is going on?"

"First of all, you know goddamned well where I have been the last four nights—and the days too, since you drive me to work."

Liam had run out of excuses for avoiding Deon on Monday. But the sex was so perfunctory it hadn't made either of them feel any better.

It had been a big shock running into Scott. But he hadn't wanted to make Deon overthink things. Even if Liam wanted to get back together,

Scott was never going to forgive him, assuming Liam ever had a chance to explain in a way that didn't end up with them tearing bigger holes in each other. He just needed time to sort himself out.

Deon's eyes were full of the same hurt they'd held when Liam found himself running out of excuses to stay at his mom's.

The look dragged out an instant apology. "I know you didn't accuse me of cheating. I'm sorry."

"So am I making you be somewhere you don't want to be?"

"No." Liam would make it be true. He reached out to squeeze Deon's hand. "I want to be with you. Look, I didn't even know Scott would take the job."

Deon jerked his hand back. "You asked the Schimikowskis to hire him?"

"Not exactly."

"What exactly?" Deon folded his arms.

Liam forced his own body language to stay open. Both of them getting defensive wouldn't fix anything.

"I have to explain this first. My mom—when Scott and I were together—my mom was holding down a job, but she was using. I was out of high school, but technically she still had me as a dependent and I couldn't get much financial aid. And I didn't want to live with her. Scott worked from two in the morning to six at night so I could go to school full-time."

"People make their own choices, Li. That doesn't make you responsible for him."

Like Liam hadn't heard that a million times, from the VA therapist to his mom to Deon. Maybe they had a point, but Liam couldn't let Scott sell his dream car without doing something. Not after Scott had worked so hard on Liam's dream. A dream that Liam hadn't even believed in by then. But that wasn't the point, though. Scott had stood by him; Liam needed to pay him back.

Liam worked his jaw. "I know that. But when I found out he needed a job—"

"Was that before or after he punched you in the face?"

Fuck. Liam winced. He should have known Deon would figure that out. "What I'm trying to say is that I needed to restore the balance. I know you don't think I owed him, but I did. And if I'm going to move forward—"

"And I'm supposed to ignore that he punched you and that you've obviously been talking to him since you 'ran into him' two weeks ago."

Deon unfolded his arms enough to add the air quotes and went right back to looking closed off and pissed.

"I didn't. I haven't called him or texted him or even seen him since you were there. I don't even have his number." It was the honest-to-God truth and Liam put all his conviction into it.

"Right. So you told him about a job here how? Skywriting?"

"No. I figured out we had a mutual acquaintance and passed it on that way."

Deon looked up like he was seeking divine patience to deal with Liam, and Liam's own temper snapped.

"So you want to believe that I'm fucking you and living with my mom and somehow sneaking out to see Scott when I have to be driven everywhere? That's your takeaway?"

Deon's shoulders sagged. "No. But I think codependence is a hard habit to break. And with him around—"

"I don't work here, Deon."

"No, your band just rehearses here and plays here."

"Exactly. Christ, I haven't spent a minute alone since I graduated basic training."

"You want to be alone?" The shock of pain in Deon's eyes went right through Liam's chest.

"No, baby." Liam stepped up to him. "That's not what I'm saying. I'm with you. I want a future with you. So I needed to balance out the past. That's all."

Deon had been with Liam through the worst time of his life and fallen in love with him anyway. Deon was hope and life when Liam had nothing left. The idea of leaving that support behind terrified him. He just needed time to sort through what seeing Scott again meant.

Liam slid his arms around Deon's waist and Deon let him, resting his head on Liam's for an instant before pulling away.

"You're either lying to me or lying to yourself, and I don't know which is worse, but I can't do this right now." Deon turned and walked away. He was almost to the street when he turned back. "Damn it." He rubbed a hand over his face. "Except I need to drive you home."

"Reeve can give me a lift."

"On his bike?"

Liam shook his head. "He has the van. Go. But—" Liam swallowed. "—call me later, okay, so I know—just call me."

Deon nodded and disappeared around the corner.

"Trouble in paradise?"

Liam spun to face the sunny end of the alley. After squinting into the glare, he made out a figure leaning on a car. Scott, ass against the hood of his Shelby Mustang, cigarette at his lips.

"Fuck off," Liam said, but he couldn't put any heat into it.

"So I guess I've got you to thank for this job."

"You're welcome."

"I didn't ask for your help." Scott dropped his butt and crushed it under a work boot. He never used to bother, just let them smolder like he didn't care if the world burned.

"You're still welcome." Liam should go in now before Dev decided Liam was going to flake out like their last lead singer. Instead he found himself saying, "Thought the bar didn't open until three."

"It doesn't." Scott stepped out of the glare and into the alley, forcing Liam to blink hard to make out his features again. "I'm staying here."

"In the bar?" That was a stupid question. That was what Scott had said.

"Yup." Scott was only a foot away now. "So look at you. The next Dave Grohl."

Warmth flooded Liam's chest. Scott loved the Foo Fighters, which made it one hell of a compliment. "Nah. Not a drummer." Though Liam had never tried. He'd learned guitar on the other side of the world, begged Ross to teach him. At first to fight the terminal hurry-up-and-wait drag of time on the base, but from the start, there'd been a rightness to the way the strings felt under his sand-dry fingers. The brand name, Seagull, scrawled on the head made him think of home, the endless scream of gulls and the smell of water.

The basics had been easy, which pissed Ross off no end. Just like when he taught Liam backgammon and Liam ended up kicking his ass all the time, until Ross wouldn't even play with him. Music, though. Mad as Ross had been that Liam picked it up so fast, neither one of them could get enough of it. Ross offering blues and country, while Liam worked out the chords to the rock songs he'd sung along to a million times. That was how he tried to remember Ross, and most of the time it was. Except when he dreamed.

Scott jerked him back to the present. "Still, got some pipes on you."

"You've heard me sing in the shower." And in bed. Of all the covers for Scott to have heard....

"Yeah, but not with a mic." Scott was close enough to touch.

Liam's body moved without him thinking, almost leaning in. Muscle memory. A trigger from the familiar scent of menthol. Of Scott.

Get a grip. You'll be lucky if he doesn't take another swing at you. Out loud Liam said, "So are we talking to each other now?"

"I'm not the one who left. Or the one with a boyfriend."

As Scott stretched a hand toward him, Liam jerked back.

Scott sneered. "Just getting the door, dude."

"Oh, right. Scott?"

"Standing the fuck in front of you, Liam."

As if any part of Liam wasn't aware of it. As if they hadn't fallen back into teasing and fighting like the past six years hadn't happened. "Can we call a truce, maybe?"

Scott stared at him with the same silent intensity that had turned Liam's crank since he was fifteen.

"Truce? Sure." Scott's voice was so flat Liam wasn't sure whether Scott was being sarcastic.

Liam decided to take it at face value. "So, since when the hell are you friends with a cop?"

Chapter Ten

ONE THING Liam was learning about music was that when they got it—not just right but perfect—he could feel it in his spine, a shock that reverberated his nuts and was damned close to sex. They had it tonight. The whole damned set, from Mac killing the riffs in the Seether opener, through the original stuff they had tucked in where the push from Reeve's grinding bass drove Liam to match it, they finally fucking had it. Even Dev couldn't complain about how this rehearsal had gone.

The audience had been on their feet since the third song and screamed applause as the echo faded. Liam shook sweat out of his eyes. Too bad the house only consisted of Reeve's grandmother and sister.

And Scott dragging a mop over the floor. But Liam had felt him watching. Despite Scott's claim that he was living at the bar, for the last couple days he'd been conspicuously absent from their morning rehearsals. Maybe since Reeve had insisted on squeezing this one in at 3:00 a.m. on a Sunday morning, Scott hadn't been able to avoid hearing them.

Chai grabbed bottled water from the glass-front cooler behind the bar.

"Water? Would you serve water if Eddie Vedder brought Pearl Jam here?" Reeve lifted his strap over his head. "Didn't you hear us? Where's the Cristal?"

"Bar's closed." Chai slammed the service gate down behind her.

"Light beer?" Reeve suggested.

"Can't serve after two," Mrs. Schimikowski reminded them.

"Can't serve you anyway, baby boy." Chai thunked the waters on the edge of the stage.

"C'mon, it's only eight more days." Reeve dropped on his ass next to the offering, swinging his legs as he uncapped a water and chugged it.

Liam tried not to miss shit that would never be possible again, but he missed being able to do that. Missed the ease, the fluid motion, the not having to worry about being betrayed by an alien limb. He felt Scott's eyes on him, as if Scott knew what Liam had been thinking, and ducked away, sliding his fingers along his strings, glancing at the scars from the skin graft on his forearm. At least he hadn't lost a hand. What if he'd been stuck jerking off left-handed for the rest of his life?

It was the kind of thing Deon said was unproductive overdramatic thinking, but Scott had always known that sometimes you had to laugh about the shitty things in life. He'd just smirk and tell Liam to look for a Fleshlight prosthetic attachment. Liam looked back out into the bar, hoping to catch Scott's eye, but he was gone.

Liam limped down the two steps to the floor and went looking for him.

"Hey." Reeve chucked a water at him. "Need to keep those vocal cords lubricated."

Liam caught it, but the unexpected motion fucked his balance enough to start him wobbling. Like he needed the reminder right now.

"Oops," Reeve said.

"Yeah, sorry, my brother's a clueless idiot." Chai folded her arms.

Joining Reeve at the stage edge, Liam uncapped his water. Thinking he could share a laugh with Scott was a stupid idea. Scott had accepted the truce, he wasn't openly hostile, but that easy place between them wasn't ever coming back. Liam should be happy with what he'd salvaged from the past and focus on the future.

He and Deon were talking, at least enough for Deon to express disbelief at a 3:00 a.m. rehearsal being the only time they could all be together with the amps. Liam had said he could come along, and when Deon had declined, Liam had suggested he have Reeve drop him off afterward at Deon's apartment so he could make an up-close inspection of Liam's instruments. Liam had meant it as funny seduction, but Deon had taken it with a huff and then silence. Liam wasn't looking forward to waking up the house when he had to go back to his mom's.

"Come up with a new name yet, or are you planning on being the surprise guest at your own return this week?" Chai kicked her brother's foot. "I still think Bag of Dicks is perfect. Mac liked it."

Mrs. S. rolled her eyes.

"Blow me," Dev spat out as he came to grab a water.

Chai smiled and said sweetly, "Kiss my go-to-hell ass."

"Anytime you want to shine that full moon in my face, babe. I'm ready. Sit right down." From his position on the stage, Dev leaned over their heads and made a slurping motion.

"Blow the Moon Out." It popped into Liam's head, words coming together in a fragment of something he remembered sung at a campfire. "I mean, as a band name."

The silence that followed made him redden. He shrugged. "Just an idea."

"No, wait." Reeve ran to the bar, vaulting up to lie on his chest and reach under. He scribbled on a napkin for a minute, then brought it over to show them. "Picture this much better, jagged black cracks in the moon, red letters with the name across it. Blow the Moon."

Dev grabbed it. "Fuck yeah. The merchandising will be hot."

"I'll get Mac." Liam pushed away from the stage.

Reeve called after him. "You going to be ready to put 'Take on Me' in the second set?"

Reeve had turned the '80s electronic pop song into a nu metal opera. It really pushed Liam's range, and for some of it he had to shift into falsetto. He had no problem screaming and growling—though he did close his eyes—but this song was hard. It was one thing when it came from feeling the lyrics and the music. This was technical, and he found himself putting a hand on his diaphragm like in the YouTube videos he'd been studying.

"I mean, if you fuck it up, it's just us, right?" Reeve pushed.

It wasn't the idea of an audience. Though it hadn't been like joining a band, he'd done open mic a few times before he'd enlisted, lying to Scott about it, claiming the need to hit the library. It had been an escape from all that expectation, from the weight of Scott shrugging off those insane work hours because Liam was going to be a rich doctor someday. From thinking he could fix his mom's life, then make it up to Scott somehow.

He'd tried being John Mayer back then, crooning a high tenor, so what was the difference now?

Scott hadn't been in the audience then.

"Yeah," Liam said. "Let's try it."

LIAM PUSHED open the door to the men's room and called over his shoulder. "Let your grandmother and Chai take the van. I'll be fine on your bike." They were all hyped after the last set, which had gone even better than the first, but now it was almost 5:00 a.m. "Just need to piss first."

He stopped just inside the door, staring into the mirror on the side wall. There was just a small circle of reflection left from the application of band stickers, and Scott's face stared back. Liam hadn't seen Scott since going in search of Mac. She and Scott had been sitting in the Mustang, sweet smoke drifting out of the open windows.

Slowly, Scott spat into the sink and went back to brushing his teeth. "I—uh—need to piss."

"Go ahead." Scott tipped his head toward the urinal trough. "Not like I haven't seen it."

There was a single stall, wide enough to be ADA compliant, but that would be stupid. After all, one of Liam's first PT goals had been to be able to piss standing up again.

"Right." Liam's voice was steadier than he felt.

Scrub, swish, spit.

Liam stepped to the trough and unzipped.

Scrub, swish, spit.

They could have been back in that tiny apartment bathroom, where getting to the toilet around someone at the sink meant a step into the shower stall or a grind across his back.

You've pissed in front of him hundreds of times, thousands. Do it and go, Liam told himself, but although he was aimed, he hadn't been able to unlock his muscle. "So, you really live here, huh?"

"Yup." *Slurp. Spit.*

"Do you just unroll a sleeping bag on the bar or what?" Liam stared into the drain.

The sink shut off. "Cot in a storage room. Chai likes having the extra security."

Footsteps. Scott would go now and Liam could finally download his bladder.

Instead Scott leaned against the door, and Liam shot him a sideways glare.

"What?" He didn't need to start thinking about anything else he and Scott had done in that tiny bathroom. Or sometimes anyplace with a door.

"I don't get it."

Liam tucked himself away and zipped, then turned to face Scott. Anticipation made Liam's skin tingle, like the tension building before a kiss. "So ask."

"Why when you can sing like that you bothered with anything else." Scott didn't wait for an answer, pulling open the door. "Be sure to wash your hands. Wouldn't want to catch anything that fucked up your voice."

Chapter Eleven

SCOTT WOVE through the Friday-night crowd with the dolly and a fresh keg of Doggie Style.

Chai intercepted him. "Getting close to maxed. Need you to help with crowd control at the door."

Liam's band was playing a set tonight, opening for Charm City Cyanide, who had a big local following and a demo out. He skirted the merchandise table and joined Ford, the bouncer working the door.

"Gonna be pissed when we close the line." Ford's bald head gleamed in the neon as he leaned down to talk to Scott.

"Fifteen more." Mrs. S. was taking the twenty-dollar cover and clicking a handheld counter.

Scott took up a post near the opposite door. There were still about thirty people waiting to get in and the line had turned into a mass of people pushing.

"Hey. I know him," a voice called, and Scott saw Eli slithering between two T-shirted hipsters with knit hats—in August—and long beards. "Scott."

A tall blond was behind him. "Who *don't* you know?"

"Who doesn't he *think* he knows?" said a guy with a dark goatee who had the hipsters muttering "Not cool, dude" as he shoved through.

"Can you get us in?" Eli wore long black board shorts and a black vest over a black mesh tank top in a club-ska mash-up that somehow worked on him.

Scott owed Eli a favor. He didn't owe the other two. Despite their jeans and band T-shirts, they looked a little too Abercrombie for Schim's and CCC.

"I'm doing a review for the *Charming Rag*," Goatee said, like that was supposed to impress Scott.

"So why didn't you call ahead?"

Schim's didn't take reservations, of course, but Chai and Mrs. S. were probably on top of local press.

"I like to get the audience feel."

Scott snorted. "And who's this?" He jerked a thumb at the blond.

"Kellan *Brooks*." Eli pointed at one of the neon signs. "Brooks Blast Energy Drinks."

Scott really doubted that connection. No way did the blond look rich enough for that shit.

Ford was running a pocket black light over a license as an obviously underaged girl bit her lip in front of him. The hipsters were already in. Scott checked in with Mrs. S., who held up five fingers.

"C'mon. But those two pay the cover," he told Eli.

Ford handed the license back to the girl and shook his head. A guy got into it with Mrs. S., claiming he'd given her a fifty and not a twenty, and Ford went to loom and flash his flesh-covered guns, so Scott took over the door. Eli and his friends disappeared into the crowd.

Later, Liam and his band were onstage adjusting their amps when Scott got sent down with a list of liquor to bring up. Rushing back up with the assorted case, he hipped the cellar door shut only to have Eli bounce off him.

"I've been looking for you. Jamie said he found you a job and you disappeared, and I swear to God if he's lying because he threw you out, I'll shave his balls with broken glass."

The scary thing was, Scott didn't doubt Eli would. If not with broken glass, then with his black-painted nails.

"It's fine," Scott yelled over the opening chords. Puddle of Mudd again. Fuck. His face heated, though there was less anger with the memory now. Scott was trying to keep his distance, but Liam was always around. And it was getting harder and harder to remember why looking for his crooked smile again was a bad idea. "I gotta deliver this." He nudged Eli with the case.

"I'll find you later." Eli slipped into the crowd.

Chai reached for the case as soon Scott was close. "Go help Tony with stage security."

Scott looked at the crowd in front of the stage.

Chai grabbed his sleeve and pointed. "Go out through the hall and come in the side. Tony'll let you in."

Tony was dealing with two guys who were whining about just having gone out for a smoke, but he stepped aside to let Scott in. This close to the speakers, everything vibrated with the sound, his bones, his fillings, even his eyes in their sockets. He swept a glance over the crowd. No mosh pit, though Chai had told him that would probably happen with Charm City Cyanide. Right then the crowd was still warming up, most of them still yelling in each other's ears and drinking from their plastic cups.

A sudden crash of percussion and then a much faster beat drove against Scott's ears. Rapid notes he couldn't even manage with an air guitar dragged the crowd's focus back to the stage. The press of their attention beat at him like a rush of exhaust from a diesel, and when Liam turned his voice loose, they were hooked.

They started nodding to the beat, an occasional fist or rock horns getting thrown up. It had nothing to do with Scott, but pride hummed through him, as sweet as any he felt when he made an engine sing. He knew damned well if he wasn't working, he'd be pressed up against the stage, staring up at Liam like the sexy rock god he was.

And shit. That daydreaming made him miss seeing the lead-up to some asshole vaulting up onto the stage. Scott leaped after him, and the greasy-haired fucker avoided him by crashing into Liam.

They both went down. By the time Scott hauled the motherfucker off Liam, the band had stopped playing, and the crowd was snarling.

"Hey," the guy yelled, despite Scott's grip on his neck. "The singer's a gimp."

Rage, sweet and pure and familiar, had Scott shifting his grip to a front headlock, ready to smash his knee into the fucker's face. Except....

Except Schim's wasn't a bad place to work and he really didn't want to start over again. As satisfying as making this waste of oxygen pay would be, it would probably fuck up the rest of Liam's set.

"Scott, I'm okay," Liam said from somewhere behind, but Scott had already transferred his grip to an arm bar and the would-be stage diver wasn't struggling much.

Tony appeared and grabbed the other side, and together they hustled him out the side door.

"Just got yourself banned, asshole," Tony told him as they let him go in the alley.

"It's part of the show," the guy yelled back.

"Not here." Tony gave the guy a shove.

Schim's had signs over the stage, in the bathrooms, over the bar. *No stage-diving, crowd-surfing, or crowd-killing. Final warning.*

The music roared back to life behind them. Scott made sure the guy kept walking. At the sidewalk, Scott grabbed a fistful of T-shirt and got in his face. "Next time you wanna call someone a gimp, stop and think about how close I came to making you one." He let him go with a shove and followed Tony back inside.

SCOTT'S HEAD rang long after Charm City Cyanide started packing away their gear, even when he stood outside blowing a cloud of smoke into the humid air.

Eli appeared out of nowhere and plucked the cigarette from Scott's fingers as he brought it back to his mouth. "Ew. Menthol." Eli handed it back.

"You're welcome." Scott nodded at the other two, Brooks Blast and Goatee. "What did you think?" He didn't know how many people still read the local arts paper, but a good write-up couldn't hurt Liam's band.

"Standard fare," Goatee said, and Brooks lightly punched his shoulder. After an eye roll, Goatee added, "The opening act had some promise, but they need to settle on a sound."

"Their singer, holy shit. If I had range like that—" Brooks shook his head.

Did Brooks Blast Energy Drinks do sponsoring? "Are you really…?" Scott jerked a thumb back at the neon.

"Yeah." Though the blond looked embarrassed about it. "But if you're looking for a free case or something, you gotta know, my old man and I aren't really on speaking terms."

"Oh." Scott dragged in another lungful.

"What's in it for you?" Eli nudged Scott sharply enough to force a cough.

"Nothing," Scott sputtered. "I like—they play here a lot."

"Doesn't hurt that the lead singer is hot as hell," Brooks put in.

An acidic spurt of jealousy clawed Scott's belly. He couldn't stop it, even if he told himself he had no business feeling like that. At best, he and Liam were just friends. It was up to Deon to protect Liam from starry-eyed groupies. Deon, who had been very obviously not here tonight, the first night Blow the Moon played to a packed bar. He hadn't been here for their solo debut two days ago either. Or picked Liam up. Not that Scott was paying attention. He just happened to be outside smoking a lot.

"Though I'd really like to talk to the lead guitar," Brooks went on over Scott's thoughts. "She was amazing." Brooks looked at Scott like he could make the whole band appear out of thin air.

"Mac," Scott said. "I haven't seen her since they wrapped their set."

"Who writes their original stuff?" Goatee asked.

"Reeve Schimikowski, their bassist. Arranges the covers too."

Goatee looked pointedly at the name over the door.

"Yeah," Scott said. "So you could call here for more info, I guess." He hoped the sudden interest in Goatee's expression meant a good story, maybe something on the front cover.

"You guys ready?" Eli asked.

"Eager to get home to Daddy?" Goatee smirked.

"Sorry if your sex life is so routine and boring." Eli grinned. "He sent me off with a weighted butt plug to make sure I behaved. I wanna get home and get my reward."

"Dude." Brooks's cheeks flashed as bright red as the neon. "I did not need to know that."

Scott's dick pulsed against his inseam. He could have done without the thought himself, given the fact that his living situation made him feel like a monk. At least he'd bought his own towels now. Better than beating off into a bar towel.

"Hey. You got a number so I can set up that modeling shoot?" Eli asked.

Scott didn't need the charity anymore. Working under the table with minimal living expenses had him stacking paper pretty fast. Enough to think about moving out of his cell. Except he kind of liked it, liked being around the Schimikowskis. Mrs. S. always had a Johnnie Walker Black for him when they toasted Pop Schim.

"I'm doing okay now," he told Eli.

"Glad to hear it, but I already told my friend I had the perfect model. Don't fuck with my professional reputation." Eli's eyes fixed on Scott's and gave him a pretty fair idea of why, despite only coming up to Scott's chin, Eli ran the show.

"Okay."

Eli typed in the number and then grabbed Scott's arm, examining where the raven wing wrapped around his wrist, almost as if Eli could see the infinity loop the feathers at the tip had replaced, the initials buried under linework. Scott had gotten the cover-up done six months after Liam left but couldn't ever stop seeing what had been there.

"I even told him some of what you had so he could work it into the book." Eli dropped Scott's arm. "Big football fan?"

"No."

"Why the raven?"

"Because it was black and looked cool."

"Yeah. Right."

Scott watched the three of them until they turned the corner, then crushed his butt under his boot and headed for the back door. Movement next to the Mustang sent his heart pumping with adrenaline, fists curling. But he knew that outline.

His fists relaxed, but his heart—that kept pounding, stupid organ that it was.

"What's the lead singer of Blow the Moon doing in a shitty back alley?"

Liam's teeth flashed as he grinned. "Living the high life." He held up his phone. "'Bout to get an Uber."

"Where's—"

"Reeve went off to celebrate with Mac and Dev," Liam cut him off.

Scott knew that trick, knew Liam did it so he made the question fit the answer he wanted to give. "You don't celebrate?"

"Felt kind of old."

Scott dug his keys out of his pocket. "I'll give you a ride, old man."

Liam grinned again. "Thought you were never going to show me your car, Batman."

Scott unlocked the trunk, and Liam lifted his guitar case into it.

After Scott pushed down the lid, Liam caressed the ridge of the spoiler. "Not a lot of trunk room."

"I never planned on moving bodies in it."

Liam snorted a laugh. "Thought you were going to start a riot tonight, though."

Scott shrugged. "I'm trying to cut down. One a year is my limit."

"I'm glad you didn't." Liam tipped his head. "As much as I appreciate you leaping to my defense."

Scott put his hand over the spoiler where Liam's had been, imagined feeling a trace of warmth from that touch. Beyond stupid. The night was hot, all the metal holding on to the warm day.

Scott coughed and stepped toward the driver's door.

Liam matched him on the other side. "Maybe riots aren't all you should cut down on."

"Yeah, because my life is so great I want to stick around forever. Besides, you know I'm too mean to die." Scott slid in and reached over to pop the lock for Liam.

Liam dropped onto the passenger seat and finished their old joke. "You just smell that way."

"Exactly." Scott turned the key. The mini torque starter engaged, and the throaty rumble purred to life. He tapped the gas to savor the sound. All the hours he'd put into the exhaust were worth it. It wasn't just the obvious things—the feel and the sound—that let Scott know she was perfect, but the way all those signals came together that made him feel like he had an extra sense. He wondered if music worked that way for Liam.

"She's gorgeous." Liam's legs spread wide, knee close to the stick.

Scott forced his eyes to the dash.

Liam leaned over him. "An eight thousand tach? Ever rev her that high?"

"Not since I replaced the block after I got her. The gauge is original, though." Scott touched the brushed chrome rim just as Liam did and jerked his hand back.

"You've had a lot done."

Scott glared at him. "I did it myself." At places he'd worked, after hours. Sometimes with help, like Jamie, but Scott had bled over this car.

"I meant your arm. The tattoos."

"Oh." Scott cut the engine and rested his hand on the stick.

Liam placed his hand on top, thumb wrapping around Scott's wrist to tap the spot where the original tattoo had been, before withdrawing. "I'm sorry." Liam shook his head.

It felt like pity, which Scott could do without. "I didn't ask—" He cut the snarl off and sighed out the anger that came with it. The bruises under Liam's eyes were gone, but Scott was dead wrong for putting them there. He reached for Liam's face and stopped an inch away. "I am so goddamned sorry about hitting you. I lost my mind when I saw you, but that's no excuse."

Liam moved the last inch and Scott's palm curved around that cheek, the rasp of stubble sending an electric shock up his arm, but he held on to the live wire because he'd never been smart enough to save himself. Damned if he ever would be.

Liam mirrored the touch, fingers rubbing behind Scott's ear, thumb at the corner of his lips. "I was pretty stunned myself. Even before you punched me. Besides—" He tried a laugh, but Scott heard how fast Liam's breath came. "—I chipped your tooth for you." He tapped Scott's mouth.

"It was an accident." Scott's lips moved against the callused skin of Liam's thumb. God, how could something that simple make Scott so fucking hard?

"Chipping your tooth was an accident. I fully intended the bottle to smack you in your face."

A tug-of-war over the last cold Natty Boh on a hot night all those years ago had turned less playful as they'd glared at each other. Then Liam had released his grip, and Scott's own strength slammed the dark glass lip into his tooth.

"Bastard." Scott breathed the word into Liam's skin.

"Not gonna argue that."

Scott had known it would happen when he opened the car door. Maybe he'd known it would happen from that first startled look at the car show.

They both moved. Mouths slammed together, hard, hungry. For an instant there was nothing Scott needed more than Liam kissing him. Not pride, not sanity, not even this fucking car. Nothing mattered but Liam. His taste, the friction and heat from his tongue, the sound—God, the sounds trapped in Liam's throat. Scott wanted it all and fuck anything in his way.

Liam gripped the back of Scott's head like he was drowning— like they both were—and Scott sank with him, trying to close the space between them.

But the hardness he felt against his belly was only the stick shift. And that wasn't the only thing coming between them.

Liam let up enough to whisper, "You're going to have to come to me because there's no way I can climb over there."

Scott pulled back but rested their foreheads together, breaths hot and thick between them. "You know it's more than that."

"I know. I just don't want to talk anymore. Please."

The Liam Scott had known—swore he still knew—wasn't one to say *please*. Sure, maybe a *please don't stop*, or *please suck me now*. But Liam usually didn't have to ask for what he wanted. He charmed it into his hands so the outcome was never in doubt.

He dragged Scott into another kiss. Jesus. Already Scott had trouble remembering why he needed to keep his hands o   Liam, but with Liam's tongue in his mouth, he was totally fucked.

Especially when Liam groaned again. Scott grabbed Liam's face and kissed back, his stomach plunging, blood beating tight and hot in his dick with every stroke of Liam's tongue.

Liam's hand landed on Scott's groin—hell, right on his dick— closing on him through his jeans. Scott broke the kiss and pulled Liam's hand off, which Scott's dick thought was an incredibly stupid plan.

Scott sagged back against his seat.

Liam sighed along with him. "Can we just save talking for tomorrow?"

What the hell. Scott had never been able to say no to Liam. "Yeah."

"Good. Now, goddamn it, McDermott, what kind of a dream car is impossible to fuck in?"

Chapter Twelve

SCOTT COULDN'T believe he'd ever convinced himself he didn't miss this. Didn't miss Liam hungry and needy and moaning into Scott's mouth. Liam pressed him into the storeroom door, bone, muscle, and sweat.

And cock. *Liam's* cock against Scott's hip.

Scott slid a hand down Liam's spine. Bare skin. The steps from the car to the storeroom were a blur of walls and kisses and yanks at clothing. Scott was pretty sure someone's shirt was still out in the hall.

His fingers brushed denim, Liam's jeans in the way. Scott shoved his hands into Liam's back pockets and grabbed as much ass as he could, dragged him closer and tighter.

Liam licked and nipped at Scott's jaw, then zeroed in on the spot guaranteed to make Scott's brain give the wheel to his dick. He let his head drop back against the door, let Liam drive him fucking insane with his teeth and tongue.

Liam gave a happy rumble deep in his throat, not a laugh, just satisfaction. His fingers got busy at Scott's fly, and oh fuck, there was a hand on his dick. *Liam's* hand on his dick, and his teeth under the notch of Scott's jaw. He needed to be closer, needed Liam in him. Liam fucking him had always been the most vulnerable but safe Scott ever got to feel.

He tilted his hips to fit them together, hiked a leg around Liam's thigh, and felt it.

His leg. Something hard, silicone or plastic, not muscle and skin. Scott stopped with his fingers pressed into Liam's ass. Liam's lips froze on Scott's neck. Not even a breath moved between them.

Scott was as sure as he'd ever been about anything in his life that Liam needed him to not care, to act like he hadn't noticed, but damn it, Scott had. He let his leg slide back to the floor, then used his grip on Liam's ass to 180 them, putting Liam's back against the door.

After one rough tug on Scott's dick, Liam raised his head. "You think I need help standing up?"

"When I blow you, yeah. You're gonna need it. Always did."

"Cocky much?"

"How sweet. You remember."

But when Scott tried to go to his knees, Liam took hold of Scott's dick again.

"I don't want just a—like this, okay?"

Ignoring the squirm of warning in his stomach, Scott nodded. On his knees, he might have been able to forget about whose cock was in his mouth, make it about nothing but getting off. But face-to-face, dick-to-dick, he wouldn't be able to pretend it was anyone but Liam. It wouldn't be just skin on the line. The break in the action had made doubts pop up like weeds through a sidewalk crack. What he wanted from Liam would never fit into some words. Better—safer—to keep things purely physical.

"You forget how to get in a man's pants, McDermott?"

"Fuck you." Scott punished him with a hard kiss and his palm barely skimming Liam's cock through the denim.

Liam met the attack with an eager grunt, abandoning Scott's dick to free his own. They both jumped at the first electric touch of their dicks brushing against each other. Liam's dick rubbed a lick of precome under the hypersensitive ridge before gliding silkily by. It was goddamned fucking perfect, and Scott hated them both for how good it was.

Wishing he was strong enough to pull away, Scott squeezed his eyes shut and dropped his head to Liam's shoulder.

"Still the same stubborn bastard," Liam breathed against Scott's ear.

"Yep."

Liam's breath hitched like he was about to say something else, but he just spat on his palm and slicked them both. Scott echoed his grip and forced himself to watch Liam's face.

Wide pupils stared right back, that always irresistible dare, a promise and a challenge. They stroked faster, fucking into their joined grip, the silky hot slide an insane contrast to the rough grip of callused skin. The sensation alone was sweet enough to scare him, but then Liam tightened his grip around Scott's shoulder and whispered, "Fuck, Scott, you feel fucking amazing," and tore something loose in Scott's guts.

Because tomorrow, hell, as soon as Liam's balls were empty, he was going to remember he had a boyfriend and a life and the chance to do amazing things and he didn't need to be tied up with Scott's waste of a life just because they happened to have been dumped in the same placement twelve years ago.

"God." Liam panted and dove at Scott's mouth.

Scott shoved a hand in Liam's still too-short hair and pinned them in the kiss.

The eventual fallout wasn't going anywhere, so Scott might as well grab on to this rush of pleasure for as long as he could, even if there was nothing left but ashes when Liam was done with him.

"Jesus." Liam groaned against Scott's lips. "You make me crazy."

Crazy was a good word for it, what with knowing the kind of pain waiting on the other side and being unable to resist diving in. Liam's hips moved in hard jerks, his tongue frantic in Scott's mouth. It was too fucking soon, but Scott couldn't stop it. It felt too good. Too much. And they might as well have been fifteen again, because Liam shot all over their hands and bellies. Just the way he grunted, the vibration against Scott's mouth, had his nuts cutting loose too. God, so fucking sweet, with the jizz-and-sweat smell trapped between them way better than the old mold stink of the storeroom.

He didn't want to let go, of their dicks, of Liam's waist, of the kiss Liam was licking more gently into Scott's mouth.

But he'd learned long ago that what he wanted didn't matter for shit.

He started to step back. Liam squeezed Scott's shoulders once and let him go.

Scott snatched up one of his towels from the crate next to the cot and tossed it to Liam. "Clean up and I'll give you a ride back to"— guilt sludged in his guts like dirty oil, but he wasn't going to ignore the truth—"to your boyfriend."

Liam made a disgusted snort. "Get on, get off, and get out, huh?"

Scott slammed down the towel he'd been using, that greasy sensation robbing him of any control of his temper. "What the hell do you want from me, Liam?"

A corner of Liam's mouth lifted in a smile. "At the moment, I'd kind of like a place to sit down."

"Christ." Scott huffed frustration at the ceiling like a smoke cloud. "Be my fucking guest." He waved at the cot. "Something else? A drink? A smoke? My left nut?" God knew Liam'd already had everything of Scott—twice—and hadn't found any reason to keep it.

But as Liam limped three steps to the cot, Scott had to ask, "You okay?" Because what the fuck did he know about an amputated leg? He couldn't see anything wrong under Liam's jeans. "Does it hurt?"

Liam grimaced as he eased himself down. "Why? Gonna kiss it and make it better?"

"Fuck you."

Liam ran a hand along his thigh, the flesh and bone one. "I'm not used to wearing it this long. But it's the other one that's feeling shaky. Haven't had sex standing up since…." He didn't need to finish. The *since I lost it* was obvious.

"Or I'm just that good."

"Yeah. That's it." Liam stretched both legs out in front of him. Another inch and the toes of his red Converse would brush the bottom shelf that held the toilet paper rolls.

Scott thought about sitting next to him, but the cot would probably dump them both on the floor. He leaned against the sink instead.

Liam looked up at him. "I really did miss you."

"No." Scott shut his eyes. "No fucking way. You don't get to do this."

"Do what?" Liam always had some brass ones.

"Don't pull that shit with those soulful eyes. You're the one who left. You're the one with a boyfriend wondering where the fuck you are. So don't act like you feel bad about any of it."

Liam dragged one heel back under the bed, then used his hands to slide the other foot back. Staring at the floor, he said, "Nobody's waiting. He dumped me."

LIAM KEPT his gaze on an oily stain on the cement floor as his admission hung in the air. He hadn't wanted to say anything, hadn't wanted Scott to go jumping to conclusions about being a rebound fuck, but he'd kept needling.

Liam had time to feel about as low as the stain on the floor as the silence stretched.

Then Scott said, "Excuse me?"

"You heard me." Bad enough to admit the first time.

"And you're just mentioning this now?"

Liam looked up. Scott was scowling—nothing new there—arms folded over his chest so that the raven's gleaming eye stared at Liam.

"Yeah?" Liam was the one who'd recently been dumped. What did Scott have to be so pissy about?

"Ratfucker." Scott rolled his eyes.

Liam had a feeling the insult was directed at him rather than Deon, but he seized on the chance to steer things that way.

"He said I had 'unresolved issues' with my past."

Scott snorted. "Ya think?"

Liam found himself cracking a smile despite how shitty the conversation with Deon had been.

"And he said he'd been my physical crutch and he wasn't going to keep being nothing more than my emotional one."

Scott sneered. "Sounds like a shrink."

"He took a lot of social science courses in college," Liam offered in Deon's defense. At Scott's blank look, Liam added, "Sociology and psychology."

Scott stared for a minute, then laughed. "Dude. You were totally fucking a social worker."

Liam's answering smile stretched thin between loyalties. He wished he could tell Scott the worst of it, about when Deon had dropped the psychobabble, his expression raw enough to make Liam's insides twist in sympathy. *"Stop lying to me. And stop lying to yourself. You're still in love with Scott."*

As much as Liam had wanted to deny it, to erase that piece of Deon's pain, he hadn't been able to. Deon had been safe and easy. Comfortable. Scott would never be anything like that. And Liam still couldn't stop wanting him.

"Yeah, I guess," he said aloud, staring back down at the stain. It looked like a rearing horse, minus one back leg. He shifted his gaze to the shelves, needing an easy change in subject. "So you really think my eyes are soulful?"

"Blow me." Scott raised a foot as if to kick Liam's ankle, then stopped. "Step on up." Liam leaned back against the cot, which felt pretty much like leaning on his rack in Afghanistan. He nudged the sleeping bag out of the way. Yup. Army green instead of the sand his had been, but basically the same thing. He shifted so his weight balanced. "So this is the guest room at Schim's?"

Predictably, Scott took that as a personal attack. "Ain't the fuckin' Hilton." He glanced around and lifted a shoulder and a corner of his lip at the same time. "Hey. At least it's better than the hole at St. Bennie's."

"I don't know." Liam pressed his elbows into the stiffness of the cot. "At least in the hole you got a mattress."

"And a bucket. Like you'd know."

Liam winced. He'd always been able to talk himself out of trouble, but Scott never could squeak by the same way. He always went down swinging. And looking at the shitpile they'd both made of their lives, they hadn't been quick to learn their lessons from the past. "At least you've got an easy commute."

Scott blew out an almost laugh. "True." Then his eyes narrowed, and his voice took on a teasing grumble. "Christ, whine about my bed, whine about trying to fuck in my car. When did you get so prissy?"

"I'm just not as flexible as I used to be." Liam smiled.

Scott's eyes widened. "Oh shit. Sorry. Christ." He took a step toward Liam, then shoved a hand into his spiked hair like he didn't know what to do with it.

"Don't. I need—" Liam was never going to stop resenting how often he'd had to say those two words in the past twenty-eight months. He let out a breath and went on. "Please just be you about my leg, okay?"

"What the fuck's that supposed to mean?" Scott's scowl was back.

Liam wished he could smooth it away like he'd used to do. A hand on Scott's neck dragging him into a kiss or using the grip to hide a caress of his skin if they were out in public. Instead he was stuck with words. "I need you to be the Scott McDermott who doesn't give a shit about anything."

Scott slid down to kneel in front of Liam. "You were always the exception to that."

Liam's stomach acid spewed a burst of guilt, sharp as a punch. *And all I did was hurt you with it.* Aloud he said, "Yeah, and you can see how much I deserved it."

Scott shot a pinched-brow look at the microprocessor knee joint poking through the denim of Liam's jeans. Scruff-covered jaw clenched, Scott made one tight shake of his head.

"Hey." Liam inched forward to brush his knuckles across Scott's face.

Scott took a deep breath but didn't turn toward Liam's hand. *"Scott's always going to be a little feral,"* Liam's mom had said once.

Keeping his voice as soft as if he really was trying to coax something wild to come closer, Liam said, "I'm the one you punched, remember? I know I've got a lot to make up for."

He sounded too much like his mom there, so Liam dragged Scott toward him at the same time Scott reached for Liam's jaw. Scott's mouth, soft lips and tingling stubble, made Liam forget where they were. Forget everything but Scott.

The reminder came when the cot flipped them forward, knocking Scott into the rolls of toilet paper with Liam on top of him.

Scott's eyes went wide with concern again, and Liam cut his worry off with an exaggerated sigh. "Ah. Horizontal at last."

Scott snorted, then smacked Liam in the head with an oversized roll of toilet paper.

Liam began the process of trying to shift off Scott, not exactly sure if the resistance on his leg was Scott's shin, knee, or the cement floor. Scott grabbed his hips to hold him still.

"Something wrong?" Scott's eyes studied him, clear and as soft as they ever were.

"No." But Liam knew Scott was aware of that difference between them, the thing that could never be the same no matter what they salvaged from the past.

Scott ran his hand down Liam's back, over his ass, onto his thigh— the stump and onto the socket.

Liam swallowed. "You totally said my eyes were soulful." He batted his lashes.

The joke worked—or Scott let it work. "Nah, they're shit brown like mine." His hands settled back on Liam's shoulders.

Liam had spent a lot of time looking for clues to Scott's feelings in the tiniest reactions of his mouth and jaw, but mostly in his eyes. They were an intense dark brown, especially now, since Liam's head was blocking most of the light from the bare bulb overhead, but in bright sunlight they had beautiful patterns of wavy starbursts. Scott wasn't always able to keep how he felt from showing in his eyes. Something Liam would never be able to admit to noticing because he was pretty sure Scott would spend a lot more time with his eyes shut just to hide that vulnerability.

"According to my license—when I had one—my eyes are hazel."

Scott rolled the orbs under discussion in a perfectly clear dismissal. "Whatever."

But Liam caught him squinting in concentration a few seconds later. Liam's spine was starting to ache from the position the shelf put them in, and Scott had to be even more uncomfortable. He pressed up on his palms and shifted onto his left side, legs under the cot.

"So what's that about, anyway?" Scott wriggled his back off the shelf, looked around for a spot to stretch out in, and then just sat, tucking up one knee to lean an arm on.

"What?" Because Liam really had no idea what Scott was talking about.

"Why can't you drive?"

"Oh. I've either got to get a car fitted with left pedals or take classes and prove I can drive with my prosthesis."

"Which lines their pockets, I bet." Scott wiped the side of his face on his jeans.

It had gotten hot in here—or maybe it was just noticeable now that a hard dick wasn't a distraction.

Scott went on. "How do they even know? About your leg, I mean."

"Man, you have no idea how much paperwork this"—he tapped his fingers against the socket—"generates. You thought Banana-Nose Joe was bad with all those packets of English homework at St. Bennie's."

Scott ignored Liam's attempt to derail him with memories. "Have you practiced at all with the prosthetic?"

Liam shook his head. "I was more focused on walking." They'd only been going to take his crushed shin at first, and somehow, after the failed attempts to fix it with pins and the endless knifing pain, he'd looked forward to getting that over with. The second amputation, after the infection that cost him his knee, that had taken everything he had to fight back from. If they were going to have a serious conversation, Liam needed to sit up. He got settled on his ass, then rolled up, catching Scott staring at the still-open waistband of his jeans.

"Well, you've got the walking part down all right."

"Yup. Sometimes I can even chew gum at the same time."

"Whoa now. Must have been taken some serious work from your PT." Scott winced. "Sorry." He cupped the back of his neck. "Uh. If he cut you loose, where are you staying?"

Liam thought having to confess he'd been dumped was as awkward as this could get, but there was more fun to come. He started to answer, then stopped. *Great job. Anything else you want to do to draw attention to the bad?*

"Actually, I've been living with my mom. Since I got out of rehab."

"Your mom?"

"She's sober now."

Scott scoffed. "Again? How long this time?"

"Really. Like for years. Even got married while I was in the Army. I've got a stepfather and stepbrothers and—" Liam stopped before he babbled about having his own room and that his stepbrothers played peewee football.

Scott stared at him for a second, then pushed up off the floor. "Guess I should probably get you home to the family, then. But I'm not walking you to the door."

Chapter Thirteen

"Do you want me to give you money for gas or something?" Liam asked when Scott made a sudden left off York Road. He tried to peer around at the gauges.

It was almost 4:00 a.m., but maybe Scott knew where a gas station was open.

"Nope." Scott pulled into a lot near the university's stadium. A couple of cars sat close to the field house, visible through the humid fog under the streetlights. "You gotta work today?"

"Weekend off. Unless someone calls in." Liam glanced around them. "If you wanted to get off again, we could have just stayed back at Schim's."

"True."

Scott against him, that wild dizzy rush that was them together. If they could still have that, maybe—

Scott turned off the engine, popped open his door, and stepped out. When he came around to Liam's door and opened it, dread skittered like a spider through Liam's stomach. Scott wouldn't do this. He wouldn't pay Liam back by leaving him out here five miles from home. The Scott he'd left six years ago wouldn't have done that. But people changed.

"Get out," Scott said, holding the door open.

Liam could call his mom, of course, or Greg, or even Deon. Reeve might still be up. Someone would come get him so he didn't have to walk back. Scott sighed, glared down, and grabbed Liam's arm. "C'mon."

Liam shook him off, then turned and planted his feet to heave himself up. "Okay. Jesus, Scott, if you wanted to be an asshole about it, you could have told me to call for a ride—" His reflexes had him grabbing the keys out of the air before he realized Scott had thrown them.

He stared at them—it. Just one key on a thick ring with a leather snap. The key to the Mustang. Scott's Mustang.

"C'mon. Before the jocks start showing up for football practice. You could drive stick before, you can drive it now."

"I don't know if I can. You don't know if I can."

"Not a lot for you to hit here if you can't."

"But the transmission."

"Will be fine. Let's go, Walsh, we're burning moonlight."

Up till now, no one had offered to let Liam try driving with his prosthesis. And as much as Liam had hated the need and dependence that created, the fear of trying and failing had been worse. It was easier to resent it and keep his mouth shut.

Liam walked stiffly over to the driver's side and sat, then used his hands to drag his right leg in and get settled. He shifted his foot from the brake to the gas, back and forth. He'd done that a couple of times in Greg's Fusion, alone in the garage. But never with any pressure on the gas, never with the car in gear.

He left his foot on the brake and pushed down the clutch to start the car and felt the rumble in his nuts. He didn't see cars like Scott did, but even Liam could tell why people worshipped Mustang Fastbacks. And Scott was letting Liam test out his ability to drive in it.

He shifted into Neutral and practiced putting pressure on the gas pedal.

"Stop being a pussy and drive the car," Scott snapped.

Liam put it back into first, took a deep breath, and eased up on the clutch and pressed the gas. The car lurched forward, bucked, and stalled.

"Goddamn it. Sorry. I don't think this is going to work."

"So you stalled it. Big deal. Start it again."

"I appreciate what you're trying to do, but—"

"Shut up and drive."

Liam blew frustration out of his nostrils and cranked the starter again.

"Right. So whatever you did last time," Scott said in a calmer voice, "don't. Go lighter."

"Not what you used to say."

"Focus."

It took two more stalls, but finally Liam was lurching around the lot and even managed to get the car into second. For a few moments he forgot why they were doing this. Just him and Scott in a muscle car, darkness drifting by outside. Like one of the stories they'd tell each other at St. Bennie's. What they'd do when they got out. Drive cross-country. See the sunset on the Pacific. The throaty engine vibrated under his ass, and he felt Scott watching him, felt the weight of his attention. But mostly it felt like freedom. Until he had to downshift again, let up on the gas too much, and stalled out.

"Not bad," Scott said.

"I suck." Liam turned to face him, grinning. "But I could so blow you right now."

"Yeah, well." Scott nodded at the lightening sky. "Gonna get pretty public here in a bit. Time to get you home to Mommy."

Liam put a hand on Scott's thigh and felt him flinch. "Thanks."

"No big."

But it really had been, even if he'd only done laps around a parking lot.

"Before, that wasn't just a rebound thing. I want—" Liam cut himself off. How could he ask for a second chance, ask Scott for anything, without explaining what had happened first? If Liam pushed, he wouldn't be surprised if Scott was the one to pull a vanishing act this time. Feral. Damn. "I wanted to be with you."

Scott stared through the windshield, silent, muscles rigid under Liam's hand. Finally he said, "For old times' sake?"

"No, not just for that. I meant it when I said I missed you."

Scott swallowed. The bob of his throat was all Liam could read in this light, no cues from his eyes or his lips. He let out quick breath, then slumped in the seat, hand going to the back of his neck. "I might have missed you a bit."

Liam bit his bottom lip to keep from smiling.

LIAM CUT off a bite-sized piece of his waffle and stuffed it into his mouth. His mom and Greg were reviewing the transportation requirements for Kevin's and Justin's Saturday activities. He stabbed a fresh piece of bacon, figured his newly manners-obsessed mom wasn't paying attention, and shoved the whole piece into his mouth. She still gave him a mom look.

The only potential issue on Liam's schedule was whether his nap would conflict with his Netflix binging. Reeve hadn't even set up a rehearsal today.

His phone buzzed against the dining table, violating the no-electronics-at-the-table rule. His stepbrothers gave him wide-eyed looks.

"Liam." His mom turned the two syllables of his name into a full sentence of disapproval.

"Sorry, might be work." Liam grabbed another forkful of waffle and pushed back from the table. "'Scuse me."

His mom sighed, but Liam was already limping away from the table toward his room. He shut the door and glanced down at his phone.

U get called 2 work?

His phone didn't know the contact, but he did. His pulse rate escalated so fast he felt it in his ears.

It's Scott btw.

Liam smiled and texted back. *No work.*

Cool. I'm down at the Eastridge corner.

Scott had accepted Liam's number but hadn't offered his own, and they hadn't said much on the drive back from the parking lot. Liam had wondered if Scott would act like nothing had happened the next time Liam saw him at Schim's.

Give me ten.

He glanced down at his cargo shorts. They covered his socket, but the rest of the prosthesis was on full carbon robotic display. He hated needing help with things, hated things he couldn't do, but he wasn't ashamed of his leg. It was just that when he wore shorts, people wanted to talk about how it had happened.

But if he wanted Scott to act like it was no big deal, Liam needed to do it too.

Liam opened his door to find his mom about to knock on it.

"Is everything okay?"

"Yeah. It's fine. I, uh, still don't have to work. I think I'm going to take a walk."

His mom's nose wrinkled, like she smelled the lie. "I can drop you somewhere while Greg takes the boys to practice."

"No. I just need to keep up my exercises and it's more fun outside."

Mom searched his eyes. "Have you tried talking to Deon? I know you said—"

"No, Mom. Talking isn't going to fix it. It's over."

"I'm sorry to hear that. He was good for you." His mom brushed at his hair. "Give it a little time. You know, sometimes things aren't as finished as you think they are."

Mom wasn't talking about Scott—would never root for him and Scott—but he still hoped she was right. There was too much between him and Scott to ever be finished. Liam ducked his head away from her hand.

His mom flicked his ear. "I know you're an adult, but you're still my little boy."

He'd wanted to hear those words from his mom for so many years, have a moment like this, but he wasn't that wishing little boy anymore. But he didn't know how to tell her that. He accepted her hug and hurried out of the house.

The Mustang idled a little way down Eastridge, but as soon as Liam turned, it rolled toward him. His skin hummed, and it wasn't all just because of the powerful engine.

"Hey."

Scott nodded and tipped his head at the passenger's seat.

Liam leaned on the trunk as he swung himself around the car.

"Leg okay?"

"Yeah." He'd hurried and the sweat was threatening to break through the vacuum seal. As he lifted his leg into the seat, Scott shot him a look, then stared out the windshield.

As Scott headed south, it occurred to Liam that he had no idea why Scott had driven up to get him. Scott had texted and Liam had snuck out of the house to meet him. He didn't know what exactly was happening between them, if they were friends or fuck buddies or what. All he knew was Scott asked and Liam went.

As Scott gunned the car through a yellow light in Towson, Liam wondered if Scott was headed for Schim's, for the storeroom and more up-against-the-wall action. Liam's balls vibrated from more than just the rumble of eight cylinders of the Mustang's engine. Too bad Scott didn't have a garage, because Liam fucking Scott over the hood of his car would definitely lead to them coming their brains out. Liam could totally manage to fuck standing up if he had the car to lean on.

He jerked out of his fantasy when Scott pulled the car over to a curb, a vaguely familiar curb opposite a gray stone church. They weren't that far from the shitty one-bedroom apartment over the liquor store. The one whose rent Scott had worked all those crazy hours to pay so Liam could concentrate on his classes.

Liam wiped his hands on his shorts, dick no longer stretching the crotch.

Leaving—running away—had seemed like the only option back then. At twenty-one, with guilt and fear and anger tangling him up until he felt trapped, he'd just wanted to get far away from everything. Despite the shit that had gone down with the accident—Liam's stump twitched in his socket—he hoped he was a hell of a lot less stupid now.

Scott turned off the engine, and silence filled up the space between them.

"I'm sorry." Liam meant it, not just as something to smooth things over.

Scott pulled the key free, and the car rolled them back a few inches as he released the brake. "For what?"

Liam took a deep breath. "I shouldn't have just taken off like that."

Scott made a disgusted sound in his throat. "Don't. God—"

Liam was going to make sure Scott heard him anyway. "I should have talked to you first."

Scott slumped in his seat. "About what? Your sudden hard-on for a uniform?"

"I needed a way to be sure I didn't just come right back."

"So you decided getting shot was a good idea? Things weren't perfect, but was it that bad? Were we?"

"I was scared."

"Christ, of what?" Scott finally looked at him.

The sunlight slashing through the car lit up Scott's eyes, making those beautiful wavy lines, and Liam read the shock and hurt in their wide-open vulnerability. He was only trying to make this better. To explain.

"I found those pills you were taking."

Scott's brows slanted in thought. "Right. Lucy Pulaski's diet pills. Man, caffeine just wasn't cutting it anymore."

Liam had felt the frantic, rabbit-quick flutter of Scott's heart, seen his eyes sink to dark hollows.

"And you know my mom—"

"Fuck." Scott launched himself out of the car, slammed the door, and stomped away.

Liam followed without the slamming, but he was having too much phantom leg pain to do any stomping.

When Scott stopped to light a cigarette, Liam caught up.

Scott stepped away from him. "Most people might notice the conversation is over."

"Right, because it takes a big man to outrun a guy with one leg."

Scott took a long drag and shook his head. "Funny how you don't want me to notice your leg until you do. Make up your fucking mind."

Oh, Liam did. Right then. In front of the Heaven's Hope Baptist Church of Govans, whose gospel music had drifted into the windows of their apartment a half block away, Liam knew he wanted Scott back in his life. Even if that life meant sharing something like the storeroom at Schim's. Liam would do whatever it took to make Scott forgive him for taking off like that. This time everything would work out. It had to. Because even when Scott was being frustratingly stubborn, even standing here getting stupid-white-boy looks from a woman who'd come out to stand on her stoop and stare at them, Liam felt more like himself than he had since he climbed into that jeep with Ross. Before his life blew up.

"Okay." Liam grinned. He couldn't help it. He'd fucked up last time, but he'd make it right. Because there was no one in the world who would ever make him feel like this.

"Fucking nutcase." Scott blew a cloud of smoke into Liam's face.

"Scott—"

"I told you I didn't want to talk about it."

"I just wanted to apologize."

"I heard you the first fifteen times. And we were fine until you got me confused with your—" Scott shifted his grip on the cigarette as he brought it to his mouth, the pause louder than any words could have been. "—mother."

"So why'd you bring me down here, then?"

Scott stubbed out the cigarette on the church gate and tucked the remainder in his pack. "I thought since the neighborhood was familiar, you'd be more comfortable practicing here."

"Practicing what?"

Scott tossed him the key.

Liam's mouth was as dry as if he'd licked the ash off the cigarette butt. He looked down the block at a pile of bikes in front of one house, at the girls playing four square with a glittering pink ball across the street. His leg—stump—burned and prickled. "I can't."

SCOTT DRAGGED out his calm, convincing voice. It was rusty with disuse, and nowhere near as smooth and seductive as the voice Liam could use to make Scott think something was a good idea. Still, Scott managed to coax Liam behind the wheel.

Liam turned the engine over, but after a few smooth feet, they jerked to a stop. He hadn't stalled it, just slammed on the brakes.

"Do you want to keep needing someone to give you a ride? Do you want to let those bastards tell you how to live your life?" Scott asked.

"Who?"

"The ratfuckers at the MVA who pulled your license."

"Oh." Liam zipped his hands around the steering wheel, knuckles meeting top and bottom as he made endless semicircles.

"Don't rub off all the leather."

"Sorry." He jerked his hands away and then settled them back at ten and two.

"What's wrong?"

"It's like trying to drive wearing stilts. It was one thing in the parking lot, but—" He dropped his forehead onto the steering wheel. "Jesus, I could kill someone."

People might think Scott was the stubborn one, but once Liam made up his mind, it took a fucking backhoe to shift his ground. Or finding the pills Scott had made damned sure to keep out of sight to keep Liam from overreacting. All the fucking way to the Army.

"I won't let you."

"Yeah? You're going to be in the car with me, everywhere I go for the rest of my life?"

Back when owning the Mustang had been nothing but a fantasy, the best part of it had been where he and Liam just drove wherever they wanted, fucking in a different hotel bed every night, leaving all the bullshit from their past in the dust. But Scott knew better now. You couldn't outrun whatever life crapped on you. You had to learn to live with it. He wondered if Liam would ever figure that out.

Scott sighed. "That's what practicing is for, so you won't need me once you get the hang of it."

Liam squared his shoulders, eased off the brake, and then jammed it down again.

"Is it the clutch?" Which was a stupid question, since it wasn't like Scott could pull an automatic transmission out of his ass.

"Yes and no. I mean, at least I can feel where I am on the clutch pedal."

"What if it was a left-foot drive? An automatic?"

"Sure. Let's try it. You got one in storage?"

"Asshole." The fact that it was close enough to Scott's own thought didn't mean he liked hearing it from Liam.

"Now you see why I'm stuck needing rides everywhere. Or moving onto a bus line."

Scott hadn't clocked it, but it had to be over a mile from Liam's house to the closest bus stop, which couldn't be good for Liam's leg. He'd seen Liam's face when he got moving in the parking lot. Giving him a little bit of freedom again had felt like a safer way of putting that expression back on his face. One that didn't cost Scott another piece of skin.

"I'll drive you back."

After they finished the clown fire drill around the car, Liam slunk into the passenger seat under the shoulder belt. "Where are you headed?"

"Gotta pick up a few things and then help Chai get ready to open the bar."

Liam sighed and slumped like a slit tire. "I would literally trade my leg to not have to sit in the damned house all day."

Scott snorted. "You could just ask instead of being such a fucking drama queen. What the hell would I do with a metal leg?"

"Then at least you'd know I'd have to stick around."

Scott shot Liam a look. "If you had the idea I wanted to make you stay where you didn't want to be, that didn't come from me."

Chapter Fourteen

SCOTT SHOVED a hand through his hair and stared into the mirror in the truck-stop shower. He hadn't buzzed the sides since he got evicted and he was out of gel. Fuck-the-world hairstyles were tough to maintain when you were living out of a bar's storeroom. It was probably time he started thinking past where he was sleeping tonight. He could see about paying out some of the tax bill before they came after what little he had dropped in the bank to cover the Mustang's insurance payment. Then an apartment, and—

He sneered at the stupid bastard in the mirror. No surprise where all this thinking about the future came from. One ball-draining session up against the wall didn't mean shit. They weren't stupid kids anymore, which meant they couldn't just keep making decisions with their dicks. For all Liam's apologies and *I missed you*s, he was dependent on someone to drive him around. If he got his freedom back and still wanted Scott around, then they'd see.

He stuck his head into the hall. The coast was clear. Trying to track down the random car part Scott had invented a need for should keep Liam busy for a few more minutes, especially since they wouldn't stock something for a '68 here.

Scott ducked back behind the door to make his phone call in private.

"Donnigan," Jamie snapped into the phone.

"It's Scott."

"Are you under arrest?"

"No."

"You assault someone?"

"No."

"Lose that job at the bar?"

"No."

"Then what do you want? I'm working."

Like Scott couldn't have already gotten to the point if Jamie wasn't snapping questions at him. "What do you know about installing a left-foot accelerator?"

"I'm sorry, did someone change my name to Google?"

"Yeah, I'll just look that up on the laptop I don't have or my text-and-talk-only phone."

"I suppose I don't need to ask why this is suddenly important."

"No."

Jamie sighed over a sound of waves slapping against fiberglass and a deep distant horn. "You get any days off from the bar when you can come down?"

"Mondays."

"No good. You got mornings, right?"

A motor whined high and sharp in Scott's ear.

"Fuck, Geist. Warn me next time," Jamie yelled away from the phone. "I gotta go."

"Somebody break the speed limit in his kayak?" Scott asked, but Jamie had already hung up.

"Shit." Scott pocketed his phone and stepped out into the hall.

Liam made a beeline for him, holding two shrink-wrapped packages. "Did you need the caps tapered or not?"

Damn it.

SCOTT TIPPED his head back to let Liam get at more of his neck. Fuck, that felt good.

The kissing and nipping stopped.

"Your jeans are buzzing." Despite it being about a hundred and ten in the storeroom, Liam's breath on Scott's wet skin left goose bumps.

"Uh-huh." Everything was buzzing.

Liam had pulled Scott in here a few seconds after they realized none of the Schimikowskis were at the bar yet. Scott thought about it being a bad idea for a few seconds and then Liam's tongue teased over Scott's lips and he didn't care how stupid it was.

"No, I mean, someone's calling you." Liam reached into Scott's front pocket and pulled out the phone. Pushing away from the door where he had Scott pinned, Liam stared at the thick boxy piece of plastic with the tiny screen. "This is your phone?"

"No money for rent, no money for fancy phones." Scott snatched it out of his hand.

"Right. Sorry." Liam's cheek showed a darker patch of red on top of the flush from the heat. "You need to get that?"

Scott hadn't bothered putting his contacts into the phone, but he knew the number: Jamie's. Scott didn't want Liam knowing about the left-foot accelerator search until Scott had something to show for it. For all Liam's *don't make a big deal about it*, he was plenty skittish about his leg. The vibration stopped.

"No." Scott shoved the phone back into his pocket and slipped under Liam's arm to move away.

"Then get back here and kiss me." Liam reached for Scott's arm, but he twisted free. "Or not," Liam said. "Who was it?"

"It's not—" *about you*. But the rest of that sentence was technically a lie, even if the phone call wasn't a reason why Liam should get that narrow-eyed jealous look.

And the urge Scott had to wrap his arms around Liam and tell him he had nothing to worry about was the reason letting Liam pull him in here was such a bad idea in the first place.

"My cop friend."

The sharp suspicion shifted to wide-eyed surprise. "Is it a cop thing? Like are you on parole or something?"

"It's fine." Scott shoved the packs of beef jerky, instant soup, and cereal he'd just bought under the cot. When he looked back over his shoulder, Liam had that still-waiting look Scott remembered all too well.

He sighed. "No, I'm not on parole. It's car stuff. I told you. He's got a classic Ford too. A '68 F-100." He tapped open the text.

Sun. 10 AM. Quinn's place. Remember it?

Scott did, and he could find it again, but he hadn't seen any signs that the guy worked on cars.

Yeah. But Y him?

Q's ex-Navy. Knows vet services. Bring the bf. Jamie texted like he was the one on a pay-per-minute plan.

Scott could back and forth with Jamie, burning up his own minutes, and still end up with no more info than he had now. Arguing about attaching the boyfriend label to Liam would be just as pointless given how obnoxiously stubborn Jamie was. Takes one to know one, Scott could admit.

As soon as he'd tucked the phone away, Liam stepped forward and wrapped his arms around Scott's waist.

Scott grabbed Liam's wrists as his hands slid down to Scott's ass. He lifted Liam's arms away. "What is this?"

"Kinda obvious, man. This is me trying to get in your pants."

There wasn't much space to retreat, but Scott backed up to the sink. "No. I mean, what is this?" He gestured between them.

Though the light through the dirty window was hitting Liam's face, his eyes still darkened in a Liam version of a scowl. "I thought you didn't want to talk about it."

The past, no. That was all long gone. The present had them—and Scott's guts—tangled together in a way that he needed to get sorted.

"I don't. Not about what happened before." All that didn't matter since they damned well couldn't change it.

"Okaaaay." The way Liam drew out the word said he didn't know what the hell Scott meant. Which sucked since Liam was the one who was good with words.

"Forget it." Scott shook his head and tried to find a way around Liam to the door.

Liam grabbed on to Scott's shoulders. Hard. Liam wasn't wiry like he'd been six years ago. He'd packed on muscle. Still, Scott could free himself, though everything on the shelves would be toast.

This grip felt like it could lift Scott off the floor. "I don't want to. I know I fucked up. What we had—Christ, I haven't been able to stop thinking about you since I saw you again. I know you probably won't ever trust me—"

"Don't." Scott meant to say it with force, but the tiny room was airless and it came out more like a whisper. It was so hot in here he couldn't think, with still more heat trapped between them where they touched, chest to thighs, where Liam held him.

"Then what? Tell me how to fix it." Liam's pleading mouth was too damned close.

Scott shut his eyes, but he was too far gone. He grabbed Liam's head and kissed him, rough and mean. Liam met him there, just as hard, grip shifting like he'd shake him.

"Fuck you," Scott panted. "You don't get to do this. You don't get to come back into my life and fuck me up again, you bastard."

"I know." Liam released Scott's shoulders and wrapped him in a hug instead.

"Things can't just be like they were." Eyes still squeezed shut, Scott rested his fisted hands on the shelf behind Liam's head.

"Okay."

But the word felt like a promise against the sweaty skin of Scott's neck. A dangerously easy thing to believe. "Stop agreeing with me, you shit."

Scott felt the laugh more than he heard it, a vibration in Liam's chest, but only a trace in his voice.

"Okay." But the amusement faded from his voice as he went on, "I get it. We're different people than we were—me literally." He bumped Scott's leg with the one that was hard in weird places.

And that was the problem. Liam had changed. But Scott hadn't. He was still the stupid ass who wanted Liam Walsh to promise he'd love Scott forever. That he'd never leave. Scott didn't have to touch his forearm to remember the infinity symbol the raven's wing covered.

When Scott didn't say anything, Liam squeezed him again, then eased the grip. "I know things can't be the same. I know it won't be easy. But it's not like it was always easy then."

Scott grunted in agreement. Bitching over errands, over whose fault the giant puddle in the bathroom was, over whether Liam really needed to drop everything to go visit his mom in rehab. Again.

There'd been that one huge fight too. Liam had brought some guy from his chemistry class home, supposedly to go over their labs, and then acted like he didn't know the guy was interested in a hell of a lot more than Liam's lab notes. Scott still wasn't sure what had made him crazier: Liam's oblivious "we're just studying" or the knowledge that the guy was exactly the smart, together, non-fucked-up asshole Liam ought to be with instead of Scott. After getting into a snarling fight with Liam, Scott had walked out after putting his fist through the wall and slept on a work buddy's couch for two nights, until he was sure he was over the urge to fuck things up in a way that would guarantee Liam went running to Chem-Lab Dude.

Scott met Liam's gaze, a steady clear-eyed stare that challenged Scott to deny the memory. He opened his hands and slid his palms down either side of Liam's spine.

If Liam was willing to accept that things weren't always gonna be sunshine and cotton candy, maybe they had a chance. With a long breath, Scott sighed out "Yeah," knowing Liam would hear an agreement to more than just the memories.

Liam's quick smile made Scott's stomach leap in stupid, stubborn excitement, and he tightened his jaw to avoid smiling back.

"So, maybe if we're both not working, we could do something, see how it goes?" Despite the smile, Liam's voice was hesitant.

Scott tilted his head. "Are you asking me out?"

"I—yeah." Liam dropped his gaze.

Scott ran a hand through Liam's hair, cradled his skull. "Hm. Dating seems kind of weird when we've had our tongues in each other's asses. But I guess we can give it a shot."

Liam punched him in the shoulder, not hard, but Scott let it push him backward. Then he put his hands in his back pockets.

Thinking of Jamie's text, Scott asked, "You work tomorrow morning?"

"No. But the band's meeting here at three because of our show tomorrow night."

Scott nodded. "I'll pick you up at nine thirty."

"At the corner."

Though Scott knew Liam was smart to keep his mom from weighing in on this until they even gave it a shot, Scott said, "So I'm your dirty little secret now?"

"God, I hope so." Liam grabbed Scott's face and kissed him.

Damn. Dirty was right. Liam tonguefucked Scott's mouth as he shoved Scott's shirt up. He squeezed Scott's pecs, working his nipples with rough strokes of his thumb. Scott's head dropped back as need rocked him, making him buck his hips into Liam's to get a little friction going, a little pressure to take the edge off.

Liam lifted his head to pant, "Can we fuck?"

Stupid questions sputtered through Scott's head. *Tomorrow? Right now? While we try this out?*

But his brain wasn't driving. "Yeah." He groaned.

"So get your pants off."

Scott yanked at his fly, then froze with his jeans and boxers around his ankles as Reeve's voice echoed through the bar.

"Scott? Damn. Where the hell are you? I totally owe you a blow job."

Chapter Fifteen

LIAM'S INSIDES went cold and hollow. His fingers tightened in Scott's shirt. "So you trade blow jobs with Reeve now?"

Scott straightened from yanking up his jeans and gave Liam that one-eyebrowed smirk. "Jealous?"

"No." Liam snapped it out to keep the fuck-yeah truth from spilling out. Maybe Liam wasn't the only one who needed to keep things secret.

"Sure 'bout that?" Scott was laughing at him. Not out loud, but Liam saw it behind Scott's eyes.

Cheeks flashing with heat, Liam tried to shove past Scott toward the door. Of course he stepped wrong.

Scott caught him, fingers vise-tight on Liam's upper arm just as Reeve slammed the door open.

"Did you see it?" Reeve demanded. "Oh, hey, Liam. You saw—" His gaze flicked between them. "Uh, fucking or fighting?"

Scott released Liam's arm. "Neither." He edged around Reeve and through the door.

"Wait," Reeve called.

"Gotta take a piss," Scott tossed back.

Reeve stared into the hall for a second, then shook his head. "Cranky motherfucker." He swung his phone toward Liam's face, voice extra nasal with excitement. "Look at this, Liam. Fucking look."

Liam tried, but with Reeve waving the phone around, it was hard. Grabbing it from Reeve's fingers, he caught the headline "Listen to This," the local arts newspaper's listings of live music for the week.

Sunday. 9 P.M. Schim's Tavern. Blow the Moon.

Too soon to say what sound the band, formed from the remains of the predictably pedestrian Backward Gaze, will ultimately claim as home, but BTM currently features genre-bending covers and a grunge metal grind on originals, all boosted by the new velvet-voiced vocalist and a lead guitar who can shred. Now's your chance to hear them before they're cool.

Recommended.

A dreamlike high buzzed through Liam's brain. The velvet-voiced vocalist in that review couldn't be him. It was the same weird disconnection he felt sometimes when he stared down at the space where his leg had been, trying to hold two different realities in his head.

Reeve yanked the phone back and smacked Liam's shoulder hard enough to anchor him in the now.

"I know. I'm seriously gassed. Can you believe Scott set it up?"

"What?"

"Dude from the paper, he called me for background, said Scott had gotten him in here on Friday and told him about us. BTM. S'cool, right? Big T or little T, you think?"

Scott got a local music critic here to listen to the band? Scott knew a local music critic?

Reeve's phone erupted with the horror movie shriek that was his ringtone. "'S Dev," he told Liam before answering. "You saw it, right? Hell to the fuck, yeah. Hang on a sec." Reeve tapped his phone and looked at Liam. "Tell Scott I owe him one."

But not a blow job. Liam nodded and turned to go.

"And hey." Reeve's voice didn't sound anything like his usual friendly neighborhood stoner schtick. "I don't know what the fuck's going on with you two, but you keep your shit from messing with the band. Got it?"

Liam swallowed back the instinctive *Yes, Sergeant* and instead answered with a smarmy salute knowing damned well that if he'd been any good at following orders, he'd—well, he'd still have two legs, for one thing.

LIAM FOUND Scott leaning against his Mustang and smoking. Scott made eye contact and then tipped his head back as if to cram as much lung blackener as possible in his next drag. The demand that Scott explain what the fuck he'd meant by "neither" dried up and died on the back of Liam's tongue.

How did Scott make everything he did look so goddamned sexy?

Liam leaned on the car next to him and reached for Scott's cigarette. Scott shifted hands and held it away. "You'll fuck up your voice."

"Right. Because secondhand smoke is good for it."

Scott exhaled away from Liam's face, then stubbed it out on the side of his boot before tucking it back into his pack.

"I didn't mean—" Liam realized how stupid his protest would sound and shifted gears. "Reeve said he owes you one."

"Wanna watch me collect?" Scott's sidelong smirk teased Liam's cheek like a touch.

The urge to smile battled the jealous burn in his throat at the thought of watching someone else—no, Reeve—suck Scott off. Of seeing Scott dig his hands into Reeve's dreads to yank him farther down on his dick. Imaginary Scott looked at voyeur Liam with lips wet and open, eyes dark and needy—

"Fuck, no," Liam snapped out.

Scott stared at him hard and Liam swallowed. Scott hadn't acted like an asshole about Deon. Even now Liam didn't know if trying to be together meant they were going to be exclusive. He didn't want to ask now. It had been hard enough getting Scott to agree to this much; Liam didn't want to push too hard.

"No, I don't want to watch," Liam said more softly.

Scott grunted, and Liam knew Scott was wishing he hadn't tapped out his cigarette. He drummed his fingers on the hood instead.

Liam gave up staring at the whitewashed bricks and looked over at Scott. "So, pretty big social circle you got now. First the cop, now a music critic?"

"Huh?" Scott stopped drumming his fingers.

"Reeve said you got some guy from the *Charming Rag* to come see us Friday, when we opened for CCC."

Scott shrugged and crossed his ankles. "I let in a guy who said he was from the *Rag*. But I did it mostly because he was with someone else I knew who I owed a favor to. Still made 'em pay the cover."

Scott's lips pushed out, his brows raised, and Liam fought a laugh at the smug expression. Scott had always bitched about the bosses he'd worked for but was downright protective of Schim's.

"Same guy asked me questions after your set, so I told him to call Reeve," Scott added. "Honestly, dude seemed like kind of an asshole."

Liam grinned. "Well, that asshole gave us a kickass review. Recommended people come to our show tomorrow."

"No shit." Scott's eyes, sunlit and shining, locked on Liam's face. "Looks like you're headed for the big time."

At that moment, Liam would have given his other leg to be able to write music like Reeve so he could write a song that would make Scott

McDermott always look at him with pride so bright in his eyes. Liam might as well have been a little kid again, wishing his mom wasn't too high to do more than glance at the art projects he brought home, to hang them up on the fridge like she did now for Kevin and Justin.

"It's just one review," Liam reminded them both.

"Gotta start somewhere, right?"

"I guess."

Scott drummed his fingers again. His blue work shirt was open over a ribbed white undershirt, the cutoff sleeves exposing every line and curve of his inked arm. Liam's fingers itched to trace the designs. The raven covering wrist and forearm, then a twisted tree with bare limbs, a mustang. Liam studied Scott's shoulder. A feminine profile, almost obscured by blowing hair, a date Liam remembered beneath it. Jenny, Scott's sister.

The cops had given Scott a few things that had been found with Jenny's body. That picture, Jenny as a teenager turning away from the camera as a long-haired seven-year-old Scott looked up at her.

A chill ran down Liam's spine. Scott's mom. His sister. Liam. Scott had been left so many damned times. And here he was, giving Liam the chance to do it again. He'd never deserve someone as loyal as Scott. Liam was bound to freak out and fuck up by leaving again. Hurt him again.

One thing the past few years had taught Liam was that he didn't have all the answers—hell, he didn't know shit. How was Liam any better than Ross if Liam took Scott down with him?

"For fuck's sake." Scott's snarl jerked Liam out of his unfocused stare.

"What?"

"You tell me. I can practically hear you grinding gears." Scott pointed at Liam's head.

Here was Liam's chance to actually be a hero. To say he'd changed his mind, admit he was a walking disaster, and tell Scott to stay far away. Instead, Liam pushed his ass away from the car, steadied himself with a hand on the hood, and turned to face Scott.

"Why'd you answer Reeve like that? Neither?"

Scott narrowed his eyes like he had no idea what Liam was talking about.

"Reeve asked if we were fucking or fighting. You said 'Neither.'"

Scott's shrug was confined to an emphatic roll of his lips. "We weren't doing either at the time."

"That's not what I'm asking."

Scott rolled his eyes. "Christ. Braids-dude really got that psych shit into your head."

"His name is Deon, and the Army made me go through all that psych shit. Had to go through a lot of counseling after I got hurt."

"Sounds like good times."

"Well, at least I can recognize an attempt to avoid answering a question."

Scott sighed and pulled his lighter out of his pocket and began passing it through his fingers. "Okay. For one, didn't know if you wanted Reeve clued in to"—he stopped the motion and used the lighter to point between them—"whatever this is. For two…." He paused and rolled the lighter over his knuckles again. "Look, you and I—well, when it's just us, things tend to go okay. It's when other people get involved that things go to shit."

Like Liam's mom. And what the hell had been the name of the guy from Organic Chem? Phil? Paul? Something preppy with a P. The one who'd referred to Scott as "your scary, abusive, controlling asshole of a boyfriend." Scott had a point.

Liam nodded.

Scott made the lighter catch, then released it. "So maybe we can take time figuring things out before dragging other people and their opinions into it."

"So actually, I'm *your* dirty little secret."

Scott's lips twisted. "'S fucking hot to hear you say it. Wanna sneak around with me?"

"Yeah." Liam leaned to kiss him.

Scott put a hand on his chest. "Broad daylight in the street isn't exactly stealth there, Army. Go celebrate with Reeve so I can finish my fucking cigarette."

By the time Scott went back into the bar, Liam and Reeve were arranging gear on the stage.

"Mac and Dev are coming in for a quick rehearsal," Liam said before Scott could ask what the fuck they were doing when the bar opened in under an hour.

"You clear that with your sister?" Scott looked at Reeve.

Reeve laughed. "Why are you so afraid of her, man?"

"Because I'm not stupid. You know Rage Mist is playing tonight."

Liam stepped to the front of the stage, and Scott held his breath. Was that metal leg gonna handle the impact if Liam jumped? After a swayed hesitation, Liam walked around to the steps. "It's fine," he told Scott as he took the stair onto the floor. "We'll break down long before they get here, and besides, Reeve says there's hardly ever anyone here before seven on weekend nights when they have a band."

Scott figured his license to toss out troublemakers didn't extend to a Schimikowski. He sighed and shoved a hand through his hair.

Liam stretched a hand toward Scott's head, but he ducked away.

Lips tight over his teeth, Liam said, "Not like you got it spiked up."

"Ran out of glue."

Liam tilted his head, raised brows clearly demanding *So what the fuck is the problem?*

Scott jerked his chin at Reeve, who was messing with the knobs on his bass. As Liam followed his gaze, Scott slipped away behind the bar.

Liam lifted the service gate, stepped through, and right on into Scott's space. "Change your mind?" Liam sounded like he was teasing, but he pressed his T-shirt flat against his stomach for an instant, a sure sign he was nervous.

"No."

Liam took that as permission to crowd up closer, driving Scott's back into the edge of the bar.

Scott put his fingers on Liam's chest to keep some space between them.

Liam glanced down. "I know we've got unfinished business, but the five-finger-palm-exploding-heart technique seems kinda extreme."

"Huh?" Scott looked at his hand. He'd been trying to keep from touching Liam more than necessary to get him to back off. The tips of his fingers jabbed right over Liam's heart, a mirror of the last movement at the end of *Kill Bill*. How many times had they watched that together?

Scott flattened his palm.

This was worse. Now he could feel the heat from Liam's skin under the thin cotton, the thud of his heart. Back when they were together, Scott had wondered if it would ever go away, the spark that made him feel so goddamned alive every time they touched. It had to fade, right? After five years, ten years? Now he knew better. It was never going away, and no one else was ever going to make him feel like this.

He shoved Liam back a step. "Seriously, dude. Did the Army not teach you stealth?"

Liam stretched his neck out to look over Scott's shoulder toward Reeve. "He's cool. He's not even paying attention."

Scott wrenched his head around to check. Reeve was messing around behind one of the amps. "Still not—"

Liam cut him off with a kiss. Tongue. Heat. Like he was going to fuck Scott right there. The jolt that rocked through him was better than any Johnnie Walker Black shot could ever hope to be.

Goddamn. Chai didn't need to worry about Scott touching the stock. Because Liam's surprise attack was giving Scott the kind of rush that was telling him to make all kinds of bad decisions.

Liam smiled into Scott's mouth, and Scott shoved him back hard enough to make the bar glass rattle.

"Cocky son of a bitch," Scott spat out, then took a quick breath, trying to calm himself down.

"Says the arrogant bastard." Liam smirked.

Scott caught himself licking his lips.

"Jesus, Scott, I'm dying here. I need to get you horizontal."

"Get a fuckin' room." Reeve shook his head as he walked by.

Scott flipped him off. *Fuck. Please don't let me be blushing.*

"That's an idea." Liam rubbed his eyebrow. "We could get a hotel."

"Something by the hour? Fuckin' romantic."

"I was hoping for just fucking, but I'll grab something out of a flower box on the way if it'll make you put out. Like that's ever been an issue."

"Fucking hate you." Scott's cheeks were on fire now. He'd come back and check the stock later. He needed a cigarette break. Another one.

Liam stopped him on the way past. "Hey, you're not like…." Liam's hand jerked in the direction of the stage, but for once, Scott couldn't finish Liam's sentence.

He waited.

"Back in the closet?"

Scott had never seen why complete strangers needed to know what made his dick hard. He didn't lie, but he didn't usually broadcast it. Made less of a chance someone would need a punch in the face for running their mouth.

"Fuck, no. Just the same old secretive dick I've always been."

"So what are you and your secretive dick doing after my show tomorrow night?"

Chapter Sixteen

"WHY ARE we here again?" Liam peered down the cement driveway to the dilapidated garage. Obviously Scott hadn't been hanging frozen in storage while they'd been apart, but Liam had never expected that his grumpy-ass boyfriend would develop a social network like a fucking Facebook addict. Cops, music critics, and now people who lived in single-family homes in a nice suburban neighborhood.

"Need to talk to someone about a part."

That at least made sense. Liam hadn't realized how weirded out this so-called date was making him until the lurch in his belly faded. Then he tripped on a raised crack in the cement and had to steady himself against the side of the Buick. This was stupid. With the time it took to drive over here, they could already be in that hotel room, be recovering for round two.

Scott shot Liam a look from over the top of the Buick's roof but at least had enough sense not to ask if Liam was okay. They fell back into step next to each other as they rounded the car.

"You nervous?" Scott asked instead.

"Why the fuck would I be?" Liam had been along a bunch of times when Scott was tracking down a part of some kind. The only risk involved was how bored Liam was going to be if they got in deep on carburetor barrels and feedback. Right now, it was enough to be out of the house.

Scott shrugged. "Big night tonight. 'Specially after that write-up."

And a lot of people might show up or they could be playing to an audience of six. Which would definitely be worse.

"Thanks for mentioning it," Liam grumbled, though he hadn't been nervous until just that moment.

"Figured it was why you were being such a bitch."

"Fuck off. It's from you giving me blue balls."

Scott had been so damned busy last night, Liam had barely had time to do more than grind on him as he passed through the narrow hall. When Reeve offered to drive him home after Rage Mist's first set, Liam had grabbed the chance to stop making himself crazy.

And now this fucking errand.

Liam expected Scott to keep going into the garage, but he turned into the backyard. Instead of a junker on blocks, there was a small bricked patio area with a grill and a glass-topped table and umbrella with six lawn chairs around it.

No parts, no car, no people.

That was until the back door slammed open. Bare feet slapped against the wooden steps as a guy—young at first glance—bounced down them, cradling a coffee mug. An electric-green silk bathrobe left most of his smooth chest bare and ended just above the leg hole of the boxers that looked too big for him. He definitely did not look like a guy interested in cars.

He sauntered right up to Liam and subjected him to a brief scrutiny; then the man's wide lips suddenly curved into a grin. "Hel-lo, sexy. I was so hoping it was you."

Liam froze.

"Are those big shades blocking most of your gorgeous face because you're so famous or 'cause musicians' rep for party drugs is well-deserved?"

"Hey, Eli." Scott grabbed the mug from the guy's hands. "This is Liam."

What the fuck was going on? Scott had always acted disgusted by guys like Eli, guys who, according to Scott, "shoved being gay in your face." Now he was friendly enough to walk into this Eli's yard and steal his coffee.

"No fair," Eli complained. "I was distracted by the eye candy."

Liam didn't know whether to be flattered or pissed off. And Scott was no fucking help. He just snorted a laugh.

Eli poked Scott in the chest. "You're disgustingly early."

"I was told 10:00 a.m." Scott avoided Eli's attempt to steal back the mug.

"Exactly." Eli rolled his eyes. "Go in and help Quinn." He gave Scott a little push. "After you bring out more coffee."

Liam watched Scott, knock-your-fucking-teeth-out-for-looking-at-me-wrong Scott McDermott, let this prissy guy put his black-polish-tipped fingers on him and order him around.

"C'mon, let's sit." Eli led Liam over toward the table.

Since Scott had already disappeared into the house, Liam shrugged and followed.

"What the fuck is this?" Liam selected a seat that put the table between him and Eli.

"A table. Where we're going to have brunch. Hopefully, this will fulfill the commitment to outdoor living I apparently made when I talked about how much fun it would be back in March." Eli flung his bangs back with a toss of his head.

Liam reached for his own hairline, missing the length that had let him—let Scott—play with the cowlick that flopped on his forehead. Liam had started growing it out as soon as he joined the band, but it had a ways to go. "Scott said we were here to find a car part."

Eli shrugged. "No reason you can't eat while talking cars."

"Had breakfast before I left."

"Both of you?"

Liam smoothed the edge of his shorts over the socket of his leg. "I'm not his mother." His own had served up some eggs before Liam made his escape.

"Christ, I hope not." Eli leaned back in his chair. "Just thinking it's not like he's got a kitchen where he's living."

Shit. Liam hadn't thought of that.

Eli went on, "You ever have a time where you didn't know where you were sleeping that night?"

When his mom was coked up, she'd disappear sometimes, but she always left him somewhere. With relatives, in a hotel room with some food. When he got older, he sometimes wondered whether his mom or someone from Child Protective Services would come for him first. "What did Scott tell you?"

"About you?" Eli's brows arched. "Nothing. Why?"

Liam swallowed. "My mom...." He thumbed away the sweat trickling into his eyebrow. "Well, it wasn't great sometimes, but we didn't end up on the street."

Eli's eyes narrowed. Liam couldn't figure out how a short guy in a chair could look down on him, but somehow Eli was managing it.

"You and Scott?" Eli asked.

The back door banged open, saving Liam from needing to answer. Scott stomped down the two steps, arms full of mugs and plates. After hipping the load of plates and silverware onto the table, he thunked a mug in front of Liam and then slid the other to Eli.

"Be right back with your sugar, you pussy." Scott tapped Liam's shoulder.

"Nah, grew out of that in the Army." Liam turned. "Besides, I can get it myself."

Scott sent back a face shrug, brows up, lips compressed, his version of a low-key *whatever, man.* "Food's just about ready."

"Thanks," Eli said.

Scott tromped back up the stairs. Liam couldn't figure out which felt more out of place in a suburban backyard, Eli in his expecting-an-orgy clothes or Scott in his almost transparent sleeveless undershirt, ripped-knee jeans, and steel-toe black boots.

When the door shut behind him, Eli turned back to Liam. "So—"

"I didn't know 'brunch' was some kind of code for 'job interview' now." Liam was tired of feeling like he'd missed the first half of a movie. "Exactly what the fuck am I applying for?"

The smile over the rim of Eli's mug suggested pissing Liam off was totally the point.

He shook his head and curled his hand around his own mug. "Am I supposed to ask your permission to date him or something?"

Eli snorted into his coffee. "God, no."

Confidence and bossiness masked how really young Eli might be. With only his eyes under the floppy black hair visible over the edge of the mug, he looked barely out of high school.

With a sigh, Eli settled his mug back on the table. "I was homeless for almost two years. That taught me we have to make our own families. Queer families. I'm not saying all straight people are assholes—"

"When are you not saying that, kid?" A familiar redheaded man came around the corner of the house carrying two lawn chairs, a big-eyed, tiny-bodied spaniel trotting behind him. "Don't believe it." He snapped open one of the chairs. "Eli's a total heterophobe."

Eli tapped his chin with his middle finger.

Recognition hit when the guy made a dismissive snort. *You two are peas in a pod.* The cop from that day at the car show. He had to be twice Eli's age. Liam guessed after a year on the street, any kind of sugar daddy looked good.

"Where's the classy part of your comedy routine?" Eli demanded.

"Did you just call Gavin the straight man?" The cop put his hands on his hips.

Eli spluttered. "Fuck you. I haven't had my coffee."

The cop grinned. "Gavin is in the kitchen with your daddy. Said you made a special recipe request. You're welcome for the chairs, by the way."

"We all contribute as we can. With brains or skill or"—Eli cast a gaze over the chairs—"manual labor."

The dog jumped up onto one of the lawn chairs, circled three times, and curled up, nose to tail, eyes fixed on the cop.

As much as Liam hated admitting he needed help, right then he was praying for rescue. The cop was someone Scott worked on cars with. Maybe if Liam threw out something about two-barrel carburetors, Scott would appear just to remind Liam he didn't know what he was talking about.

"Liam. This is Jamie."

"Yeah, we kinda met before." Jamie gave Liam a semifriendly once-over and stuck out a hand. As Liam shook it, Jamie added, "You staying clear of tent poles now?"

Liam forced himself not to reach for his nose.

"Now how is that any fun?" Eli demanded. "Assuming we're talking about the fun kind of tent poles?"

Liam shoved himself away from the table and stood. "I need to talk to Scott."

"Who knew talking tent poles was so stirring?" Eli said.

Without bothering to comment, Liam stomped up the stairs, his uneven steps making his frustration hotter.

The door opened into a kitchen that smelled like breakfast in heaven. Coffee, eggs, peppers. And bacon.

A solidly muscled guy with salt-and-pepper hair and wiry scruff stood at the stove and stirred a giant pan of home fries. A vaguely familiar man with model-type cheekbones leaned against the counter, and Scott—fuck—all Liam could see of Scott was his ass. His perfect ass. The ass Liam's dick should be in, except they were stuck at this stupid little party.

Liam reached for Scott's belt loop, then put his hands in his pockets to avoid temptation. Fuck if Liam would be able to stop himself from groping that ass if he put his hands on Scott. And these guys already acted like they were two beers away from a gangbang.

Scott straightened and put a pitcher on the counter. "This the one?"

The guy at the stove glanced over. "Yup."

Liam knew the second Scott saw him, knew by the slow blink and the quick bite of his bottom lip.

"Hey." Scott's voice was husky, close enough to I-just-had-a-dick-down-my-throat to make Liam's cock go from aware to half-chub.

"I need to talk to you." He started to back Scott into the hall.

The guy at the stove looked over his shoulder. "Food in five."

Out in the hall, Scott jerked open a door, and they crowded into a bathroom tucked under the stairs.

Blame sexual frustration, blame the humidity making his leg ache, blame too many goddamned people who acted like they knew all about Scott. Liam snapped.

"What the fuck happened to keeping this just between us?"

Scott had the goddamned fucking nerve to smirk. "Well, you shoving me into the bathroom for a hand job might be a giveaway."

"This isn't about—" Liam caught the direction of Scott's stare a few seconds before the throb of blood in Liam's dick forced him to pull at his shorts. "That's not why. Why the hell are we here?"

"I told you. For a part."

"The Mustang runs fine. What's so goddamned important it can't wait?"

"Until after we fuck for old times' sake?" Scott folded his arms.

"No. Jesus Christ, Scott." Liam took a step forward, brushing against Scott's sharp elbows, the forearm with the raven's wing spread to cover that old tattoo. Liam looked up. Scott's mouth was twisted in a sneer, everything about his expression saying he didn't give a shit except for his eyes. "No," Liam repeated softly. "Because I want to be with you. I don't want a hand job or just a fuck for old times' sake. I thought you wanted that too, and I'm trying to figure out why you would drag us to some big gay brunch thing when you said you didn't want to drag other people into our business."

Scott blew out a long breath. "I didn't know it was going to be a thing. Jamie, the cop—I told you about him, that he's into classic Fords—he said Quinn would know something about what I'm looking for."

"That guy in the cargo shorts in the kitchen?" Liam couldn't keep the disbelief out of his voice. The guy stirring home fries seemed way more likely to know about lawn care and dad jokes than a part for a classic car. God knew Liam had met enough gearheads to know the difference.

"Yeah. He's ex-Navy."

"What the fuck does that have to do with it?"

"Okay, don't be pissed, but I'm trying to figure out how to refit a car with a left-foot drive for you."

"That's the part you're here for?"

"Yeah. Jamie said Quinn knows some stuff about veterans' services, so…." Scott shrugged. "And you said you wanted me to not give a shit about your leg. Seems like it would be easier for you to feel regular about it if you weren't always stuck in your house waiting on a ride."

Liam wished he'd stayed the fuck outside, letting Eli make him feel shitty for not realizing that Scott was probably hungry. That was nothing compared to the riot of guilt worms spawned in his gut when he realized Scott had been trying to help. Not just that, but Scott had listened to what Liam wanted and was trying to make it happen. He let out a long breath, and his lungs weren't all that was deflating. The way his nuts twisted as his dick shrank put an ache into his thighs. He reached behind to open the door and sidestepped into the hall.

"Why didn't you tell me I was being an asshole?"

"You got there eventually."

"Thanks." Liam bumped their shoulders together as Scott passed him, heading back through the kitchen.

Scott with friends was a new concept. Liam had the uncomfortable suspicion that he was jealous. He'd never had to share Scott before.

As they approached the kitchen door, Liam asked, "So how long have you known these guys?"

"I've known Jamie awhile, mostly from swap meets, and then we started working on our cars together. Quinn and Eli I met right before I got the job at Schim's. Or, I guess, before *you* got me that job. I never did figure out how you worked that."

The kitchen was empty now. Liam stopped at the back door. "I figured Beauchamp—you know, the one who passed out at the car show?—was with Jamie, and he obviously knew you. So I tracked Beauchamp down."

Scott shrugged, eyes down. That was Scott-speak for *Don't know, and I feel embarrassed about not having the answer*. Liam also knew that was only another shrug away from *Don't know, and if you keep asking I'll be pissed about it*, so he dropped the subject.

When Liam pushed open the door, there seemed to be about thirty guys in the yard now. He almost backed into Scott, but David Beauchamp stepped toward him like Liam had conjured him up.

"EMT Walsh. Pleasure to see you again. I simply had to find out if you were able to run your quarry to ground." Beauchamp's gaze shifted over Liam's shoulder. "May I presume—"

"David." The name came at a volume that was just audible over the background chatter, but it had the effect of a drill instructor's bellow.

Beauchamp froze midsentence as his Top moved to stand behind him.

No way could Liam have forgotten him. Pacific Islander features and warm brown skin along with massive biceps tattooed in a traditional Samoan pattern were memorable enough; coupled with the size of the rest of him, Beauchamp's keeper was unmistakable.

"How's your nose?" the man asked. "Don't think we got to names at our last meeting. Tai Fonoti." He offered a hand.

Liam made his way down the rest of the stairs to take it. "Better, thanks. Liam Walsh." A quick head count showed the number at ten, counting him and Scott. The table was crowded with food, dominated by a two-foot-square pastry box.

Though Scott didn't take part in the introductions, Liam could feel the silent presence behind him, a little off to one side, literally having Liam's back as they followed Beauchamp and Tai toward the table.

"Nothing personal, Beach," Eli was saying as they approached. "I just ran out of chairs."

Tai folded his arms over his chest, and he had to know it made him look even bigger. "We weren't invited?" He looked over at Beauchamp.

"I brought pastries as an apology," Beauchamp offered with a shrug and wide innocent eyes that wouldn't fool a toddler. "But when I called Gavin—"

"Leave me out of this, please, Beach." Mr. Cheekbones was seated in one of the lawn chairs.

"C'mon. Secret codes like 'chai' and 'rooster' and you don't expect me to want a seat at the denouement?" Beauchamp seemed to be appealing to Liam for assistance now.

Soccer dad—Quinn—stood up. "We've got some old plastic chairs in the garage. And a card table."

"Don't bother." The rumble from Tai made every hair on Liam's body stand at attention. "We won't be staying." One hand clamped around the back of Beauchamp's neck. "And David certainly isn't going to want to sit down."

Beauchamp's mouth opened, but then he licked his lips and shut it again.

Eli leaned against his chair back. "You know, I want my guests to feel right at home," he purred up at Tai. "If you feel the need for an immediate response, take it upstairs, second door on the left."

Tai's gaze swept the table and then fixed on Eli. "Everyone's good here?"

"They will be," Eli said.

Tai nodded and steered Beauchamp at the back steps, passing close enough for Liam to hear the muttered "Oh shit" from Beauchamp.

Scott cleared his throat. "Is he gonna…?"

Liam turned to see him finish off his words with an open-palmed gesture to mimic a smack.

"Definitely." Eli drew out the words in an even more exaggerated purr.

Quinn grabbed a big handful of Eli's hair and yanked his head back to plant a hard kiss on his mouth.

"And everyone's okay with this?" Scott went on.

"Is there a reason why you're not?" Eli asked him.

"Not personally, I guess." Scott shrugged.

"Welcome to the freak show," Jamie muttered from his spot next to Mr. Cheekbones, then jumped. "Ow." He glared at the man.

"As long as it's safe, sane, and consensual." That came from a cute guy in glasses, neat goatee, and wavy hair sitting by Eli.

The blond on his right stood up and came around the table to pump Liam's hand like he was going to try to sell Liam something. "Hey. Big fan. Can't wait for your show tonight. We'll both be there."

"We will?" The dry tone suited the goatee guy's hipster look.

The blond winked. "Don't worry. He'll be there. I know the way to his heart."

"Blow jobs?" Dark brows arched over the rims of his glasses.

"Berger cookies," the blond said. "I'm Kellan. The wiseass is my boyfriend, Nate."

"Kellan *Brooks*," Scott put in, like the guy's last name was particularly significant.

"Sit down," Eli urged.

"Where are your two little chicks, Mother Hen?" Jamie asked him.

"At work, why? Missing their jailbait asses?"

As he eased into a chair, Liam swore he heard Jamie's jaw snap shut.

"I'm going to live tweet some of your show tonight. Instagram it too. You've got an Epiphone Casino, right?" Kellan barely paused for breath. "You got it strung hard tail or trapeze?"

Liam had just gotten a flaky layered custard thing up to his lips. Damn. It smelled amazing. "Uh—trapeze." Liam remembered the early lessons Reeve had given on the electric hollow body, though the process of restringing it seemed way above Liam's current ability.

"Cool. Fucking gorgeous axe, man, but I just can't handle the deep-set neck." Kellan moved his fingers as if he were sliding up and down the frets. "Fucks me up."

"I haven't needed much range with the melody line—"

"Your voice has it, though. Holy shit, it's fucking amazing. What's your lead guitarist play? I couldn't see the body over the security dude's—"

"Hey, babe," Nate cut in. "You think you could hit Pause on your fanboying for a few and let him eat?"

"Sorry, man." Kellan put a hand on Liam's arm, then jerked it away from the contact with the scars and skin graft. "Uh—oops. Hope I didn't hurt—"

"It's over two years old. Plus there isn't much nerve sensation left." As the words left his lips, Liam felt Scott's stare against his cheek. Liam hadn't told him anything about what had happened beyond those two words at the car show. *Army. Afghanistan.* Not a lie. But pretty damned far from the whole truth. The pins and needles of paresthesia rippled up from his phantom foot. He fought the urge to stomp the ground. Not that it would have helped.

"Where'd you serve?" Quinn asked.

"OEF. Paktika. 365." The reduction to its base elements—mission, location, length—was usually enough to shut down questions.

It worked with Quinn, though Liam caught a nod that passed between Quinn and Jamie.

When the sound came, it could have been some typical Sunday morning home improvement project. But it wasn't quite as normal as a hammer against drywall. A blunt impact on flesh made a different but still recognizable echo. Scott shifted in his seat, picking up and putting down his coffee without drinking any of it. As the rhythm of impact increased in pace to jackhammer speed, Liam buried his embarrassment in a mouthful of pastry and cream. It was one thing to see the cuffs on Beauchamp's wrists and watch the dynamics, knowing that some people got their kink on that way, but it was a whole different thing to hear it. To hear it and know what was going on. And to who.

"Mimosa?" Mr. Cheekbones offered the pitcher to Liam.

He nodded.

As the other man filled a glass, he said, "Somehow we seemed to have missed our opportunity for introductions. I'm Gavin. Should you happen to feel a wet nose at your ankles, don't be alarmed. It's just Annabelle searching for any dropped crumbs."

Like that sound from an overhead window wasn't alarming enough. Jesus.

Liam glanced around the table. Jamie grinned and muttered something in Gavin's ear. Eli had shifted and thrown a leg over Quinn's lap, and Nate was licking something off Kellan's thumb. To Liam's left, Scott was rigid, knuckles white around the fork resting on his half-empty plate. Liam wondered which impulse Scott was fighting harder. The one to get as far away from the gut-churning awkwardness or to go tearing into the house and take on the guy built like a pro linebacker. But Beauchamp didn't need protection, right? That was how it worked, as far as Liam knew.

"So, Scott." Eli grinned. "Cut or uncut?"

Scott's fork scraped against his plate. "'Scuse me?"

Liam heard the warning of imminent violence in Scott's tone.

Eli held up a hand. "Not you. Your preference in dicks. I got into this thing with my friend Casey about circumcision, and—"

"Seriously? Nobody's got a problem with what's going on?" Scott's voice cracked with anger.

Eli swung his leg off Quinn's lap and straightened in his chair. "Some people have a problem with the fact that you and I—and everybody else at this table—likes dick."

Kellan raised a finger.

"And one of us also likes pussy." Eli paused for an eye roll, but he smiled at Kellan. "Plenty of people think it's disgusting."

"Pussy?" Jamie interrupted. "Ow." He turned to Gavin. "You're lucky you didn't kick the dog."

Gavin sipped his mimosa.

Eli went on over the interruption. "That just having to know we're queer is reason enough to treat us like shit."

Liam got where Eli was going with it. And yeah, it was his house. Still, it didn't make it any easier to listen to somebody's dungeon games over brunch.

When Scott took a deep breath, Liam knew Scott was catching on too.

Eli nodded. "Now I, for one, enjoy having my ass paddled to bruises before Quinn shoves his deliciously cut cock up—"

Nate spluttered out his coffee, while Quinn choked on his, turning deep red before catching his breath.

"—and I'm goddamned if I'm going to let anyone make me ashamed of who I am, how I love, and in adult company, how I get off."

Scott ran a hand through his hair, as if trying to get his 'hawk to stand up. "Yeah." He nodded. "Okay."

The sound of open-handed blows against flesh stopped as abruptly as it had started. A few houses away, a lawn mower snarled to life.

"It's still fucking weird, though," Jamie muttered to Scott, then winked at Gavin. "Ha. Missed that time."

"YOU TRACKED this down in one day?" Liam stood in the driveway next to Quinn while Jamie and Scott set up a removable left-pedal accelerator in Quinn's Buick.

Quinn shrugged. "It's still summer for another week. And I already set up my classroom for the year. But it was easy enough." Quinn's gaze felt like a laser drill into the side of Liam's head. "Would have thought the VA would be a logical start."

It would have been, if Liam didn't try to limit his VA contact to a minimum. Seeing people who'd been wounded in combat reminded him that he hadn't come by his scars honorably, just through the stupid conviction that he had all the answers.

"What makes you an expert?"

"I spent a chunk of the last year of my Navy career in the hospital in Bethesda. Some of it in a coma."

Liam turned to meet Quinn's eyes and then wished he hadn't. The guy looked like he could see straight through to the back of Liam's head to dig out all his faults and lay them out for people—for Scott—to see.

"Maybe it was different back then. Almost twenty years of war changes things. Lots of paperwork and waiting now."

"Hm." It wasn't an agreement.

Liam stepped around the hood and got another eyeful of Scott's ass as he lay over the seat. Maybe Eli would offer them a room to work things out since he was so accepting. At least now Liam understood why Scott liked Eli. From their first night together at St. Bennie's, Scott had accepted Liam, without conditions, without judgment. Liam knew, with a certainty that ran deeper than bone, that Scott wouldn't care about Liam's scars or stump. Scott would always accept Liam in a way he didn't deserve.

"For fuck's sake, McDermott, it's just practice. He's only going to the end of the driveway." That was Jamie, who was out of sight as he leaned in the passenger door.

"Just two holes, and I promise to fix them." Scott's voice was muffled.

"No," Jamie shot back.

"How big a hole?" Quinn asked.

"It's a fucking hole, Q. To the outside. Wet feet, rust."

"Fine. I'll hold it, then," Scott said.

"It's got vinyl grip on the base. It's designed to stick to the goddamned carpet. Stop being pathetic." Jamie popped up on the outside of the passenger door and slammed it shut. "Try it out." He jerked his chin at Liam.

Liam should be focused on the car, but then Scott crawled out of the other side and lifted his undershirt to wipe the sweat off his face, revealing wet skin sprinkled with dark hair. The lines of muscles on Scott's abs made Liam's mouth water. He bit his cheek to keep from pitching a tent right there.

He focused on the deep scowl making a V on Scott's forehead, but then he wanted to kiss it and force it away with a bad joke.

"Saddle up, cowboy," Jamie called from the other side of the car. "While we're young."

Scott hovered as Liam swung himself into the driver's seat one leg at a time, glancing down to make sure his prosthetic wasn't pushing on the gas pedal or brake. As soon as he settled in and put his hands on the wheel, panic knocked the breath out of him. He couldn't figure out why. It was just a regular dashboard, nothing fancy. Certainly not a jeep. And this sensation wasn't anything like that watery-guts sensation of taking fire, the skin prickle of waiting for the impact of what you couldn't hear in time to duck away from to tear through armor and flesh.

Scott crouched and ran through everything about the system that Quinn had already shown them, that the new pedal was connected to a bar that would depress the car's accelerator for him.

Liam practiced shifting his left foot from the accelerator to the brake. It didn't feel nearly as awkward as it should, and he had a hell of a lot more control than he did with his prosthesis. Scott looked up at him, lips curving in a twitch of a smile. Liam wanted to grab him and run back to the Mustang, not just so he could kiss a bigger smile onto Scott's face, but because he'd finally recognized the breathless dread. And it had nothing to do with PTSD or jeeps. This was all him. Always had been. He'd chase something, like getting out of foster care and back with his mom, becoming a doctor, or being able to drive again, but the closer he got to having it, the less he seemed to want it. The only time he hadn't wanted to run when he got close was with music.

And Scott.

Because that was all that mattered. As long as he got to have music and Scott, everything else was background noise.

His breath came easier now. He took a deep one, started the car, and popped it into Reverse.

"Just give me a second to get in." Scott shut the driver's door and started around the hood, but Liam had already taken off the parking brake and started idling backward down the driveway.

Scott took two steps after him and froze, his hard stare way more expressive than the finger he held up.

Liam shifted his foot to the brake at the end of the driveway. Compared to trying to work out the right pressure on the pedals with his prosthesis, this was cake. He craned his neck around and then backed into the street. He'd take a lap, like Quinn had suggested, since getting one of these for himself was going to run three bills.

Despite that initial panic, by the time he made it to the corner, his cheeks hurt from smiling. He could do this. His chest opened wide on a deep breath. He could have sworn it was the first time since the accident that he was doing something by himself. He knew it wasn't technically true. It was only that everyone trying to help had felt like being buried alive. He cut his eyes to the passenger seat, suddenly wishing he hadn't left Scott in the driveway. Scott would understand what Liam meant. He'd know how it felt—how Liam felt.

He pulled back into the driveway and rolled to a stop. Jamie, with his hands on his hips, was talking at Quinn. Scott stood off to one side, leaning against the garage door. As Liam cut the ignition, Scott arched that one brow.

Liam grinned at him.

Scott nodded and pushed away from the peeling wood before disappearing around the corner of the house.

By the time Liam managed to get himself out of the car, Quinn and Jamie were in Liam's face with descriptions of the different kinds of left-foot setups, permanent, portable, adjustable. Quinn entered Liam's email into his phone, promising to send along a form he could use to apply for help paying for it.

"Though I'm guessing you won't have to worry much about labor costs for installation," Quinn added with a wink.

Scott wasn't in the yard. The dog was curled up asleep on a chair, and the table had been cleared. As Liam started for the house, Gavin met him on the steps.

"I take it your drive was a success?" he asked as he maneuvered around Liam. The dog shook herself awake, jumped down, then yawned before trotting over to Gavin. She cocked her head at Liam.

The expression was so similar to Gavin's when he'd asked his question that Liam pressed his lips together against a laugh. Then he realized Gavin was waiting for an answer.

"Yeah." Liam bent to offer a hand for Annabelle to sniff. "It's surprisingly easy to get used to using my left foot."

The dog made a quick survey of his hand, almost as if she were only being polite, then sat and cocked her head again.

"Uh, she's cute," Liam added for something to say.

"I'm sure she appreciates the sentiment." Gavin smiled, and the corners of his eyes crinkled.

Liam had no idea how someone like Gavin ended up hanging out with the rest of these guys.

Jamie strode into the backyard. "'Ey, Montgomery? You 'bout ready? I gotta be at work at three."

Liam looked sharply at Gavin. Gavin Montgomery? Like one of *the* Montgomerys?

Gavin met Liam's stare and shrugged apologetically. "I'm nothing more than a piece of flotsam that washed up on a fortunate shore."

Jamie snorted, and Annabelle bounced to her feet. "C'mon, then, Flotsam. I don't want to be here when Jetsam starts another free show. Text him later."

Gavin bent and scooped up the toy-sized spaniel. In a soft voice, Gavin said, "There's nothing they won't do to help if you ask."

Liam pointed his chin at Jamie. "So, um, thanks."

"Save the thanks for Quinn." Jamie fluffed under the dog's ears. As he and Gavin headed for the driveway, Jamie cranked his head around to add, "And Scott."

Chapter Seventeen

FOR SOMEONE who'd just had a pretty big problem solved, Liam was in a bitch of a mood on the drive back to the bar, and Scott was tired of silent glares.

He shot a glance over and then looked back at parkway traffic. "What's up?"

"I'm fine."

"Yeah, right. You're fine."

Liam's breath huffed out. Scott started a mental countdown to when Liam would crack. *Five, four, three, two—*

"I'm jealous, okay?"

"Jealous?" Scott gave an involuntary jerk of the wheel and then dragged the Mustang straight again. "Of what?"

"You and all your friends. I know it's stupid. But you weren't exactly socialized before."

"Well, at least I was housebroken." Scott rolled his eyes. "And they aren't all my friends." The memory of Eli grabbing Scott at the door to mutter in his ear *"Please work out your shit. I'm counting on you guys"* had him pressing the accelerator to whip around some asshole putzing along in the middle lane. What the fuck business was it of Eli's? God knew they'd all be geezers by the time he and Liam worked out their shit. "I told you. I only really know Jamie."

Liam grunted an acceptance.

"I didn't expect it to get out of hand like that."

"Or for anyone's hand to get used like that." Liam's voice had a trace of humor.

"Jesus. I didn't know what the fuck we were supposed to do."

"Me either. I mean, I saw his wrist cuffs—"

"Is that what those things mean? I just thought that was some sweet leather, out of place on his preppy ass but—"

"Yeah. It's kind of a sign for that stuff."

Scott slowed as the traffic merged down to two lanes by all the mansions set way back from the road. He tried for casual as he asked, "You—uh—into that?"

"Nah. Met guys on the base who were into it. I didn't know there were people who lived it twenty-four seven."

Scott stared down at his hands on the wheel. That stupid, instinctive punch at the car show aside, he couldn't imagine hitting Liam, even if Liam wanted it. And as for Scott—shit, he knew Liam didn't need leather or chains to keep Scott anywhere Liam wanted him, the bastard. Liam had invisible hooks, deep under Scott's rib cage. Worse, Scott wasn't sure he wanted them out, even if he could figure out how to remove 'em.

Liam tapped at his phone as they waited at the light for a left on York Road. "All set." He shoved the phone under Scott's nose.

Scott focused enough to see an email from the Best Maryland Inn confirming a reservation for tonight. Swallowing the urge to head directly for the address and to hell with showing up to haul kegs at Schim's, Scott managed a nod and a "Cool" that didn't sound too forced.

After tucking a cigarette between his lips, he dragged out his lighter. The cool rush of smoke took away the anxious stink of hot tar and rubber. He exhaled out the window and took another drag before he remembered. With a guilty glance at Liam, he tossed the barely started smoke out the window. "Sorry."

"It's your car. I've never asked you to not smoke."

"Yeah, but you're singing tonight." Scott was still trying to wrap his head around the fact that the Liam he'd known forever could front a rock band, hold a crowd of metalheads spellbound with his voice.

"Still didn't have to do that."

Given the price of a pack, Scott was half-tempted to open the door and grab the still-burning stick. But then the light changed, so he just rolled his head on his neck and made the turn, changing the subject as he did. "You ready for tonight?"

"The show or later?" Liam's tone told Scott all he needed to know about the big grin on Liam's face. "That reminds me." Liam pointed at the Royal Farms gas station a block away. "Can you stop there? I've got to pick something up."

Scott said he'd wait in the car and watched Liam stride off into the little convenience store. Maybe it was what Scott wanted to see, but Liam's steps looked confident, more like the rolling swagger Scott remembered. Obviously, being able to drive again was going to make Liam's life much easier.

Scott took advantage of the time to get in a smoke, climbing out of the Mustang to lean against the driver's door. A green '71 Stingray pulled in a space away. The girl who got out first gave Scott an assessing stare, so he made sure to give a friendly nod to the bearded guy with her. Last thing he needed was to get into it over that kind of nonsense.

He tapped the cigarette out against his lighter when Liam came back out, then tucked the half smoke away. Liam popped the tab on his twenty-ounce Red Bull as he approached the car. He stopped with a hand on the door and chugged. Scott watched Liam's throat bob, mouth watering as he thought about how that sweaty, bristly skin would feel on his tongue.

"Problem?" Liam asked. "Shit. I should've asked. I'll finish the drink out here."

"Just get in the car." As good as he'd gotten the exterior and engine, the interior was another story. A cigarette burn—not even his—marred the driver's seat, and the left rear seat had something melted and baked into the backrest. "It's fine."

Fuck if he ever wanted to have a car so mint he'd freak out over someone drinking in it. Like those guys who kept their classic cars under cover all year, hauled them on trailers to shows so they stayed like they were factory-new. Why have a car and not drive it?

Liam tossed a fresh pack of Newports on Scott's lap. "They don't sell singles, and I figured I owed you one."

If Liam was going to insist on keeping score, Scott had to learn how to take the win instead of arguing about it.

"Thanks." Scott nodded at the Red Bull. "That your preshow ritual?"

"Not really."

Something in Liam's voice made Scott sneak a glance at him before he pulled out of the lot. Between the grin and the expression in Liam's eyes, Scott's dick was ready to jump the gun. He squeezed the wheel and focused back on the traffic.

Liam went on, "I was hoping there'd be another reason to stay up tonight. Want some?"

They had to stop for another light. Liam waved the can under Scott's nose. Scott tugged on the leg of his jeans. "I've never needed much help staying… up."

The force of Liam's smile hit Scott right on the side of the face and made his jeans even tighter.

IT WAS just sex. Scott readjusted himself, then bungeed the keg onto the handcart. Good sex. But he was building himself up for it like some virgin on prom night. Yeah, it was always good with Liam, but Scott's brain—and his balls—were waxing it up with a shine of memories that were too damned good to be true.

And Liam wasn't helping. He hung around after the band did all their setup and sound checks, looking at Scott like they were already alone, until Scott was ready to drag him into the storeroom to see what they could manage up against the wall, and to hell with the Best Maryland Inn. Scott still stopped to wipe the sweat off his face with his T-shirt before dragging the keg upstairs.

He recognized the uneven rhythm on the stairs before he heard Liam's voice. "Jesus, Scott. Keep your shirt on."

Smug bastard. Scott turned, pretending to continue to wipe his face, and let his other hand hitch his threadbare jeans a little lower on his hips.

"Fuck. That's not fair."

Scott let the shirt fall back down over his stomach. "Fair?" He stalked over to Liam. "Fair like the way you keep looking at me?" He grabbed Liam's waist. "Fair like you following me down here when I'm supposed to be working? How 'velvet-voiced' do you think you're going to sound after I shove my dick down your throat?"

Liam kissed him, grabbing the sides of Scott's face, as if Scott wanted to be anywhere but there, where he could taste Liam, breathe Liam—God—feel the stroke of his tongue send a shock to Scott's balls. He could stay right here forever. Until the pressure built and he couldn't.

Fuck waiting.

Scott dragged Liam under the stairs. A quick hand job now was the only way Scott could survive the night. As he reached for Liam's fly, a grin against his mouth told him this was exactly what Liam had been planning when he came down here.

Scott lifted his mouth enough to whisper, "Christ. How did I forget how pushy you are?"

"Because you like where I push you to."

"Damn right."

The door to the cellar banged open above them. "Scott. You're bringing that keg up today, yes?"

If it had been anybody but Mrs. S., he might have snarled something back. Instead, her voice acted like an ice bucket on his balls. "Right now, Mrs. S."

As Scott stepped back, Liam raised an eyebrow at him.

"Not one fucking word, Walsh." Scott started wheeling the cart to the foot of the stairs. "Or you can figure out how to fuck yourself at that motel."

Schim's had filled up since Scott had gone downstairs. They were three deep at the bar, and people were already trying to stake out a spot close to the stage, though the band wasn't playing for another ninety minutes.

As Scott straightened up from switching out the keg, he saw that a table near the end of the bar now had a sloppily lettered Reserved sign slapped on top. For the band? There were three chairs tilted to lean against it. The traveling bands usually sat in their vans until they came on. Reeve was helping his sister behind the bar; Mac and the drummer had disappeared as soon as they'd set up.

Reeve pulled a glass of Blood Orange Ale and snatched a twenty from the guy he put it in front of. "Scotty, my hero. You gotta thank that Brooks guy—wait, introduce him to me. He's been tweeting and instagramming about the band, and just look at this place. How the fuck did you get in with him?"

Scott tore his gaze away from the sign and scanned the crowd for Kellan. "Don't see him yet. And I'm not *in* with him. He likes the band." He nodded at the reserved table. "You set that up for him?"

Reeve tapped at the cash register and stepped back to the bar to give the guy his change. "No. But please, man, whatever's going on with you and Liam, can you just keep a lid on it until after the show? He's skittish enough."

Liam hadn't seemed freaked at all ten minutes ago.

"What happened?" Scott turned his full attention on Reeve.

Reeve shrugged. "We had a set list and now he's tweaking out about it."

As good as Reeve's songs and Mac's playing were, any idiot could tell nothing mattered as much as Liam's vocals. Scott crossed his arms. "So change it."

"You know, if we hired a manager, I'm pretty sure I'd have known."

"Am I the only person working here?" Chai hip-bumped her brother out of her way. "Scott, bring up some more Jäger and schnapps, those Moon Shots are going fast."

Chai had repurposed a cocktail recipe into what she was calling Moon Shots in honor of the band. She was stressing the Jäger to the customers, but Scott bet there was more of the cinnamon and orange schnapps in the cocktail shakers.

"Jäger and schnapps, coming up." The sooner he dropped it off, the sooner he could find out what had Liam's shorts in a bunch.

Of course, nothing was ever that easy. As soon as he dropped off the case, Chai sent him down for another keg. By the time he was dragging that behind the bar, Reeve had vanished. Well, Liam was a big boy who didn't need Scott to hold his hand—or fight his battles.

Chai grabbed his arm and, through yelling and sign language, told him to pour out a tray of her premixed Moon Shots. He handed the tray off to the waiting server and tried to get a look at the reserved table, but a crowd of girls at that end of the bar were holding up their phones for selfies. He pressed a palm against the bar for leverage as he tried to look around them.

"Scott. Hey." Eli put a hand on Scott's shoulder.

Scott saw the kiss coming and managed to duck out of the way.

Eli laughed. "So who do I have to blow in this place to get a drink?"

"Me." Chai folded her arms. "So you might be out of luck."

"Name the time and place, gorgeous." Eli batted his eyes.

Chai shot a look at Scott, her brows raised in an *is-this-guy-for-real* question. He shrugged an answer.

"What are those pretty things in the blue plastic shot glasses?" Eli said.

"Moon Shots. One for five, two for eight." Chai's pricing had led to her raking in two-dollar tips all night.

"Gimme four. And keep the change." Eli slapped a twenty on the bar.

Chai tipped her head toward the jug she was pouring the shots out of, and Scott set them up.

Chai had moved on to the next customer, so Scott had to hand her the cash.

"Remind me to train you on the register tomorrow, and cover for Ford at the door so he can take a piss. And don't punch anyone tonight."

He hadn't punched anyone on Friday. He'd wanted to, but he'd only dragged that would-be stage diver outside. He saluted Chai and headed for the door. The reserved table was still empty.

"Thirty-five more," Mrs. S. said from behind her cash box.

Ford handed him the pocket black light and gripped his shoulder. "Thanks, man. Be right back."

The cover was only ten tonight. Chai and Reeve had argued over it, Reeve saying that would scare people away from an unknown band and Chai claiming they needed to act like they were worth it if they wanted people to care. Mac had said, "She's right," then disappeared before the argument started up again.

There wasn't a line now, but as they checked IDs and collected the cover, people bunched up, which was why Scott didn't have any warning before he looked at the next customer and found himself asking Liam's mom for ID.

She looked older, her skin tighter, lines deeper on her face, but there was no mistaking that look of stunned disapproval. "Scott? Liam never mentioned you working here."

Scott forced a swallow past the tightness in his throat and nodded. "Mrs. Walsh."

"It's Becker now." A quick hand movement indicated the tall middle-aged white guy next to her. "My husband, Greg."

What was he supposed to say to that? *Nice catch? I never expected to see you off coke for more than a month?*

Scott kept right on nodding. His throat wouldn't let him talk anyway. Least now he was pretty sure he knew the reason for Liam's sudden twitchiness. And the reserved table.

"And this is Deon."

Of course it was. Marilyn Walsh—Becker, that was—produced Liam's ex-boyfriend with a flourish like a magician executing a trick.

"We've met." Deon pushed the words out in a tight voice that didn't give Scott any clue about what the fuck was going on.

Chai's warning echoed in Scott's head. *And don't punch anyone.*

"What's the holdup?" someone called from the crowd behind the Beckers. And guest.

"Thanks for covering." Ford was back. "There a problem?"

Scott passed back the black light. "No problem at all." He pushed past Deon and stepped outside. "They're with the band."

Chapter Eighteen

"I SAID I was fine with it. I just thought we should start harder and faster." Liam watched Reeve stick the set list onto the curve of the Epiphone Casino. Once they were onstage, everything would be fine. It was just the waiting that was killing him. He wanted to start now.

Mac's eyes were closed as she sat with her back to the van's wall, fingers sliding up and down her fret board.

Reeve handed the guitar back to Liam and checked his phone before issuing the latest report from his grandmother. "Amma says we're thirty away from capacity, but it's slowed down."

"Holy shit." Dev leaned over from the passenger seat and snatched the phone from Reeve's hand. "That's, like, what? Almost three hundred people?"

"Two-twenty is our limit."

"Okay, so two hundred. For us, man. Can you believe it?"

According to Dev and Reeve, Backward Gaze had been lucky to draw thirty people on their own, and when they'd opened for other bands, they'd been heckled. Liam was glad he hadn't been around for that.

"Cool," Liam agreed as Dev passed him the phone. As Liam turned to hand it off to Reeve, Scott's name seemed to jump off the screen.

Under Reeve's grandmother's text about them approaching capacity was a second text. *Anybody seen Scott?*

Liam jabbed at the screen as he pushed the phone under Reeve's nose. "Did something happen to Scott?"

Dev made a disgusted sigh. "Dude. Could you be more of a thirteen-year-old girl?"

"Speak for yourself, asshole." Mac slipped a joint out of her shirt and lit it before closing her eyes again. She took a couple of hits before leaning to offer the joint to Reeve, who shook his head. Liam accepted it gratefully.

He didn't know if the weed was that good or he just wanted it to be, but he felt better by the time Mac passed it to him again. Scott was probably just dragging a keg around, Reeve was right about the opener, and they were going to crush it tonight.

He couldn't wait to get on the stage.

"We got this, right?" Reeve asked them.

Mac sucked a last hit. "Aye, aye, chief."

LIAM CHECKED his mic, then stepped back, nodding in the direction of the soundboard. The stage lights made it impossible to see much more than shadows after the first ten feet. He didn't need to see or even feel the crowd to know it was there, though. The expectant energy poured onto the stage, vibrating up his bones—even the ones made of carbon fiber—to fill his head with a rush of excitement. He wanted to feel like this all the time.

It was like sex. No, it was like sex with Scott. But the sparks from this intense connection were shared with a bunch of strangers.

Not all strangers. Right at the edge of his field of vision, Kellan's blond head and height stood out. As Kellan raised a phone and thumb, Liam spotted Nate next to him.

Liam wished he could see Scott.

He let his fingers brush the frets to get ready for the first chord and heard the whisper of that friction echo in the amp.

Reeve tapped his mic and the crowd's volume dropped. "We want to dedicate this first song to my grandfather—"

"Shut up and play something," someone yelled from the dark, followed by shuffling and shushing.

Then Chai's voice rang out from the bar. "Pop Schim!"

There were enough regulars familiar with the ritual. Echoed toasts followed, lots of people raising those little blue shot glasses.

Reeve went on. "And to everyone who's sacrificed to serve this country. Including our lead singer, Liam Walsh."

That had not been part of the set list. Liam jerked his head around to see Reeve pointing at him as the crowd cheered. Liam mouthed *What the fuck?* at him.

Just holding the guitar was all the memory he could handle of Ross. Hard enough to get through the lyrics of "Rooster" without picturing Ross crawling toward him. Now Reeve had to go and make people want to see if Liam got all tripped up with emotion?

He wanted to tear off the Epiphone's strap and get the fuck out of there, but Dev tapped his sticks with the cue and Liam's fingers settled on the strings instead.

Reeve's bass hummed deep while Mac's Gibson started the mournful whine. Reeve's and Mac's voices were naturally an eerie half step off each other on the backing vocal.

The audience crooned along, though an impatient voice started the lyrics and got shouted down.

Liam exhaled, then opened his chest to hit midrange, and everything was perfect again because it was about the music. The crowd screamed at the end of the first phrase, and Liam focused on that energy, slitting his eyes against the light, and poured the feeling back into every note. On the second verse, the audience screamed at every one of the trills and riffs Mac slid into the peaks and valleys.

He felt it all in his chest, the music somehow coming through him from someplace else. He barely flinched at the line about a dying friend, and by the time they were on to the Puddle of Mudd song, he wasn't thinking much at all.

The last song before the break was one of Reeve's, "The Art of Quitting." Starting off with a drum solo that proved why Reeve put up with Dev's shitty attitude, the bitter lyrics were all about betrayal. Reeve swore it wasn't a romantic breakup but about the old lead singer and guitarist quitting the band.

Liam spat the verse in a harsh whisper and then opened his throat to scream the chorus. Had he ever been that angry himself? If he'd written the song, he'd feel like he was up here naked. Scott probably understood the feeling better. No shit. Liam had been the whining bitch the lyrics talked about, the one who threw everything away.

There was another instrumental section before the bridge, no melody, just Dev and Mac and Reeve passing around solos. He faded back as much as the small stage would let him, ducking out of the spots, grabbing a bottle of water out of the crate behind Mac. The warm fluid barely hit his throat before he felt it—a hard stare focused on the side of his face. Not someone watching the band. Just him. Scott?

He wanted to shade his eyes and peer back, but his cue was coming, the build of chords setting up the venom in the words of the bridge to the last chorus.

Since he didn't have to play the guitar until the chorus, he held the mic in both hands. "And when you're crawling, broken, bleeding." He opened his eyes.

Fuck, not Scott. *Deon* glared from next to a poster-covered column ten feet back.

Liam shut his eyes again to get through the rest. "Don't come to me." His voice broke with emotion, exactly the way Reeve had wanted, but this was fear, not rage.

What the hell was Deon doing here? And what the fuck had happened to Scott?

IT WAS hard to slink close to the wall when you were hauling a case of liquor bottles through swaying bodies, but Scott was giving it his best shot. There was only so much hiding out in the storeroom he could get away with. He shifted his grip to step around two big guys who were throwing horns at the band—Liam's band—and came face-to-frowning-face with the one he'd been trying to hide from all night.

"It was a surprise to see you here, Scott." Marilyn leaned in to yell in his ear, but he still caught that assessing stare he'd become all too used to when surrounded by social workers.

He considered pretending he couldn't hear her over the drum solo, but that would just make the moment last longer. "Yes, ma'am. I have to get back to work." He hefted the case so she'd have to notice it.

"Liam mentioned he'd run into you at the car show, but not that you had a job here. Is there a reason he wouldn't tell me?"

'Cause you're his mom, not his girlfriend was what Scott wanted to say, but he didn't. He also didn't push through Marilyn to get to the bar. "Have to ask him."

"Scott, goddamn it. Where's my liquor?" Chai probably could be heard even next to the amps, and Scott had never been happier to see anyone as she jostled Marilyn out of the way.

Scott held on to the case and followed to take refuge behind the bar.

"Who's that?" Chai put her mouth close to his ear as he unpacked the bottles.

"Liam's mom."

Marilyn was still at the service gate, watching them instead of her son.

Chai shot over another look as she made change for a drink. After slapping the cash in front of a customer, she grabbed Scott's ear again. "What's her issue with you?"

Scott snorted. "Long fucking story."

Chai glanced down at his hands and Scott followed her gaze. His left pinky had been caught in a chain and almost ripped off one time, but he didn't think that was what she was staring at. The light over the register showed up the scrapes on his knuckles, skin lost to contact with the rough cellar wall.

Not on purpose, though. He'd almost lost control of a keg earlier. Hell, his knuckles were often more swollen than not, though it was usually from trying to work a wrench inside an engine instead of contact from something like a wall. Or a jaw. He'd never hit anyone who hadn't attacked first—except those two times with Liam. Shit. Maybe Marilyn was right to look at him like he was a monster trying to steal her innocent child.

"No punching, right?" Chai shoulder-bumped him.

"No punching."

A burst of screams and applause was followed by Reeve's amplified voice. "Yeah. All right. Thank you."

More screeches from the crowd.

"Thank you," Reeve said again. "Stick around. We'll be back in ten."

Liam probably needed a few minutes to soothe that voice of his, to wipe off the sweat, and do whatever else musicians did when they took a break, but Scott had to know what the fuck Liam's maybe-not-so-ex-boyfriend was doing here. Marilyn had abandoned her post at the service gate.

Scott started off in that direction, but Chai yanked him back with a grip on his T-shirt.

"Not you." She pushed him toward the taps. "Pour what I tell you. Two Blood Orange."

Pouring beer into plastic cups didn't require a lot of focus. Scott peered through the taps. Between the height and the braids, Deon was easy enough to get a fix on. He handed off the cups.

"Two Doggie Style, one Salty Crab."

Scott froze with his hand on the Salty Crab tap watching Liam land awkwardly as he charged off the stage and headed straight for Deon.

The beer splashed over his hand, and Scott released the tap—along with the breath he'd been holding. No way was this turning out to be some joyful reunion with hearts and flowers and shit. Liam's jaw was tight enough to crack a molar, and he looked more likely to strangle the dude than to hug him.

Scott finished the order and slid it to Chai. Marilyn joined Deon and Liam. Based on her hand movements, she was trying to calm things down.

With every breath squeezing past the tightness in his throat, Scott sidled to the Honeydew Jalapeño, then back along to the Bare Ass Blonde tap, while Chai kept snapping orders. Thank fuck she'd kept him from doing something stupid. They weren't kids at St. Bennie's anymore, and Liam didn't need Scott fighting his battles for him. Liam had goddamned been to war.

Or maybe at the ripe old age of twenty-seven, Scott had wised up to the fact that the only person in the world more stubborn than him was Liam fucking Walsh.

Liam shook off his mom's hand while shaking his head and stomped toward the bar, proving Scott's point for him.

He stalked up to the service gate. "Can I get a couple of waters for the band?" He stared straight at Scott, though Chai was closer.

"Earth to Scott. Where're those Bare Asses?" Chai cut in.

Scott made the handoff. Out of the corner of his eye, he watched Marilyn come up behind Liam. Loud enough for Scott to hear, she said, "Deon was the one who encouraged you to audition. He drove you to all of the practices. Why wouldn't I invite him?"

"I told you why." Liam's sigh was weighted with frustration.

Filling the next order took Scott out of earshot, but when he stepped back, Liam was ducking his head away from his mom. "His decision, Mom. Hey, Scott, can I get those waters now?"

Scott turned and opened the fridge door. He was a good six feet away, but Marilyn's voice easily cut through all crowd noise. "Don't tell me you're back together with Scott?"

One of the plastic bottles almost slipped out of Scott's hands, but he pinned it against his chest.

Liam's answer came quick and loud and full of disgust. "I'm not."

That was exactly what Scott wanted him to say. What they'd agreed on.

Yet Liam's answer still knifed a gash under Scott's ribs so deep he fought the urge to reach down and stuff his guts back in.

Instead he thunked the four plastic bottles of water in front of Liam and Marilyn.

"Well, at least there's that," Marilyn said.

"Here you go."

"Thanks." Liam's hand shot out to grab one, and Scott jerked his fingers back so they didn't touch, accidentally or otherwise.

Marilyn met his gaze. "Scott."

Just his name. Was it supposed to be an apology? A greeting? A drink order?

Or a challenge?

"Ma'am? Can I get you something?"

She shook her head.

Liam scooped up the waters. "Mom, I gotta go. Thanks for coming." He tapped her shoulder with his free hand and headed for the alley door.

"Scott. Two more Blood Orange." Chai slapped the wood next to him.

"Coming right up."

SCOTT PAUSED to catch his breath as he hauled up the keg of Blood Orange. He'd been running stock most of Liam's second set. This last fucking keg felt like double the weight. As Scott wheeled it through the service gate, he shot a glance toward that reserved table. Marilyn and her new husband were still there. No Deon. Thank fuck.

The only thing he'd heard from Liam since he'd told his mom that of course he wasn't back with Scott was a text. Not that Scott understood what the hell it said. It was two little boxes with question marks in them—what Scott's cheap phone showed him when someone sent him an emoji—followed by the word *later* and a question mark.

As Scott hooked up the new keg and rolled out the tapped one, the music slammed to a stop and Reeve called out, "Thank you. We are Blow the Moon. Good night."

The more the crowd screamed and clapped, the more the corner of Scott's lips tried to lift in a proud smile. They were still clapping when Scott got back from dropping off the empty keg.

"Well, shit." Chai met him at the service gate. Scott followed her gaze to where the crowd was all waving their lighted phones at the stage.

She huffed out a sigh. "He's going to be fucking impossible after this."
Pointing at the back door, she said, "Go get them."

"Huh?"

"They want an encore."

Scott had to tighten his jaw to keep his scowl in place as he ducked
out through the side to Reeve's van. After three bangs on the back door,
Reeve popped it open.

"For Cthulhu's sake, keep it in your pants, man."

"They want an encore," Scott snapped, looking anywhere but at
Liam, though he couldn't help catching a glimpse of Liam's excited face.

"No fucking way." The drummer lunged forward.

Scott shrugged and backed away, using his key to get back in the
side door rather than the one by the stage.

He detoured into the storage closet and shut the door behind him.
This was his life. Even if he wasn't living in this particular little shitty
box, tiny apartments were all he was ever going to be able to afford. He'd
always be working at some nowhere job until his temper got the better of
him and he had to go find another one. But Liam. He could do anything.
He had a good job. And now he had this singing thing. Even his mom
wasn't dragging him down anymore.

Maybe leaving Scott *was* the best thing that had happened to Liam.
Scott should be a little less selfish and remind Liam of that.

But goddamn it. He wanted this one fucking night. And he was
gonna have it.

He slipped back out.

The band was doing a Breaking Benjamin song as the encore. A
solid ballad, Liam's voice soaring over the music, so warm and clear
Scott felt like he ought to be able to touch it. Even Chai was standing
still to listen.

The yearning in the lyrics—in Liam's voice—made Scott want to
promise him anything. Worse, it made him wish for those days when he
believed that they'd always be a part of each other's lives. In the song,
Liam pleaded with everyone to stay, and as sure as the headaches coming
after all those Jäger shots, Scott knew he'd never be the one to leave. He
forced his fisted hands to unclench and shoved back the hair that had
fallen onto his sweaty forehead. Any more of this and he'd be charging
the stage like a lovesick groupie.

The traffic at the bar was down to the last few people determined to end their night passed out in vomit. He leaned toward Chai's ear.

"Spare me for a smoke break?"

"As long as you're back in five for the last rush. You know it's raining?" She jerked her chin toward the front window.

"Whatthefuckever."

LIAM EASED himself down onto the van floor and took the handful of fast-food napkins Reeve shoved at him.

The napkins cleared away the sweat and rain, but he was still shaking and nauseous.

"That was fucking awesome." Dev pounded Liam on the shoulder before moving on to Reeve. At least Dev had enough sense to not put a hand on Mac.

"What the fuck?" Dev went on. "Did that really just fucking happen?"

"Weren't you there?" Mac asked dryly.

"Dude. Fuck. Dude." Dev kept on ranting and alternatively thumping on the backs of the seats, Reeve, and Liam.

Liam tried to find the anchors the therapist had talked about. Rough recycled paper napkin across his face. Check. The sound of Dev celebrating. Check. Smell of rain and pot and sweat and metal and fire—no. He moved the napkin closer to his nose. No fire. Just because the frenetic riffs Reeve had woven into the end of the encore reminded Liam of that out-of-control slew of the jeep, the sickening lurch, and the fanatic leer on Ross's face as he twisted the wheel....

Not real. Just music. Just some hard-core jams that felt like they were slipping into chaos. He'd never rehearsed them because he just wasn't that good on guitar yet. He pressed the napkin into his nose and mouth.

"Dude." Dev gripped the back of Liam's neck and shoved him toward the back door. "Liam, don't heave in the van."

Liam pulled away. "I'm not. It's just fucking hot."

"Panic attack. This'll help." Mac handed him a freshly lit pipe.

"I'm fine." But he took a hit. At least it slowed his breathing.

"Hang on. It's out." Mac leaned over with her lighter. "You really okay?" she murmured.

"Yeah, thanks."

He was surprised to realize he was. The sickening sensation had faded. Now if he could just stop sweating.

"It's cool." Reeve let out a deep breath. "It was pretty wild."

"We're going out, right?" Dev said. "We gotta go out. After-party or something."

"Even you could probably get laid tonight." Mac took her pipe back.

Dev was in such a good mood he only laughed. "Damn straight. Uh—no offense, Liam."

"Fuck." Liam scrabbled for the phone in his pocket. What if Scott had texted him back? He couldn't be mad about what Liam had told his mom. Scott was the one who suggested they keep things on the downlow. But there was nothing. "Fuck," he said again.

"You coming with?" Reeve nudged Liam.

"Thanks. I've got other plans." *I hope.* He was about to stuff the phone back into his pocket when it buzzed. He looked down and sighed before putting the phone to his ear. "Hi, Mom."

Dev laughed again. "Awesome plans, old man. Have fun."

"Hi, honey. I just wanted to tell you that Greg and I are waiting near the front door for you."

"You good getting home, then, Li?" Reeve asked.

"Hang on a sec, Mom." Liam tapped Mute. "I'll be fine. See you guys Wednesday at Reeve's, right?" He used a hand on the wheel well to shove himself to the back door and pop it open.

"Can everybody make it tomorrow instead?" Reeve said.

"Seriously?" Dev asked.

Liam had been planning on staying in the hotel—in bed—hell, balls-deep in Scott until checkout.

"Bar's closed. We can leave all the gear and get out of here and not have to set up again."

"Got work until closing," Mac said.

"So later, then? Like be here by ten?"

Liam supposed their dicks might be raw by then. He hadn't really thought much past just getting them there. "I can make it."

"Yeah," Mac agreed.

"I guess." Dev shrugged. "But I'm gonna be hungover."

It had stopped raining but the air was so wet it might as well have been. As he shut the back of the van again, he remembered Mom was still on the phone.

He unmuted her. "Sorry. We had to get some stuff settled."

"With the band?"

Her question started the acid pump in his stomach again. Probably should have eaten something between energy drinks. The epic level of caffeine might explain how he'd gotten so freaked out.

"Yes, Mom."

"I'm so proud of you, honey."

"Thanks." He didn't know if he was walking or swimming through this humidity. Using his shirt to wipe off first his face, then his phone, he snuck a look to see if Scott had texted.

"Is something wrong?"

"No."

"You sound distracted."

Yeah, he should have been more grateful about the praise. And maybe it would have meant more if she'd ever shown up for anything when he'd been younger. Or if he wasn't so focused on Scott that nothing else mattered right now.

"I'm just tired."

"Me too, honey." She laughed. "It's way past my bedtime these days. Do you need to wait for the roadies to give you your guitar?"

He rubbed his face again and started walking around the side of the building to the front. The mist kept the streetlight confined to a tight bubble around the pole. After a car whooshed by on the wet pavement, he answered, "We don't have roadies."

He rounded the corner and stopped. The bricks were black with shadow, but a tiny light glowed as it swung through the air, brightening as someone sucked the end of a cigarette. The figure was nothing but a dark outline, but Liam would know Scott even from under a blindfold. He'd always know him.

"Mom, can I call you back?"

"No. I need to know if we're driving you home."

Liam's feet pulled him toward Scott. "I'm good."

"Greg needs to be in early for a meeting, so we'll see you at home."

"Uh-huh."

The tip lit Scott's lips as he pulled in smoke. One hand rested in the pocket of his jeans, a booted foot pressed back against the bricks. Fucking James Dean bad-boy pose, and Liam had never seen anything sexier. That was until Scott pursed his lips and blew the smoke straight up.

Liam's mouth went as dry as if the cloud had hit his face. "Uh—I'm going out so I'm gonna be late," he managed to get out.

"Have fun."

Liam pocketed his phone.

"Going out, huh?" Scott took another drag. The cigarette was almost down to the filter.

"With you."

He couldn't have forgotten, right? This was just Scott being mad about Mom and Deon.

"That so?" Scott flicked the cigarette away. In that moment the street was quiet enough to hear the cigarette hiss in a puddle.

Liam's breath felt like it had hissed out along with it. "You're mad."

Scott raised his brows like he was thinking it over, then nodded. "Well, I *am* breathing."

A huffed laugh slipped past Liam's lips. "Yeah. It is kind of your default."

"So twenty-seven years old and still lying to your mom?"

"What the fuck? I thought that's what you wanted?"

"Yeah, well, I'm also kind of an asshole."

Liam's fingertips were burning with the need for just a quick touch of Scott's skin. He brushed his shoulder, but Scott shrugged him off.

Scott stared over Liam's shoulder for a second. "And that's also kind of my default."

Chapter Nineteen

SCOTT TURNED the key and pulled it, eyeballing the mostly empty motel parking lot. For a guy down a leg, Liam could move damned fast when he wanted to. He was already unlocking the door to the room by the time Scott swung out of the car.

He popped the hood and pulled the distributor cap free of its clips, which ought to discourage anyone planning to take the Mustang for a joyride. Liam was on him as soon as Scott came through the door, and he was pathetically grateful for it, for the sensation that wiped out the need to keep his guard up. The whole goddamned surreal day had been an endless tease. First feeling so over his head with Eli's freaky friends, then the torture of Liam up there seducing everyone with his amazing voice, to finally—Jesus—finally Chai telling them to get the hell out, she'd close alone since their eye-fucking was making her twitchy. The craving for this went deeper than any time he'd been desperate for a cigarette. Given that sometimes he'd been eyeing half-smoked butts on the sidewalk, that was pretty desperate.

It wasn't all in his balls either. Every inch of his skin was hungry for the contact, and when Liam's mouth crashed into Scott's, electricity shuddered down his spine. He opened his mouth and let taste and tongue and breath fill him up. Liam drove him against the door, and Scott's hands shot to Liam's shoulders, pulling him closer. Fuck the bite from the doorknob stabbing into his back. Fuck the whole goddamned world. They had this.

And he was ten kinds of stupid. No matter what bullshit Scott told himself, one night was never going to be enough. All the fucker had to do was kiss him and Liam was in Scott's blood like sweet, sweet nicotine. The rush and lust and freedom and sureness deepened with every pump of his heart.

Liam jerked back. Scott hauled him close again.

"I'd say I was impressed, but I know that's not your dick," Liam murmured onto Scott's lips.

"Huh?" Scott let him go. Then he felt the hard plastic between them, well above his hip. Yeah. That would have been impressive. "It's the distributor cap from the Mustang." He let Liam step back, and the bumpy black cap dropped to the floor at their feet.

Scott scooped it up and put it on top of the dresser next to the TV.

One corner of Liam's mouth lifted. "I know you love that car, but you sleep with pieces of it? Is this a security-blanket kind of thing?"

"Fuck you. I pulled the distributor cap so no one could steal it."

"Oh." Liam nodded, his lips now wide with his full knock-the-wind-out-of-you smile. "That's smart."

Scott ignored the sudden wish to wag his tail for more compliments. "So we going against the door again? Thought the whole point of this was the bed."

"Then get your ass in one." Liam's smile vanished, and Scott tried to not miss it.

Instead, he yanked his T-shirt over his head and sat on the edge of the bed closest to the bathroom to take off his boots. When Scott stood to shuck his jeans, Liam ripped the covers off the bed. Scott hooked his thumbs in the waistband of his boxers but hesitated. Liam hadn't so much as taken off his shirt. He did pull lube and two boxes of Trojan Ultra Thins out of the small backpack he'd brought.

Scott raised an eyebrow as Liam sat, then put the lube and both boxes on the nightstand.

"Someone's planning a big night." Scott toed out of his socks.

"Thought we both were."

"You think you got six rounds in you?"

Liam dropped on his back and shot a hand out to grab Scott's thigh. Teasing fingers drifted under the thin cotton leg of his boxers, grazing the bottom of an asscheek, then moved to slide along Scott's taint, brush his hole, thumb under his balls.

Liam's upside-down face stared up as Scott's dick thickened, then rose.

"I think." Liam let out a long breath, creating an extra prickle of sensation on Scott's skin. Liam rubbed with finger and thumb, and Scott's knees wobbled.

"I think," Liam said again, voice low and deliberate and echoing against Scott's skin, "I'm gonna give it my best to get six rounds in you."

Scott gave in and pushed his hips forward, eager for more.

"Now"—Liam pulled his hand away—"get these off so I can get my mouth on you."

Scott dropped the boxers and spread his legs as Liam moved his head closer. He tried to lock his muscles to prepare for the first touch, but just the damp heat of Liam exhaling almost had him falling forward. Liam knew it too, the ratfucker. His cheek curved against Scott's thigh, and a laughing breath teased his skin.

"Want to get on the bed now?" Liam asked.

"Why are you being such an asshole?" Scott climbed onto the mattress, kneeling around Liam's head.

"Afraid you can't handle the competition?"

Scott stretched forward to unfasten Liam's jeans.

Liam dropped a hand to cover Scott's. "Did a lot of sweating on stage. Might be kind of ripe."

Scott pushed the hand away and got his own inside to grip the velvety skin. "Fucking summer in Baltimore. Who isn't?" Scott leaned in and got a mouthwatering whiff of Liam's dick. Yeah. There was the sex-sweat smell, but it was Liam too. Familiar and good and—Scott wrapped his lips around the head and flicked his tongue over the salty slit. Oh fuck yeah.

He hadn't wanted to rush, but this was Liam. It was the two of them together, and there was nothing like this. No way to do anything but race toward the end so they could do it again. He started a greedy, hungry suck.

Liam gasped. He clutched Scott's hips and dragged him down, sucking on just the tip, and if Scott's mouth wasn't full of dick, he'd have been begging for a little more, promising anything for just a little more heat. A little more wet. A little more tongue.

Then oh God, there it was, and Scott had to pull off to catch his breath. Liam's laugh vibrated against his dick, and Scott growled in his throat. They knew everything about each other. They'd learned this on each other, and there was no flick, lick, or squeeze they hadn't done on each other first. They were as competitive as hell too, so when Liam started pushing a finger in, it was *on*.

He went deep, lips almost to the base, and then tried to get at Liam's balls, but the barely open jeans and tight boxer briefs got in his way. Liam didn't cooperate at all when Scott tried to shove them off.

He lifted his head. "You planning to fuck with these on?"

Liam didn't answer, but Scott knew him too well. Read the hesitation in Liam's body as well as the pressure from his mouth. Scott's balls might kill him later for it, but he swung off and flopped on his back next to Liam.

Liam looked at him then stared at the ceiling. "I'm not—" He swallowed. "—not ashamed of it."

Yeah, right. Scott kept his mouth closed.

"There's also… to do the skin graft for my forearm, they took a big patch from the inside of my thigh."

"Uh-huh."

"I wear shorts all the time, I swear. It's just—"

Scott scrambled up and straddled Liam's hips so they were face-to-face this time. He put his hands on Liam's shoulders and waited until Liam looked at him. Really looked at him, not that fake "I'm listening" bullshit that fooled so many other people.

"Don't think for one fucking second that I gave one shit about your skinny, pasty legs once I got a good look at your sweet, fat cock." Scott dragged his palms down from Liam's broad shoulders to his pecs. "Though I gotta say I always liked these too." He pressed and rubbed. "Feel pretty good. How they looking these days?"

Liam's fingers bit into Scott's biceps. "You really are a major fucking asshole."

"Thanks for noticing. Now will you take your pants off?"

Liam grinned. "Make me."

As soon as the words left Liam's mouth, Scott had him in a headlock, pinning Liam's flesh leg by wrapping it with his own and shifting his weight on top of Liam's chest. He and Liam had scrapped like this plenty in those two years they'd lived together. Just like back then, Liam had better upper-body strength, but Scott had had years of honing survival instinct on his side.

Scott had been quick to come to Liam's defense, but Liam could always hold his own. First with the punks back at St. Bennie's, and Scott was sure he'd been tough with those insurgents or whatever they were in Afghanistan right until they bombed him.

"Nice, genius." Liam's voice was strained. "Now how you going to get the clothes off me?"

"Could wait until you pass out." Scott tightened his choke hold.

"You into necrophilia all of a sudden?"

Scott huffed a laugh into the side of Liam's face and saw him shiver. "You give or do I have to get serious?"

"Serious?" Liam gasped.

"Yeah." Scott forced Liam's head close and, with calculated precision, tickled the back of Liam's ear with the tip of his tongue.

Liam jerked and squirmed and threw his hips, almost bucking Scott off.

Scott did it again.

After another bout of gasping and bucking, Liam tapped out, three quick pokes on Scott's forearm.

Scott let him go.

Liam tore off his shirt and flopped onto his side. "Cheater."

"Since when are there rules?"

Liam rubbed his throat. "Tickling is always cheating."

"Don't be ticklish, then."

"I'm going to fuck you so hard."

"Big talk for a guy who won't take off his jeans."

Liam glared. And he kept on glaring as he climbed off the bed and brought his hands to his waistband. Scott stared right back.

Liam's chest was more cut than Scott remembered it. Made Liam's shoulders look broader than ever. Light brown hair still dusted his pecs, but there was more hair on his abs now. And damn, those abs. Scott had never seen cuts like that except in a picture. Liam must've been doing a lot of working out while learning how to use that leg. That made him think of Deon, but Scott shoved the thought away. Because Liam was peeling down his jeans.

The strip they'd taken off his thigh was a perfect rectangle of dark pink. Yeah, if Liam hadn't explained what it was from, Scott would have thought it was weird. No one had scars in such perfect lines. The boxer briefs and jeans hit the floor, and Scott stared.

He'd seen it that first day, when they sat on the picnic table at the car show, seen the metal rod into his sneaker and the robot-like calf and knee joint. But this was different. Scott hoped to hell Liam hadn't been bullshitting about needing Scott not to care about his leg.

Because even though it looked like it still hurt like a bitch and Scott had no idea how the fuck it worked, it didn't make any difference. Liam had always meant more than just his body. Been more. Scott didn't care what pieces were missing any more than he knew what the color of

Liam's eyes was called because what had mattered had always been the way Liam looked at him. The way they were together was so much better than just Scott on his miserable own.

He stared at the leg and the scar and the place on Liam's arm where the skin patch had gone. Stared good and hard, then nodded.

"So, that thing come with turbo-fuck mode?"

"Nah." Liam's grin told Scott he'd gotten it exactly right.

After sitting on the bed and kicking away his jeans, Liam added, "I've just had to get creative sometimes."

"Show me what you've got, then." Scott stretched out next to him.

Liam rolled on top of him, solid weight and welcome heat making the tightness burning Scott's jaw and chest ease. His dick was happy about it too. Especially when Liam lined his up so they were rubbing together. Satiny skin dragged against Scott's own, hot and stiff.

If cracking open his ribs meant he could get Liam closer, Scott would have done it in a heartbeat. He tilted his hips and wrapped his legs around Liam's ass.

"Fuck, that feels good," Liam breathed against Scott's mouth. "Always so fucking good with you." Sex had never been the problem between them. Pretty far from it.

"Yeah." Because like it or not, it was the truth.

Liam kissed him. Not rough or hard but intense. He might as well be already balls-deep in Scott from the way it felt. Like they weren't in two separate bodies but reaching together for something in the same skin.

He rocked up, trying to get Liam's dick inside where he needed it, needed the heat and the stretch. But Liam didn't cooperate, the stubborn fuck.

Scott freed his mouth. "C'mon. Do it."

Liam grabbed Scott's thighs, pulling them farther apart, and that did the trick. Liam's cock stroked the crack of Scott's ass, the pressure on his hole making him wiggle down for more.

Scott squeezed his cheeks together, forcing a gasp out of Liam.

"Don't do that. I'm trying not to fucking lose it here," Liam grumbled.

"And I fucking want you to lose it. Get the fuck in me."

What Liam meant with that eye roll, Scott didn't care because Liam was finally shifting off and grabbing the lube. Scott could count on his thumbs the number of guys he'd let fuck him since Liam left, and both of them had been in that first shitty year of feeling… nothing. Just empty. Hell, he hadn't been able to get a rage on.

What that had taught him was that sex couldn't fill empty and that he was a tight-assed bastard when it was anyone but Liam. But Scott wanted it now. Right the fuck now and no dicking around with fingers either.

Liam slid one in, a quick, deep burn. Scott couldn't keep the grunt from passing through his lips.

It wasn't awesome, but it wasn't Liam's dick either. That's when it got better fast.

When Liam stopped and went for more lube, Scott flipped onto his hands and knees.

"Uh…." Liam put a hand on Scott's hip.

"What?" Scott looked back over his shoulder.

Liam's hair was just getting long enough to do that wave at his forehead. Glaring down, he stuck out his stubborn-as-fuck jaw, looking like he had as a teenager.

Scott waited.

"So, I can't exactly kneel and get much push."

It surprised the truth out of Scott. "I honest-to-God forgot about your leg right now."

"Wish I could." But there was a quick smile behind Liam's words. "Roll back over." He stood next to the bed.

As soon as Scott's back hit the mattress, Liam grabbed Scott's hips and hauled him to the edge. His legs dropped open around Liam's as he leaned in.

"I'm still gonna make you forget everything but my name." Liam dragged his stubble across Scott's.

It should have been corny, or at least said like a tease, but somehow Liam managed to back that up with his stare. Instead of rolling his eyes, Scott swallowed. Christ. One fucking night as a rock star and Liam could already bring it.

Scott cleared his throat. "Lots of talk and no action."

Liam arched his brows and opened a box of the Trojans.

Scott stared at the ceiling as resentment burned hot enough to threaten his hard-on. They'd never used condoms before. Never thought they'd ever need to. And though it mattered more sensation-wise for the one doing the fucking, it mattered a hell of a lot to Scott right then. He hated that now that they were together again, there'd still be something between them. A load in the ass could be a mess, yeah, but he'd always loved falling asleep with Liam still in him. Though the feeling had turned out to be a big fat lie, Liam shooting in him had made him feel like they were closer, that Scott was somehow safe.

The lube and the condom made the first touch at his hole cold. Liam pushed, and Scott tried to relax.

Liam pulled away. "Let me—"

"No." Scott grabbed the arm pressing on his thigh. "C'mon."

It was easier the second time. Still burned like a bitch, but it was good too.

"Jesus, you're tight." Liam's eyes were shut, lips pinched like he was working out some chemistry equation.

Scott grunted, then managed, "Cut the sweet talk, Walsh. You're already getting laid."

Liam laughed, and it was definitely better. It was them again. Liam rocked a little, pushing deeper, and Scott's body remembered how this worked, remembered how fucking amazing it felt. He arched toward Liam for more.

"Oh. Fuck." Liam's head dropped back and his hips pushed forward.

If Scott's voice didn't feel as sharp as glass in his throat, he'd have agreed. Then Liam held on tight and slammed them together, balls slapping up against Scott's ass, and it was all Scott could do to remember how to breathe.

Liam's fingers bit down to the bone as he panted. Scott managed to crack open his eyes.

Liam smiled down at him. "Hey."

"Hey."

"We good?"

"Fuck, yeah."

Liam started moving, and Scott met every thrust until they were crashing into each other, the smack of flesh echoing in the empty room. Liam added the strength of his arms, forcing Scott onto his dick, as if he wanted to be someplace else.

He never wanted it to stop.

Liam fucking him was the only time Scott ever felt like he could just let go of everything he kept such a tight grip on. Anger, fear, and that bone-deep knowledge that no matter what he'd always end up alone. He could let that all go, because it was the only way to let himself be fucked. And it still scraped and stung more than a little because they—he'd—rushed it. But oh Christ, it felt so good.

Like some damned mind reader, Liam groaned. "So fucking good with you, Scott."

Yeah, right. Like a hole wasn't a hole. Scott knew better. But he also knew that the piece of silicone in his duffel bag stuffed under the cot back at Schim's didn't touch him like this. Maybe Scott could move it to hit all the right spots, but it still didn't get to everything that ached for pressure the way Liam's dick did.

"Harder. C'mon." Scott arched his back. Because if Liam didn't start going deep enough to get his dick in Scott's throat, he might actually say some of that crap out loud.

Liam shifted his grip from Scott's hips to his shoulders. When he leaned in for a kiss, he bent Scott's knees up to his ears. The angle made a devastating rub inside and a white-out fuzz of pleasure behind Scott's eyes.

Scott grabbed on to Liam's back, kissing like he needed it to breathe because that was safer than words, safer than begging to let Liam know what he needed.

Liam lifted his head. "Sorry, can't balance."

Someone might as well have dumped ice water on him. Scott let go instantly. Here he was pissing and moaning about them using condoms, and Liam had to worry about managing on one leg.

Scott took a deep breath, then swallowed. "So, who do we gotta talk to about making those things more fuck-friendly?"

"I'll put it on my to-do list." Liam braced himself against Scott's chest and straightened up.

Scott propped himself up enough to get a look at Liam's stance. His right leg was out at an angle, thigh braced against the mattress edge.

"Jesus, don't look like that. I didn't say I was stopping." Liam took hold of Scott's hips again. He rocked a little.

Scott's breath caught at the return of friction. A second ago he'd have sworn his dick was just going to pack it in, but now his pulse throbbed from base to tip, and by the time Liam started fucking him again, it had roared back to desperate need.

Liam shifted to short hard thrusts, using each one to drive in a word. "Just. Can't. Kiss. Like. This."

Then he rolled his hips, and that was fucking it.

"God." The word burned Scott's throat as it was torn out of him. Before he could tell Liam to do that again, he did. Over and over. Short hard thrusts and that fucking roll.

Scott got a hand on his dick, jacking himself fast as he rode the build to the top.

Liam pulled him into each thrust, grip tight enough to hurt, as if Scott was the one who kept trying to leave.

Need made him crazy. Stupid. Pathetic. "Don't stop. Please, Liam, don't you fucking stop."

"Yeah. Not gonna," Liam promised.

For that moment Scott could believe him. It was goddamned impossible to feel this good and still be alive.

He jacked himself faster, tighter on the head. Right there. Jesus.

"God, you feel so fucking good." Liam's sexy voice, the one that seduced everyone in that bar, panting for Scott.

It was more than his nuts could take.

"Oh fuck." He came like his life depended on it, body jerking, the shocks so sweet they hurt. A spray across his chest, one to his neck from an even harder spasm, and then the last shudders all over his stomach.

He'd just managed to open his eyes when Liam started fucking him again, lips parting as he stuttered out a "Christ, Scott, fuck," and then Scott got to watch him lose it, those smooth strokes lost in tight little slams of his hips.

So fucking hot. Liam dragged a shaky hand down through the jizz on Scott's chest before easing out of him. "I gotta…." Liam waved at the bed and Scott shifted his hips over.

"Thanks." Liam sat, then flopped back before rolling toward Scott.

"Fuck." Liam kissed Scott's neck where one of his shots had landed. "Mmm. That was fucking impressive."

Scott swallowed.

"I can kiss you now."

Scott turned his head to meet him. The bitter taste clinging to Liam's lips reminded Scott of all the ways things had gone sour last time. Neither one of them had any reason to think things would be different this time.

His distraction must have come through in the kiss because Liam raised his head.

"What?" Liam studied Scott's face, then sighed. "You always do that, you know."

"I'd say what, but you're gonna tell me anyway."

"Jump to the worst conclusion, like everything's all black-and-white."

Considering Liam claimed he'd left six years ago because he thought Scott was turning into a speed junkie, saying that took some balls. But he wasn't wrong.

"So what if I do? Lots of times I'm right and it is a fucking disaster."

"And a lot of times it isn't." Liam shifted so that his head was on Scott's chest. "Christ, I missed you so fucking much. You have no idea. I was so stupid."

Scott lifted a hand, hesitated, and then rested it on Liam's head. His hair was growing out fast, the untamable waves silky against Scott's fingers.

Liam leaned into the touch like a cat. "You don't have to believe me, but I've never stopped being in love with you."

Scott wanted to jerk his hand back. He wanted to shove Liam away, to hurt him so he would stop saying lame shit that didn't fucking matter because they couldn't stay in this hotel room forever and all the bullshit out there would find a way to pull them apart again. But damn it. Couldn't he just have this one night of lying to himself?

"You're pissed. I can hear it in your heartbeat." Liam rolled onto his back. He dropped a hand over his face. "I want this to work this time. It will. We just have to figure out what to do."

Scott knew what he should say. *You could tell me and everyone else the truth for once. Not what you want it to be, but how it really is.* Then maybe it wouldn't be so easy for it all to go to shit. But Liam was too damned stubborn to do anything he didn't want to or to admit that everything wasn't gonna be like he thought.

Scott rolled off the bed and hunted up his jeans. "You figure it out. I'm going outside to have a smoke."

Chapter Twenty

IT HAD to be the first time in his life Scott appreciated all the damned smoking laws, since it gave him an excuse to retreat—escape—outside. August heat hit like a wall after the cool of the room's AC. It was raining like it meant it now. Not a downpour, just steady solid wet. The roof hung over the strip of sidewalk in front of the motel rooms so he managed to get a cigarette lit, but run-off and bad drainage soaked his bare feet.

He leaned on the doorframe and blew his exhaust into the rain, then let his head fall back against the rough wood. Christ. He'd always been too dumb to know when to stop fighting. No different now. He was totally fucked whether Liam had his dick in him or not.

Right from that day when Liam goddamned Walsh had winked his nonswollen eye and asked if Scott wanted to fight or fuck like it was all the same to him, he'd been under Scott's skin, good and bad. Liam was there in the jittery need when it had been too long without a cigarette. The curl of satisfaction under his ribs from the sound of a perfectly tuned engine. The dangerous thrill of opening up the Mustang on I-95 at 3:00 a.m., touching a hundred and hoping all the state troopers were asleep.

Covering that tattoo hadn't fixed it. Scott should have known he couldn't shake the bastard. Might as well stop trying and take what he could get.

And when the inevitable happened, when things got too real—things like having a boyfriend who was always scraping by because of his hair-trigger temper and control issues and whatever the fuck had made him unfosterable—Liam would chase off after something else.

It would hurt like hell, but this time he'd see it coming. Besides, if there was one thing Scott could handle, it was pain.

He clung to the two-by-four behind him, made himself stay and finish his cigarette before going back in to spill his guts. A deep hit helped relax his hunched shoulders, his clenched fingers. Yeah, he could do this. He tossed the butt into the wet and spit after it before ducking back into the room.

"Hey." Liam was in the bed they hadn't fucked in, curled on his side and facing the door. His leg stood next to the bed, and Scott's eyes traced the shape under the blanket, picking out the sudden drop just past Liam's hip.

"Hey." Scott reached for the light switch, but then he spied a hunk of black on Liam's pillow. After a second of alarm—gun? dried blood? tarantula?—he realized it was the distributor cap, half hidden by Liam's grip on it.

Scott snorted a laugh. "What the hell?" He put it on the nightstand and flipped off the light.

"Not like I can chase you right now." Liam's voice was tired and cranky.

"I'm not going anywhere." Scott sat on the other side of the bed and pulled off his jeans again before adding, "I never did."

Liam looked over his shoulder. "Scott—"

"Don't. Just… gimme a minute."

Scott swung into the bed, pulled the covers up, then scooted across the mattress to snug himself behind Liam's back. It wasn't as weird as he'd thought it would be, feeling only part of Liam's right leg against his own. After a minute it just felt like holding Liam.

Liam sighed and relaxed. Scott rubbed his face against the back of Liam's neck, breathing as deep as he ever did when smoking to get a hit off Liam's skin. To steel himself.

It would be easier like this. Without looking into Liam's eyes. Scott locked an arm around Liam's chest to keep him from turning over and kissed the top of his shoulder. Definitely bigger, broader than he'd been six years ago.

Nut up, McDermott. Now or never. He took a breath.

Liam tangled their fingers together and brought Scott's hand to his mouth, kissing across the knuckles. Jesus, Scott had forgotten how sensitive Liam could make his hands feel. Liam settled Scott's hand back over his chest and sighed again.

"I shouldn't have said that. About leaving." The words were about as easy to get over his tongue as it was to roll an engine block up a hill. "I don't want you to feel like you have to keep apologizing for it."

Liam squeezed his hand. "Okay. But—"

"Christ." Scott butted his forehead against Liam's shoulder. "Just shut up and let me say this."

"Okay." Liam's chest moved sharply, though whether in a silent laugh or swallowed frustration, Scott couldn't tell.

"I get why you're always saying you're sorry. You need people to like you and they do."

Another squeeze from Liam's hand.

"You even made me like you, and you know what an asshole I am. I hate everybody."

The ripple in Liam's chest was softer this time, more like a laugh.

"So here it is. Yes. I'm in. I want to try and make it work, whatever that means." Scott swallowed. "For however long that is. It doesn't mean I'm not going to wonder if today's the day I wake up to you gone. But—" He sucked in a quick breath. "—I love you. And my life doesn't suck as much when you're in it, so if—"

Liam's chest lifted their hands in a deep breath. And another. Scott flopped his head onto the pillow. The ratfucker had fallen asleep on him.

LIAM WAS back in the jeep with Ross. Except sometimes when he looked over it was Scott. No, it was Ross saying, "Not gonna happen, Lawman." Had to be Ross. Scott couldn't know the unit had turned his initials into a nickname.

So it was Ross, and the jeep was accelerating past the telephone poles farther from the base against the hot, dry spring wind, and though he'd swear he was right there in the jeep with Ross again, part of him kept insisting that this time he could change the outcome because he knew what happened next.

"How is being locked up better?" Liam said, but no, he'd already said that.

"I warned you," Ross said.

"I knew it," Scott said.

"Think you've got all the answers," Scott/Ross said.

The jeep started to slide. "Sorry, Lawman. I can't go back." Ross's calm expression was worse than the crazy one.

Liam screamed but no sound came out. Or maybe it did and no one could hear it over the screech and grind of metal. Time froze, let him catalog every dizzying lurch in his guts as the jeep rolled; then Liam was airborne, free of the chaos for just an instant. Black, red, dust, smoke, fire, and pain made an endless loop in his head. This time it wasn't Ross crawling toward him, crawling from the fire like the Terminator. It was Scott. Scott calling his name. Scott needed him and Liam's body wouldn't work and he couldn't get there.

"Liam. Hey. Wake up."

He was pinned down. Maybe this time they'd have to cut off his arm. How could he play guitar with one arm? That was how Ross would punish him.

"Liam."

He fought to get free, kicked and shoved at what held him down.

"Damn it. Liam!"

Liam woke up with a jolt.

Scott was there. Not on fire. Scott held Liam's shoulders and shook him hard, lifting him up and dropping him onto the mattress.

He wasn't back in Texas. The weight on him was Scott.

Scott's eyes glittered as he peered down. "You with me now?" There was enough light to see the pinch of worry in his brows and the lines around his nose.

"Yeah." Liam took a deep breath. He was sweaty as hell and wasn't sure he wouldn't puke, but mostly he was relieved. Fucking dream. He didn't actually remember anything between when they started to roll and when he woke up in the hospital. But he'd heard enough that his imagination took over.

He thumbed the scar on Scott's eyebrow, a touch to let them both know Liam was really here, but Scott pulled back farther.

Liam squinted. "Is your mouth bleeding?"

Scott shrugged, then let go of Liam's shoulders. "You punched me." Scott ran his tongue over his lips. "Guess you got me good. So we're even on sucker punches."

"Goddamn it. I'm sorry."

"I'm fine." Scott slid off Liam's hips and settled on one side. "How are you?"

"Okay. Usually leaves me more nauseous. But," he added before Scott decided Liam was a total basket case, "I haven't had a dream like that in a long time." Sweat glued him to the sheet.

One side of Scott's mouth quirked up. "Guess I just bring out the best in you, huh?"

Was Scott really going to use a fucking bad dream as a reason why things couldn't work?

Feral didn't even begin to cover it. Scott was even more skittish than he'd been when Liam had met him. Not that Liam could blame him.

He forced himself to sit up and get his foot on the floor. He needed to piss and get this fear-sweat stink off him. But when he thought about everything that would mean—strapping into his leg, hoping the rim of the tub wasn't too high for him to navigate, then taking the leg back off once he'd made it into the tub—it was too fucking much. But he really had to piss.

"Shit."

The sheets whispered as Scott shifted. "What?"

"I didn't bother to bring a crutch."

The air-conditioning made him shiver. Behind him, Scott hmmed. Like he always did. Like he knew Liam would cave. Spill out what he hated to admit.

"And I could put my leg on but it takes time, and it's a pain in the ass when I really gotta pee."

"Gotcha." Scott scrambled across the bed and slid off to stand next to Liam. "Not saying I wanna carry you, but I'm pretty sure I can figure out how to be a crutch if you tell me."

Liam replayed that in his head, but it still sounded the same, as matter-of-fact as when Scott had explained why he'd brought in the distributor cap. Problem and solution. No hidden disgust or frustration at Liam's helplessness.

"Okay." He used Scott's forearm to steady himself as he stood. "Get on the other side of me. And let me put my arm around your shoulder."

Scott looked at him through half-lidded eyes. "Considering I let you put your dick up my ass, I think I can handle an arm on my shoulders."

Liam wanted to punch his arm, but he needed all his balance. "Then you put your arm around my waist to help me hop."

"Got it." Scott latched on, then wrapped his fingers around Liam's wrist with his free hand.

They managed to get to the bathroom with less lurching than Liam had expected. Probably because they were close to the same height.

Liam balanced with the help of the toilet tank and tried to free his other arm from the grip Scott had on his wrist. "Thanks. I can take it from here. There's stuff to hang on to."

Scott let go of Liam's waist but shifted his other hold from wrist to elbow. "So you just call me when you want a ride back? What am I, an Uber?"

Scott's smirk chased away the last of the horror from Liam's dream.

"Hey. If watching me piss is your kink, have fun." Liam lifted the lid and the seat, then hesitated. He probably should sit rather than wobble and spray the floor.

Before he could turn, Scott wrapped both arms around Liam's waist, then pressed against him, solid, steady support.

"Everything about you is my kink and you damned well know it." Scott rested his chin on Liam's shoulder.

Liam leaned back and grabbed his dick to aim. A naked Scott pressed against his back wasn't at all like the impersonal touch of a nurse or therapist all those times he'd needed help to get him through the most basic stuff of living. He didn't feel helpless. Scott holding him felt like love even though he'd never said it out loud. Not once in twelve years. Maybe he'd never say it.

Liam had always believed in all the ways Scott showed him Scott loved him. That they'd gotten this much back, that Scott was here, Liam would have to believe what that told him too.

Despite having had way too many people involved in his body functions those first few weeks in the hospital, having it be Scott watching him, holding him was somehow intimate.

"So go for it." Liam pulled Scott's right hand down. "Aim for me."

Scott's breath hitched against his ear, but when he spoke, his voice held all the usual detached sarcasm. "Water sports, Walsh? Now that *is* kinky. Maybe you want to give Beauchamp a call."

He cupped his hand around Liam's dick, though.

Liam shut his eyes, dropped his head back against Scott's shoulder, and let go of the muscle holding in the stream. The splash echoed in the tiny space, but the hitch in Scott's breathing sounded right in Liam's ear.

"Shake for me?" Liam grinned, knowing Scott would hear it in his voice.

Scott's laugh rumbled against his back, but he did it.

Liam cupped the back of Scott's head. "I need a shower. Wanna come in with me?"

"Beats the truck-stop stall. I'm in."

I'm in. Scott's words slid around in Liam's brain looking for a memory to crash into, but since Liam was working hard on not remembering right now, he shook his head.

"What?" Scott stood next to the tub as Liam sat on the rim to swing himself over.

"Nothing. Just something I forgot." After getting the spray going, he pulled himself up with the handrail attached to the back wall. "I could seriously use one of these at home." Then Liam wanted to kick himself. Scott didn't have a home and didn't exactly feel welcome at Greg and Mom's.

"Shouldn't be too hard to install." Scott tugged on the bar as he stepped in.

But if they could make this work, they could get an apartment again. With what money? The EMT station at the fairground would be closing after October.

The water smelled rusty, but there was decent water pressure. Liam hopped farther into the spray to make room for Scott.

Scott shot a hand out to grab Liam's hip. "Maybe play pogo stick on a different surface."

Liam looked back over his shoulder. "Aw. He cares."

Scott squeezed the flesh he was holding, then let go.

Smooth, Walsh. Push him away harder next time. Liam grabbed the tiny shampoo bottle. "Wanna wash my hair?"

Scott took the bottle without a single smart remark. After dragging his hands through Liam's hair a few times, Scott said, "So, how much do you remember?"

Liam went from relaxed to red alert in a heartbeat. Which, if he had to guess, was now approaching a hundred beats per minute. "From the dream?"

Scott made a noisy sigh. "No. From before you fell asleep. After I came back in from smoking. Rinse." He pushed Liam's head under the spray.

The rush of water blotted out sound and gave him a second to think. When he ducked back out, Scott was muttering, "…worst timing ever, I swear."

Scott tore open the soap and rubbed it across Liam's shoulders, working up a lather, then working over the muscles, soothing and relaxing with deep pressure. Scott's thumbs swept up to massage the base of Liam's skull, easing away tension and a headache Liam had just begun to feel.

"So?" Scott's hands moved down Liam's spine.

"Mm." Liam tried to think back while making a big detour around his dream in the middle. "You said something about the distributor cap, about you never being the one to leave."

Scott's fingers skidded for an instant, and Liam swore he heard Scott's teeth snap together.

Liam went on. "And you said something like you knew why I always apologize."

You even made me like you.

"Then you said you liked me."

Scott's hands froze at Liam's hips. A choked laugh vibrated through their echo chamber.

"Yeah. That's about it." There was a pause before Scott went on in a voice huskier than Liam had ever heard from him. "Then I said I wanted to try and make this work. Us."

Liam forgot everything and spun around. Scott barely managed to keep them both upright.

Liam rested his hands on Scott's shoulders. "Seriously?"

Scott rolled his eyes. His arms were wrapped tight around Liam's waist. "Right. 'Cause I make a habit of spewing my feelings for a joke."

Liam wouldn't exactly call it spewing feelings, but he'd take the win. He grabbed Scott's face and kissed him.

Chapter Twenty-One

ACCORDING TO the red numbers on the motel's digital nightstand clock, it was 4:17 a.m. Even if it had been twenty-one hours since Liam had really slept, he was wired. They were lying facing each other, and every time Liam remembered what Scott had said about giving them another chance, a wave of excitement and expectation rushed through him, and like the ocean, the supply seemed endless. He kept touching Scott's face, studying the starburst patterns in his eyes in the light of the bedside lamp.

"Dude. You're freaking me out," Scott said, but he smiled when he did.

"Sorry. I'm just happy. I missed you so much. I need—" Liam cut himself off. *To keep reminding myself it's real* didn't exactly fit. If he was going to imagine perfection, they wouldn't need to be hiding out in a hotel room. He wouldn't have to worry about how freaked out his mom was going to be.

Scott arched his scarred brow in invitation for Liam to finish, but he shook his head.

"Okay." Scott's eyes got more focused, intent. "Well, I need to tell you some stuff."

Since Scott wasn't someone to overshare, Liam's heart sped up.

"Not life-or-death, relax." Scott tugged at the thick part of Liam's cowlick. "It's why I have to live at the bar right now."

When Scott first mentioned the settlement, Liam knew immediately that's how Scott had bought the Mustang. He wasn't surprised about the lawsuit. Scott had told him how unbearable things got at St. Bennie's before he ran away.

"I didn't know I was going to owe taxes on it. Ratfuckers keep adding a penalty every month as long as I still owe 'em. When I make a regular paycheck, they take out so much I can't live on it. Least not here in the city. So I'm saving up to get that monkey off my back. I know it's not going to make things any easier for us."

Liam's stomach squirmed with a fresh hatching of guilt worms. He'd come to appreciate Scott's refusal to sugarcoat things, even when it kept him from saying things Liam wanted to hear. After the million broken promises making up Liam's childhood, he'd clung to the fact that what Scott said, you could damned well believe. He'd never make a promise he wouldn't keep.

Liam just couldn't be like that. Couldn't use honesty like a weapon to keep people away. But he owed it to Scott to come clean about some of the half truths Liam had been hanging on to. Even if the whole truth meant he didn't look the way he wanted Scott to see him.

"I didn't get hurt in Afghanistan," he blurted out before he changed his mind.

Scott tipped his head a little, but that was the only reaction to the confession that had scorched Liam's throat like acid.

"It wasn't an IED. It was an accident. Off base. And it was my own fucking fault."

Scott propped his head up with a cocked elbow. "I gotta hear how you tore off your own leg and set your arm on fire. Go on."

Liam shook his head. Of course Scott would take Liam's side. It only made this harder. "That skill set was above my paygrade."

"What was your paygrade?"

In trying to keep from having to admit his own blame in the mess, Liam hadn't told Scott anything except Army and Afghanistan.

"I was a sixty-eight whiskey. Combat medic."

Scott's eyes widened. "Damn. No shit?"

"Yeah."

"So you did become a doctor."

"Not really the same."

"Right." Scott bit at a piece of his thumbnail, then turned his head to spit it at the headboard. "You were more important, keeping people's guts in place while getting shot at."

"A couple times," Liam admitted. Mostly it had been boring. The only really scary time had been when Ross took two pieces of shrapnel in his thigh on a patrol. Damn, that had been a lot of blood. And yelling. And dust and noise. Liam hadn't known where anyone was, who might have been behind him as he tried to stop the blood pouring out.

"After our 365, we were supposed to get two years at home base. But they cut it to one."

"Ratfuckers." Scott spit away another piece of nail.

"My buddy Ross comes to see me two nights before we're supposed to deploy. Drags me out of my rack to say goodbye."

Scott didn't interrupt with questions, but Liam found himself offering more explanations.

"Ross, you'd have liked him. Check that. You're too much alike. You'd have hated each other. I guess it's why I got along with him. It was his second tour and he taught me guitar and backgammon and how to make better food out of the crap from the MREs." They'd been at a combat outpost on Liam's birthday, and Ross had managed a chocolate frosted cookie out of creamer, sugar, and cocoa packages, caramelizing it over a book of matches.

Liam swallowed hard at that memory. He was sure Scott would get it. Being in a placement like St. Bennie's wasn't exactly like being part of an infantry platoon, but the frustration and boredom and rules and monotony that could make a friendship intense were.

Scott nodded. "So he drags you out of bed to say goodbye."

"Yeah. He was freaked about going back. We were going to be doing more direct action, relieving a brigade that had had a lot of casualties." Liam didn't have to close his eyes to see it. The moon glinting off the black of the jeep, Ross with a hand on the door. "I thought he was going AWOL. I thought I could talk him out of it."

Liam glanced down at the rectangular patch of grafted skin on his forearm. He'd been such a cocky son of a bitch. "I *knew* I could talk him out of it. Just fucking knew it."

Scott put a hand on Liam's face, thumb brushing gently across his cheek. Startled, Liam looked up. Scott wasn't super touchy unless they were having sex. Not like Liam, who sometimes felt like an addict jonesing for some human contact. And when it was Scott and skin-to-skin, it was as if someone had pumped some Demerol into his IV. Scott didn't reject Liam's handsiness, at least not in private, but he couldn't ever remember Scott reaching for him like this.

"Go on. It's okay," Scott whispered.

"He told me not to, but I climbed in his jeep. It was his own, civilian, not the Army's. I tried to reason with him. How was going to military prison going to be better?" Liam turned his face into Scott's palm for a few seconds. "I'll never forget the way he looked when he said, 'You don't get it. I'm not going anywhere.'"

Scott moved closer, resting his forehead against Liam's.

"He offered to let me out, but I said I wasn't going to quit on him. I still really thought I could change his mind." Liam took a deep breath and got the rest of it out. "I should have known then, but it wasn't until he started swerving all over the road that I got what he meant."

"Bastard should have just used a gun and not dragged everyone into it."

Liam didn't stop. "He rolled us into a telephone pole, and the engine caught fire. He was killed. I woke up in the hospital. At first they thought they could save my leg, but the operations didn't help. The first amputation was below my knee, but then I got an infection. I was lucky not to get a dishonorable discharge. No one was supposed to be off base."

Scott kissed him, pushing Liam onto his back. Stretching out full-length, weight pressing him down, Scott cupped Liam's face and sucked gently on his lower lip, then drew Liam's tongue into his mouth. Scott kissed like he was trying to inhale Liam, breathe him into his lungs. It wasn't the urgency of need. This was… tender. And when Scott lifted his head and their gazes locked, Liam understood what Scott was telling him.

That he was glad Liam was alive. That Scott loved him. And nothing else mattered.

He shouldn't worry about what Scott said. It was all right there.

Everything Scott wasn't saying hit Liam like a blow to his sternum, a real physical pain. When he could breathe again, the words just spilled out.

"There's something else I have to tell you. And it's really going to piss you off."

Scott raised both brows.

"When we were together before, I sometimes skipped classes—those classes you were working two jobs to pay for, so I could meet this guy at a coffee shop. Not like dates," Liam hurried to explain. "He played guitar and I sang. Open mic. Acoustic stuff, nothing like the band. Jesus. I felt like shit because you were working so hard and then you started taking those pills—"

Scott rolled over onto his back. He was shaking. Shit. Was he crying?

Liam pressed up on his elbows to look. The asshole was laughing. Liam had kept that horrible betrayal locked away, and Scott thought it was funny?

If he'd had a right leg, he'd have rolled and kneed Scott where it would hurt. He settled for elbowing him in the gut.

"Ow." Scott jerked up and his laughter faded.

"What is so goddamned funny about that? It's why I left. I was—" Liam swallowed. Great. Him crying was all this mess needed. "You were doing all this so that I could be a doctor and I didn't even know if I wanted to be one anymore. You were risking your life taking pills, and I was skipping out—"

"I knew."

"What?"

"I knew about the singing." Scott didn't sound pissed off. "You had a six o'clock class. I was home from the garage, grabbing a shower before I went to bed to get up for the UPS job. I'd been hoping to get a little action, so I hurried. I was just drying off when I heard the front door shut. I ran out and saw you left your book bag. Figured I could at least chase you down and give it to you. But you weren't headed for the bus stop."

Liam collapsed onto his back and put his forearm over his face.

He felt Scott shrug. "When I saw you meet that guy, yeah, I was pissed." A breath of a laugh. "Was about two seconds from charging in after you and breaking things. But then you guys started setting up. I watched for a bit. Then you started singing and I knew."

"Knew what?" Liam pulled his arm back down and looked over.

Scott shrugged again. "That music is what you are."

Liam put his arm back up in time to catch the moisture leaking from the corners of his eyes. No review about a velvet voice, no crowd wanting an encore, nothing was ever going to mean as much as Scott understanding that.

Fuck it. Liam ground the heels of his hands into his eyes. "God, I love you so fucking much." His voice shook.

Except for a thick swallow, Scott was silent.

Liam smacked Scott's shoulder. "Why didn't you say something?"

"Figured if you wanted me to know about it, you'd tell me. Not like you needed my permission for it."

"Scott." Liam pulled himself onto Scott's chest. Tentatively, Liam swung his hip so that his stump rested on Scott's thigh. He didn't flinch. One hand came up to rest on Liam's hair, just as tentatively as Liam's move had been, like Scott did need permission. Liam gave it, pressing into the touch. Scott stroked his fingers through Liam's hair. "Jesus, Scott."

"Then you were gone." There was no accusation in Scott's voice, only a statement of fact.

"I didn't want to leave you."

Scott huffed at that.

"No. Really. It wasn't you I was getting away from. It was me. The Army—I signed up because I knew it was the only way to make sure I couldn't head right home because I missed you. It was like trying to outrun myself." And no way would he ever be able to make it up to Scott for how much Liam had hurt him with that stupid decision.

"So. How's that working out?" Scott's hand drifted through Liam's hair again.

"I've had to slow down a bit." He moved his stump.

"Guess so." Scott breathed out against his hair.

Liam was afraid of the answer, but he forced himself to ask anyway. "What do we do now?"

"You promised me six rounds. Gonna have to step it up. Checkout's at eleven, right?"

SEX COULDN'T fix everything, especially when it wasn't sex that was the problem. But goddamn, it felt good to push his dick inside Scott again.

The way they were spooned on their sides meant all the thrust came from Liam's hips. He swore Scott's ass was tighter from this angle, even when Liam hitched Scott's leg up higher to get deeper into that sweet, hot friction.

Liam buried his face in Scott's neck, wanting more of Scott in him, around him. Scott. The name echoed in Liam's mind in time with his thrusts, but he kept it locked tight in his throat. He inhaled the sweat and shampoo smell on Scott's skin, and the refrain went off again. Blood, breath, bone, Scott was in every bit. And the best part of all, Scott still wanted Liam, still wanted to be with him even after everything he had done. Scott turned his head, and Liam kissed him, diving in for more sensation, more heat, more Scott.

It didn't matter—and Liam would never ask—but sometimes he had this fantasy where he was the only one who ever got to have Scott like this. That Liam was the only one Scott let himself need like this. That Scott only ever lost that edge between volcanic rage and glacial distance with Liam.

Liam arched his back and went harder, driving grunts out of Scott's throat while his ass clung and dragged on Liam's dick. Every stroke wound Liam up further, his balls burning as they drew up. Liam's muscles ached from thrusting, from holding back when he needed to come, and he snaked his hand under Scott's leg and started jerking him off.

Neither of them could seem to stop kissing, though by this point it was more like openmouthed breathing at each other with tongues.

Liam hit the point of no return. He couldn't have held it back if someone had a gun to his head. He'd have to make it up to Scott with a killer blow job, but then Scott gasped and jerked against him, ass clamping, and thank God, because Liam was already spilling into the condom, barely aware of the pulse of Scott's dick against his palm, the thick creamy stream that pumped out to lace Liam's fingers.

Coppery blood hit his tongue, and Liam knew he must have bitten Scott's lip. Liam raised his head as he rocked them through the aftershocks until Scott dragged Liam's hand away.

Their entwined hands rested on Scott's chest, so Liam felt the hard slam of Scott's heart slow and calm.

Scott pulled Liam's hand up and kissed his sticky knuckles. "Damn. Thought I was gonna shoot from just fucking."

"Yeah?" Liam grinned and jiggled his dick in Scott's ass. "Goals, baby."

"*Almost*, you smug son of a bitch."

Scott almost never directed that particular endearment at Liam, since they both knew Scott meant it literally in Liam's case. Shit. There was a lot they still needed to talk about.

Liam propped his head up on his cocked elbow and looked down at Scott. "Sorry about your lip."

"From you punching me or going all zombie flesh-eater?" Scott swiped his tongue across the little tear.

"Both." Liam dropped a kiss on Scott's swollen bottom lip. "I hear girls pay good money to get their lips to look that fat."

"Pretty sure you just had your hand on my dick, and do you even know any girls like that? Think Mac or Chai spends a lot of time worrying about how fat their lips look?"

"No," Liam admitted.

"You're so full of it, Walsh." But there was a warmth in Scott's teasing that Liam had been missing.

Scott had always claimed being the little spoon made him claustrophobic, but right now he tucked their hands under his chin and sighed.

Liam shot a glance at the clock—as if he needed that with the crack in the drapes showing dark gray instead of a black sky. He couldn't let them leave this room, this bed, until he knew when he'd get to fuck Scott again, to hold him and know Scott had really forgiven him.

"Don't fall asleep," Liam urged.

Scott jerked to attention. "Why? Is it—do you think you'll have another—" He seemed to be trying to find the word to describe it. "—dream?"

"No. It doesn't usually happen twice in a night if I get out of bed. But, how are we going to do this?"

Scott groaned and wriggled onto his back. The groan might have been from Liam's dick sliding out of him, but Liam suspected it had more to do with the choice of conversation. Liam peeled off the condom and dropped it on the floor behind him.

"Guess we've moved right past dating again." Scott tucked his hands behind his head.

"I don't know. I kind of like the idea of taking you out—"

A sharp arch of Scott's eyebrow made Liam rethink the phrasing.

"—of us going out, like to dinner or something."

Scott snorted. "Yeah. Can you see that? I don't even think I own a shirt I could wear in a restaurant that doesn't have plastic tables bolted to the floor. 'Sides, how is going out together keeping other people out of our business?"

"Maybe other people's opinions weren't as much the problem as—" Liam swallowed hard. "—as I was."

Scott studied his face, then brushed fingers through Liam's hair. "I'm thinking I may not have been the easiest person to live with either."

"You mean the way you go from zero to a hundred in two seconds flat when you think something's wrong?"

Scott's jaw jutted. "That," he admitted through clenched teeth.

Liam settled his head on Scott's shoulder.

"It's not just people this time, though. There's the band," Scott pointed out.

"That ship has sailed. Reeve already knew. Mac doesn't bother with that kind of stuff. Dev figured it out. By the way, he's not homophobic, just a dick. And Chai's the one who told us to leave tonight."

"I don't mean that way. You think all of those rock bros would be throwing horns for you if they knew you liked banging dudes?"

Liam's guilt worms started a fresh session of squirming. Was Scott right? He hadn't really thought that far. "The guy from Judas Priest is out and—"

"He already had his millions, and his millions of fans, when he did. I watch you sing. I watch them watch you. Don't blow this on—"

"On you?"

Scott lowered his eyes and made a disgusted sound in his throat. "Now who's taking things to extremes? It's not about me."

"I never thought I'd make money at singing. I don't care about that. I just want to—"

He wanted him and Scott in a house—maybe not one like Eli and Quinn's—an apartment would be fine, but if there was a garage, that would be nice. Scott could work on cars, and Liam could sing, and they could fuck and fall asleep and do it all again tomorrow. That wasn't asking for much, was it?

"—be with you," Liam finished. "Everything else is bullshit."

Scott looked at him like Liam had lost his mind. "Seriously? That's your plan? Love wins and we skip through the daisies? Why don't you call your mom and tell her where you are?"

"Well, what do you want?"

Scott rolled over on his side. "What does that matter? It's never mattered before."

Liam felt Scott pull away like something was being yanked out of him no matter how deep the roots. He grabbed Scott's shoulder and forced him to turn back. "This. That's what I mean. Why is it all or nothing?"

Everything about Scott's face said the conversation was over. Rigid jaw, thin lips. The expression he wore when he was about a second away from rage. Except his eyes. Maybe Liam was full of it, but he swore there was something pleading about Scott's eyes. Something that said he wanted to be wrong.

Liam let go of Scott's shoulder. "You said you were in. That you wanted to try to make this work. Did you change your mind?"

"Fuck." With that explosive breath, Scott shut his eyes, as if he knew they had given him away. "No."

Liam waited.

Scott finally met his gaze. "No, I didn't change my mind."

"So why can't we decide what that means? Be together how we want."

"Because we both know the world doesn't work like that. We don't get to pick."

"Works for those friends of yours. They make it work. Christ, they even spank and God knows what, and then have brunch and still work on cars and whatever and—"

"All right."

"Huh?" Liam needed to hear that again because it sounded like Scott had actually given in.

"Just stop talking."

"So I won?" Liam wasn't exactly sure what he'd won, what he'd gotten Scott to agree to, but at least Scott wasn't actively resisting him.

"Still talking." Scott rolled on his side again.

"What about—"

"Yes. Whatever it is, yes, if you'll stop talking."

Liam curled around Scott and smiled into his shoulder. "Thanks. I'd love a wake-up blow job."

"Ratfucker."

Chapter Twenty-Two

SCOTT SOMEHOW managed to not act like a complete idiot when Liam's band practiced at the bar on Monday, mostly by staying in the storeroom. But when they ran through that encore again, Scott couldn't help himself. He slunk around one of the pillars and watched.

Jesus, Liam was hot. The way he sang made Scott remember every bit of how it felt to have Liam wrapped around him, dick hitting all the right places in Scott's ass until he was ready to pop.

From her table near the bar, Mrs. S. spotted him. "Scott. Come sit down."

Liam's head turned toward Scott like some kind of hunting dog. That sexy voice hitched in the middle of a word but then finished the line.

"Break," Reeve called, and the feeds from the guitars and drums dropped away. He sighed into his mic. "Guess we've lost Liam."

Liam shook himself. "Sorry."

Des or Den—whatever the just-a-dick drummer's name was—rubbed the back of his hand over his forehead, stick still in his fist. "Good. That mean we're done?"

"No. Still want to run that instrumental section."

The drummer groaned. Mac nodded, her fingers moving up and down the neck of her guitar.

"I thought we all were ready to go next level." Reeve swung to look at the drummer.

"Yeah, yeah. Just be sure *Next Level* gets on my tombstone." The drummer—Dev—toweled off his face.

Liam adjusted his mic and winked at Scott.

A wink should not have been able to hit Scott in the guts like that. Maybe his balls, since they'd been raring to go from the second Scott saw Liam's lips so close to the mic.

When Liam strummed a chord, Reeve put a hand on his shoulder. "Not you, lover boy. Go, get it out of your system." Reeve shooed Liam off the stage. "Maybe next rehearsal we can get a little focus."

Liam grinned and stepped down from the stage.

"Yeah," Dev called. "When you don't have dick on the brain."

Scott's hands clenched. Maybe Dev wasn't a homophobe, but that didn't mean he got to run his mouth without a beatdown.

"Better than having a dick for a brain," Mac said. "Like you," she added in case there was any doubt who she was referring to.

"Hey." Liam stood in front of Scott.

"Hey." Scott shot another look at Liam's bandmates. Reeve strummed a chord, and Mac picked through a few notes.

"So." Liam stepped forward and Scott backed up. They weren't a secret anymore—not even from Mrs. S.—but Scott still wasn't ready to put on a show. 'Sides, the way it felt right now between him and Liam—like just touching him would set off a shower of sparks faster than a dragging muffler—he didn't trust them to not put on one *hell* of a show.

Scott let Liam back him into the hall, then turned and bolted for the storeroom, Liam close behind. Scott slammed the door shut, then pressed Liam's back into it.

Sparks weren't the problem now. Liam's breath hit Scott's cheek, Liam's face so close, and that look in his eyes made something jar loose inside Scott. Something under Scott's ribs that fought him for control and the only way to keep it locked down was to dig fingers into Liam's hair and kiss him. Hard.

But they had to breathe sometime.

"Fucking missed you," Liam got out between pants when Scott let him breathe.

"Saw me this morning."

"It's after midnight. Technically that was yesterday."

"Whatever."

Liam cupped Scott's face. "Not whatever. I missed you."

Scott swallowed, wishing there was a way to hide from the way Liam was looking at him. It made what was trying to get out of him more frantic. It wasn't a violent outburst he was trying to control, not anger. This was soft and needy and wanted to believe the look in Liam's eyes would always be there, that Scott would always matter, and no way could he let that out.

Because even if he believed in Liam, he didn't have faith in the rest of the world not to fuck everything up.

"Technically do you want a blow job or not?" Scott dropped to his knees.

"I didn't mean I just missed sex—oh fuck."

In the time Liam started and abandoned his protest, Scott had him unzipped and in his mouth.

"Fuck, Scott. F—ungh." The back of Liam's skull hit the door with a loud enough *thunk* to be heard over the violent riffs of the band's encore. Urgent fingers petted the shorter sides of Scott's hair as he licked the head of his cock. "Yes."

There was only so much he could pack into a blow job, but Scott gave it his best shot. He worked his way down, licking and sucking, drawing more and more and more of Liam into his throat, telling him he wanted, needed Liam inside him. He cupped Liam's balls, drew them out, and rolled them over his fingers as he swallowed around the thickness, making his eyes water, telling Liam Scott would always take care of him. When Liam's hips bucked a little, Scott encouraged him with a deeper bob, promising to fucking worship the rock god Liam was on stage because that was part of who Liam was now.

They moved together, the frenzied pace of the music driving them on. Scott dropped his hand to rub at his dick, which was so hard it had its own heartbeat swelling and pounding and hurting.

"Oh shit." Liam's fingers tightened on the sides of Scott's head, then released. "I'm—fuck—" Liam shoved frantically at Scott's shoulders.

The vein riding Scott's tongue pulsed; then Liam came, as bitter as the damned Imperial IPA they had on tap, thick and hot. Scott swallowed it all as Liam jerked and gasped and shuddered over him. Lips throbbing, he kissed his way down the shaft as Liam kept muttering "Fuck, Scott, fuck" and rubbing his fingers over Scott's skull.

Then again, maybe sometimes he could pack a lot into a blow job.

Liam let out a long breath and then cupped Scott's neck, rubbing a thumb across his lips. "You didn't used to like to—"

Scott licked the salt and bitter from Liam's finger. "Yeah, well. Things change."

"Not everything."

Scott rolled to his feet while managing to keep from looking at Liam, which helped him get a grip on the softness that was trying to slip free again.

"What's wrong?" Liam asked because he knew Scott too damned well and there wasn't exactly a lot of room to hide in here with two people.

Scott tugged at his jeans. "Nothing." He sat on the edge of the cot.

"Nothing a little payback won't fix?" Liam suggested.

Scott wasn't about to turn down getting his dick sucked, especially not by Liam, but he scanned the room quickly, trying to figure out what would be best for Liam's leg. Obviously it bent, but how comfortable was it for Liam to kneel? Even sitting on the cot was an accident waiting to happen.

"Aren't you going to miss your ride?" Scott said. The music had stopped.

"Are you saying you won't give me a ride?" Liam hit him with another one of those winks. It was just as effective as it had been when they were kids.

Scott threw a hand up at the room. "You gonna pull a decent-sized mattress out of your ass?"

"I could ride *your* ass standing up all day."

Scott pictured himself clinging to the sink while Liam pounded into him, and clenched his ass on nothing. What would be worse, Liam trying and getting pissed off or Scott letting Liam make that stupid decision for himself?

"Maybe, but that means I gotta wait around with my dick in my hand. Unless you got a spare cock somewhere." The instant the words left his mouth, Scott wanted to take them back. All he could think of was the dildo hidden in his rattiest boxers at the bottom of his bag under the cot. This was what happened when he said shit without thinking it through.

"No." But Liam's grin said he'd read everything that just went through Scott's face. "Do you?"

Turned out Liam could kneel without much trouble, just a click and knock against the cement when he went down. Which was why Scott was leaning with his back to the sink, hands clutching the rim like it was a lifeline out of hell while Liam sucked his cock and worked the dildo in his ass, when someone pounded on the door.

"Yo, Liam. The Epiphone's in a case on the bar," Reeve called.

Shit. What if his grandmother was standing next to him?

Liam flicked his tongue around as he pulled off Scott's dick. "Thanks," he yelled back like Scott's cock wasn't wet and bobbing right in front of his face.

"So, you gonna need a ride or you good?" Reeve's voice wasn't as nasally coming through the door.

Liam looked up at Scott, eyes dark and full of an intensity Scott was a little afraid to name. His whisper brushed over Scott's dick. "Am I good?"

Scott nodded.

Liam smiled and twisted the dildo. Scott bit his lip. Ratfucker.

"You gonna give me a ride?" Liam whispered again.

"I fucking hate you," Scott spat out. He'd done okay so far limiting any sound effect. Until Liam went fast and hard with the silicone dick, and Scott had to slap a hand over his mouth to muffle himself.

"I'm good. Thanks. Scott'll drop me off. Later."

"Totally dick-whipped, Liam." Dev's voice was low. "But fucking go for it, man."

Liam did. And Scott was sure he was going to pass out from trying to swallow the sounds Liam was yanking out of him with his mouth and tongue and the pressure of that dildo. Damn it. Scott knew exactly where he wanted it and even he couldn't do himself this well.

Liam pulled off. "Say it again."

Scott only had to think about what Liam meant for a second. "Fucking hate you."

Liam smiled.

"Stop again and I am so kicking your ass, Walsh."

The words were almost swallowed up as Liam went down on him again, but Scott swore he heard "Love you too."

COUPLE DAYS later, Scott hugged the bricks of the alley for what little one o'clock shade that provided and smoked the day's third cigarette. Usually he managed to keep it to five a day, but he needed to think.

The junker would run eight hundred and fifty, though Jamie said they could maybe talk the guy down to eight hundred since Scott would be picking up the tow fee too. It needed new brake lines and pads, for sure. The parts to get it running plus the tow would eat up all of what Scott had socked away from working under the table at Schim's. In two more weeks, he'd have had enough to settle up with the government and maybe even get out of the storeroom. If Eli came through with his six hundred, Scott might be out of the hole enough to swing first, last, and security deposit on something decent enough that Liam would want to move in.

Instead he was considering going back to scratch so Liam could have a car fitted with a left-foot accelerator.

He knew it was crazy. He was crazy. Even now some mean little voice told him to keep Liam trapped, so he still had to rely on Scott or his mom or Reeve or whoever to get around. But he couldn't do that to Liam.

It was the worst thing Scott could imagine, worse than the damned tax bill because Scott would still be able to pay that off soon. Liam could never buy his way out of not having a right leg.

He took a last drag and flicked the butt away as a white delivery-style van pulled into the alley, late-model, maybe last year's, with green cursive on the side and a rose. If someone had sent Chai flowers, Scott was going to have such a good time tonight.

Then Liam swung down from the passenger side, a plastic grocery bag swinging on his arm and a big fat smile on his face. Scott tried to scowl, but he was happy to see the bastard too. Liam hadn't been to the bar since Monday. Even now he was supposed to be working some event at the fairgrounds, which Scott supposed was the case considering Liam was dressed in that mailman-like uniform Scott remembered from the car show, and starchy button-downs weren't his usual style.

Liam held up the bag. "I brought lunch. Meatball subs from Mancini's."

"And one turkey, double meat." A woman stepped down from the driver's side, dressed like Liam except she had on slacks instead of the shorts he was wearing. A long black braid dangled over her shoulder, and her skin was a dark copper-brown. She had a smile almost as bright as Liam's with whiter teeth.

"Kishori works with me. She needed to run a delivery for her family's florist before we clocked in, so she picked me up and we picked up lunch." Liam handed out the sandwiches like it was a picnic at the beach.

"Nice to meet you, Scott." Kishori unwrapped her sub and took a bite. "Sorry." She held a hand over her mouth as she chewed. "I work two jobs and I'm starving."

Scott nodded at her. Liam was going to end up needing to explain shit to his mom if he kept bringing random people in on it, though he wasn't going to ask Kishori if Liam had told her they were boyfriends. He probably had. That was Liam, caring and sharing. Scott stared down at the white-wrapped bundle sealed with deli tape, a big M in black grease pencil that he'd swear had been written by the same guy who used to take their orders six years ago. His letters had unexpected extra loops.

Did Liam seriously think Scott needed reminding of all the Mancini's subs they'd eaten back when they had that apartment?

"I gotta work until ten tonight. It's the State Fair." Liam sounded apologetic, as if Scott had been begging to see him. "Don't suppose you could take off to pick me up then?"

"Breaks aren't really in my contract. Especially not on a Saturday night."

"And I'm working another double tomorrow." Liam sighed and rest a hand on the bricks near Scott's head.

"Thanks for the sandwich." Scott wasn't sure what he was supposed to do here. Liam couldn't expect they'd hit the storeroom with his coworker standing right there, shoving turkey in her face. Maybe he should have invited them inside anyway.

"You're welcome."

Liam stood staring at Scott and Scott stared back. Then he got it. "Yeah. Been missing you too."

Liam's smile lit up his face again. "I took the extra shift so I had Monday off."

"Huh. Funny how I'm not working Monday either."

"Yeah. What are the odds?" Liam's face got closer and Scott was pretty sure he was going to let Liam kiss him in the alley at fucking one o'clock in the afternoon.

"Hey, Li," Kishori called.

"Shit." Liam stepped back. "We gotta run and drop the van back off."

That had Scott wondering how much schedule and ride juggling had gone down to make this casual stop. Liam hadn't even taken his own sandwich out of the bag.

Liam pointed at the sandwich in Scott's hand. "Try and get something in your system besides tobacco or salt."

Scott rolled his eyes. "Soon as you quit living on caffeine." Considering Liam's worrying over Scott taking a couple of dexies, Liam had some fucking nerve to be pulling a Brooks Blast Energy Drink from the bag as he walked away.

It wasn't until the van had backed out of the alley that Scott got the idea that Liam had meant a drive-by with sandwiches as a date.

Scott stepped inside, stowed his sub in the fridge, then went to call Jamie about the junker he'd found.

LIAM JERKED awake. Panic blasted adrenaline through his system. Even before he opened his eyes, disorientation hatched swirled questions through his head. *Am I late? What day is it? Where the fuck am I?*

He blinked, and sunlight stabbed into his eyes.

Then cigarette smoke curled up his nose, and everything was all right. Scott. Familiar and safe. More home than the ranch house with Mom and Greg could ever be.

As the jolt of fear faded, he latched on to more bits of real world. The Mustang. Sunrise in his face. He'd fallen asleep while Scott was driving him—where had Scott driven him?

Pins and needles, sharp as fire, raked through his leg. He stomped, still too bleary to remember it never did any good.

"Hey." Scott stubbed out his cigarette, sending a fresh whiff up Liam's nose.

"Where the fuck are we?"

"Beach." Scott pointed his chin at the windshield.

Through sun blindness Liam managed to glimpse sand, seagrass, and diamond-bright water. A seagull screamed overhead, trying to reboot the dream he'd fought free of. "Where are we at the beach?"

"Delaware."

Liam nodded, though it didn't exactly make sense yet. He rubbed his face. He'd been working double shifts at the fairground over the weekend. He'd begged Kishori to bring him down to the bar after they closed up Sunday and—

"So when I said let's do something on our day off…?"

Scott shrugged. "You said you liked the beach a couple times."

Liam hadn't been since—his brain had to squint to pinpoint the fifteen-year-old memory—since Mom's sisters had taken him. Back when they had contact with Mom's family.

Scott turned and reached into a plastic bag on the back seat. "Water or a Brooks Blast?"

"Duh."

Scott handed him the red-and-gold can. "Sorry it's a little warm." He dug in the bag again. "Here." He tossed a Tastykake honey bun in Liam's lap.

"God, I fucking love you." He tore the plastic with his teeth and then dove in for a sweet mouthful washed down by the fizzy vanilla energy drink. He leaned his head back for a second and then grinned at Scott, contentment stretching along every nerve. "Nice date, by the way."

"Fuck you." Scott huffed a laugh. "Better than your lame drive-by with subs."

"Totally. Points for romantic setting."

"Shut up."

A sidelong glance showed Scott's lowered lashes and pursed lips. He was ridiculously cute when he was embarrassed. He didn't blush much, but that look through his lashes got Liam in the chest every time.

Liam took another bite then a swig from the can, blending two—no, with Scott here that made three—of his favorite things in the world. "But I'm subtracting for the potential for sand in seriously uncomfortable places." Eager for more of the cool air, he popped the door open, then stared down at the sand covering the broken, faded asphalt of the road that cut through the sea marsh around them. And then at the foot shell filling his right sneaker. "Shit."

"What?"

"I've never asked about sand with my prosthesis. I know the knee part is splashproof but not submersible. But sand's gonna get in some places, and I sure as fuck can't replace anything that gets damaged."

"Won't the Army—"

"Covered the first one. Top-of-the-line. But that's it."

"Shit." Scott smacked the dashboard, open palmed. "I didn't think."

"Yes, you did. You thought about bringing me here and my favorite Tastykake."

Scott faced him. "But not about whether you could actually get out of the car."

Liam tangled his fingers in the long pieces of Scott's hair and dragged him closer until their foreheads touched. "You did exactly what I asked you to. You didn't give a shit about my leg. So let me worry about that."

Scott swallowed, then nodded against him.

Liam rubbed the back of Scott's neck. "You're going to hate me saying this, but this is how I know we're going to make it this time."

Scott pulled away. "Why, because I drove you to Delaware to eat a Tastykake in my car?"

"Exactly." Liam bit his lip, then jumped in all the way. "Because we're both saying what we want and actually listening to each other." Before Scott could start bitching about Liam talking like a social worker, he added, "It still counts as a date, so I'm still going to put out."

"You'd better." Scott reached into his pocket, then shoved a crumpled receipt at Liam. "I put $5.89 into getting laid, man."

Liam grabbed the paper. "Sprang for condoms too. What a gentleman."

"Shut up and eat your breakfast."

The empty plastic bag gave Liam an idea. He stuffed his sneaker and foot into it before tying the plastic ends off around the post above his ankle. Scott watched, then rummaged in the trunk.

He came back and handed off a roll of duct tape. "Will this help?"

"Yeah. I can clean it with alcohol after." Liam stood outside the car, then took a step onto the sand. It was a whole new balance game, but the bag should keep the worst of the sand out.

A half mile to the north, a few houses shimmered at the horizon. To the south, nothing but marsh. Aside from the seagulls, they were alone. Scott carried a sheet as they left the little piece of road pointing at the ocean. He'd really planned this. Happiness bubbled up until all Liam's blood felt carbonated. Only worry about what could happen to his C-leg held him back from tackling Scott to the sand and kissing this joy into him.

Scott spread out the sheet. He didn't hover, but waited until Liam knelt and got himself onto the sheet before joining him.

"How'd you find this place?" Liam leaned back on his elbows, then just sank onto the sand. Cool on his back, warm on his front and the sound and the smell and Scott. He'd never been so close to perfect before.

"Asked at the place where I got breakfast. There's a boat launch into the river about a quarter mile back." Scott stretched out next to him. "Going back to sleep?"

"No. Just—thanks for this. I haven't been anywhere for fun since—since before."

"Not like it's Ocean City or anything."

"No." Liam rolled onto his side. "But you're here."

"Jesus." Scott rolled his eyes.

"Will you punch me if I say you're cute when you're embarrassed?"

"Say it again and find out."

Liam laughed and shifted around, letting the sand shape around him.

Scott made a few throat-clearing sounds. Just as Liam was starting to get a little freaked out, Scott said, "About you going places, I mean, on your own. I'm—you're getting a car with a left-foot accelerator."

"I'm what?" Liam pushed away from the sand.

"It's not right. You shouldn't feel all trapped into hanging around, needing a ride."

"Trapped? Like, you mean, with you? For fuck's sake, Scott. I thought you—we—"

"Now who's going from zero to a hundred? I want this to work. Us. So when we get an apartment—"

Liam launched himself on top of Scott. "It's our second date and you're asking me to move in?"

Scott had latched his arms around Liam's ribs as he landed. Now Scott dropped them to his sides. "Asshole."

"Sorry. I'm just—you—" Liam kissed him.

It was too much, too big for words. Scott saw a future for them. Scott trusted him—them—enough to want to live together again. The carbonation in his blood crossed into his brain and God, everything was going to be good again. Scott held Liam's shoulders, mouth opening for him, the stroke of tongues rippling sensation down Liam's spine so he had to get closer, get more.

When he stopped for a breath, Scott's eyes were lit up with those sunbursts, wide and soft and hopeful. "Is that a yes?"

"To an apartment, yes. To you buying me a car, no. You need the money for the IRS."

"Chai's not planning on firing me yet. Even if we get something close to a busline, you need to be able to get around. To get to work.

Because we both know the shit is going to hit the fan when you tell your mom."

Liam slid off onto a hip.

"Or were you planning on never bringing it up?" Scott went on.

Liam rolled onto his back and ground the heels of his hands into his eyes, which got sand in them. "Fuck."

Scott was right. It definitely would be a shit show. To make it worse, he'd have to admit he'd lied when she asked. She might like to phrase things in her recovery-speak way about Scott's anger addiction and learned helplessness, but Liam knew it was more. To her, Scott was a reminder of someone who'd been there for Liam when she couldn't be and she'd never forgive Scott for that. The sand was cold against his back and scratching the hell out of his corneas.

Liam blinked hard to get the sand out. "No. Just putting it off. Like maybe until moving day?"

Scott leaned over him and brushed the sand away gently. "Hey. I'm not going to push. That's between you and your mom. But we gotta make it so you can get around. You shouldn't have to be dependent on me either."

A car had always been at the top of Scott's wish list, and Liam understood the freedom it represented to Scott. Being able to drive himself would make Liam's life easier though.

"Okay."

Scott arched a brow.

"*We* can look into getting me a car," Liam clarified. "And us an apartment. And eventually telling my mom. But two things are not up for negotiation."

"Is this like a prenup or something?" Scott smirked.

"I don't know, are you proposing?"

"No." Scott's stunned expression made Liam laugh.

He thought about it for a second. About making promises in front of a clerk and some witnesses. Scott's cop friend and maybe Reeve. Maybe someday.

But even getting married couldn't make this any more real, wouldn't change how Scott was the only person who let—no, *made*—Liam be whole. Scott's honesty didn't let Liam fake anything. His anger forced out the darker feelings Liam always wanted to hide. Loving Scott would always come with some pain, and it was good because it kept Liam from being numbed into niceness.

He had to say it. "I really fucking love you. You get that, right?"

Scott's mouth twisted like he was disgusted, but his eyes stayed bright and happy. "Yeah." He ducked his head and kissed Liam's palm. "Me too." Shifting onto his belly, Scott stretched out on the sheet. "Christ. This dating shit is exhausting. I need some sleep before I drive back."

It was stupid, but Liam would miss him while Scott was asleep. But Liam pressed himself up. "Go ahead. I'll wake you up in an hour or so."

"Hey. Almost forgot. What are the two nonnegotiable things?"

"I get to make music."

"Of course." Scott grunted like it was the only possible answer.

"And I get to be with you."

SCOTT SCRUBBED the sweat off his face and neck in the storeroom sink and patted around with a towel. He didn't think he'd even have time to feel the dips and ridges in that cot before he was asleep.

It had been one hell of a night. Chai had him filling drinks and running stock and working the register and security. Mostly security. Delayed Autopsies went in big for costumes and theater, so they had some weird-ass fucking fans. The face tattoos alone were enough to give him nightmares.

His phone chirped with a text.

U up?

He sat on the cot to answer Liam. *Booty call much?*

The phone rang a second later. "What's up?"

"Hey."

Scott couldn't afford the minutes for phone or text sex, but as soon as he heard Liam's voice, it was obvious that wasn't the reason for the call.

Liam sighed. "Christ. I really wish you were here." His voice sounded like it had been wrung out to dry.

"Rough time at work?"

"Nothing special."

Scott waited. Phones hadn't ever been their thing, so he didn't know if this would work the same way it did in person.

After a few quick breaths from Liam, Scott got his answer.

"You know how I said I didn't get that dream often."

A jolt of adrenaline pulled Scott up off the cot. Liam thrashing, punching, trapped in the kind of night terror Scott had gotten when he was younger, and no one was there now to pull him out. There was nothing Scott could say or do to fix it, nothing for the adrenaline burst to do but make him nauseous and leave him pacing.

What could he say? "Right."

"Stupid, I know. Just a dream."

But they both knew that wasn't true. Liam had been soaked with sweat, muscles shaking when Scott pulled him awake.

"Scott."

He couldn't have the phone pressed any closer to his ear without putting it through his skull.

There was a wet sort of click, like Liam had swallowed. "I need—"

Scott didn't make him finish it. "I'll be right over."

On mostly empty streets, it was a fifteen-minute drive. Scott made it in under ten. It wasn't until he was parked in front of the house he'd seen Liam come out of that the parade of complications marched through Scott's head.

He grabbed his phone.

"I'm here. You want to come out?" The house was one-story. Maybe Liam's bedroom was in the front, easy enough to make it to the door.

"Not really." Liam's voice had an uncertain waver in it that squeezed Scott's ribs like a giant fist.

"I don't suppose you're wearing your leg."

"My room is the back left as you face the house."

Scott tucked the phone in his pocket and rested his forehead on the steering wheel. Because what Scott's night really needed was a creep around the outside of Marilyn Walsh Becker's house at three thirty in the morning. He did it anyway.

Liam opened his window as Scott walked up. The ledge was about the middle of Scott's chest—if he'd been able to get that close. There was a prickly bush in the way.

A shirtless Liam leaned out. "Aren't you supposed to throw pebbles?"

Scott stared at him. "You want me to hit you with rocks?"

"Never mind."

This was why things got so fucked-up. Scott could not make himself stop and think shit through when Liam was involved. Liam needed him, and here he was. Those diagnoses had been wrong. Scott didn't have poor impulse control. He had poor Liam control. Light flashed in the cloud-filled sky. Two Mississippis later, a long roll of thunder beat on the bones of Scott's ears.

Right then, poor Liam control was going to get Scott wet. "So what now?" Scott whispered.

"You could come in." Liam jerked his thumb at the room behind him.

"Seriously?" Despite himself, Scott tried to get closer. The bush drove tiny needles through his jeans up to midthigh. Scott wasn't thrilled about risking his boys in a climb. "A neighbor's probably already called the cops. I'll be lucky to not get shot."

The light flicked on in the room behind Liam. "Liam, honey. Are you—what are you doing?"

Marilyn appeared behind Liam's shoulders and stared silently at Scott as another rumble echoed and mumbled to a stop.

"Scott," she said finally on a long-ass sigh.

He nodded. "Mrs. Becker."

"Perhaps you could use the front door if you'd like to visit." Her too-pleasant tone dug in sharper than the thorns on the bush.

He should have worn a fucking ski mask.

Chapter Twenty-Three

MOM LEFT his room with a sighed *We need to talk*. Liam grabbed his crutches and swung himself at the door with the biggest jumps he could manage, terrified that by the time he got to the front steps, Scott would already be a blur of taillights.

But when Liam yanked open the door, Scott was on the cement stoop, chewing on his thumbnail with his other hand tucked in his pocket. Liam's chest loosened enough for him to catch his breath. Maybe he was just as bad as he accused Scott of being, quick to see disaster in everything. He needed to remember how it had felt on the beach. Just them. Everything else was bullshit.

Scott stared at his boots. "So, I should go."

"No. You should stay."

Scott looked up at him, brows wrinkled in confusion.

"I put it off, but that was wrong," Liam explained. "And this isn't just about me. We're not giving anyone else the power to fuck us up." He reached for Scott, and when Scott didn't retreat, Liam pulled him into the house. "You were invited in. Let's have some coffee."

No confusion now, just that one brow arch Scott did when he didn't have a good answer right then. He'd damned well better hope that he never lost control of his facial muscles. God forbid Scott have to actually say what he was feeling.

One bonus to Mom being in recovery was that there was always a pot of coffee ready. She didn't have a lot of fancy stuff in her kitchen, but her coffee maker was like something from a spaceship. It even ground the beans. He poured them both a mug and, since he was fucking exhausted, let Scott carry the coffees to the dining table so they could sit down.

"Sorry about that," Liam offered, curling his hand around the mug while low thunder vibrated the fillings in his molars.

"You control the weather now?"

"You know what I meant."

A murmur of voices, Mom's and Greg's in the hall, was followed by the flush of a toilet and a bedroom door creaking closed. Then Mom cut through the dining room on her way to the kitchen. Oh shit. She could not seriously be planning for the *We need to talk* to happen now?

Her coming back in with her *Progress, Not Perfection* mug and pulling out a chair answered that. Liam snuck a sideways look at Scott in the chair next to him. He didn't look angry, but Liam knew that blank face. It meant he was keeping something locked in. Sometimes the look meant he was a second away from grabbing Liam and kissing him until he couldn't breathe. But usually it was an indication that he was about a second away from exploding into punch-a-hole-in-the-wall rage.

Liam wished he was the optimist Scott always bitched about him being. It was just that life had made Liam used to working without a net. Tonight it seemed like it was one hell of a long way down. He took a step out onto the high wire and squeezed Scott's thigh under the table. It was like trying to reassure granite.

Scott and his blank face stared down into his coffee. Liam wasn't even sure he was blinking.

Mom took two long sips on her mug, then put it down and looked right at Liam. "You could have told me the truth. I specifically asked if you were back with Scott."

"Because you would have approved?"

"Of course I wouldn't."

Liam tried to keep his voice calm. "I'm twenty-seven years old. I don't need you to approve of who I date."

"Obviously. But you're not acting like you're twenty-seven. You're acting like a teenager sneaking a boy into your bedroom."

Scott slumped back against his chair. "Gotta award the points to Mom there," he sneered.

"We didn't—*I* didn't want you to know. Because you've always been down on him. On us." It took everything Liam had been learning about controlling his voice to not sound like a whiny brat. "You think either of us wanted to deal with more of that?"

Mom rested a hand on the table, palm up. Something out of her substance abuse counselor classes, probably. "If you think something is right, you don't lie and hide, Liam. What does that tell you?"

Scott made a sound in his throat, something like a growl, but whether he agreed with Mom or not wasn't clear.

"You've never had anything good to say about Scott. What does that tell *you*?" Liam didn't give a shit what his voice did now.

Mom folded her hands in her lap and looked at them before meeting his eyes again. "I admit that when I was using, I saw him as competition for your attention. I used your support to enable my addiction, and he pulled you away from me. I know I wasn't your mother when you needed me to be, honey."

There were tears in her eyes and in her voice. Liam swallowed. "It's okay. You were sick." The words spilled out, easy and familiar, like they had his whole life. But tonight, the aftertaste was more bitter than the coffee.

"And, Scott, I owe you an apology for my behavior then too. Liam's enabling must have put a lot of stress on you."

Scott shoved away from the table, grabbed his mug, and strode off into the kitchen. Liam held his breath. Any moment there'd be a shatter as the mug hit the sink, the floor, the wall. He waited for the slam of the back door, but everything was quiet.

"I get it, Mom." Liam's ears still strained toward the kitchen. "But that doesn't explain what your issue is with Scott now."

"Because I can see that this isn't healthy for either of you. If you'd go to the Nar-Anon meetings, you'd see the patterns."

"I'm not a fucking pattern, Mom. Neither is Scott."

She shut her eyes and picked up her mug, but Liam didn't see her drink from it.

"Scott has never addressed his addiction to anger. Until he understands his powerlessness—it will impact his life and the life of anyone who loves him."

"Jesus Christ, Mom. Scott would never hurt me." He managed to not rub the bridge of his nose. There was still a bump there. But he wasn't lying. That punch had been a startled reaction. For all the times Scott had been angry enough to break a dish or punch through plaster, he'd never aimed at Liam. "Besides, I think he's controlling his anger pretty damned well right now."

The vibration of steps behind him told him Scott had come back out of the kitchen to stand behind Liam's chair. "Got a lot of practice of you hating me, Marilyn. Twelve years of you telling him I'm a piece of shit and ruining his life."

Mom shook her head. "It's not that I dislike you, Scott. I know you've faced a lot of challenges in life, and I'm sorry that my addiction added to them." She turned to Liam. "And you know this has nothing to do with your sexuality, honey. You may be twenty-seven years old. But I can't stay silent when I can see you walking into disaster."

"Disaster?" Liam wished he had his prosthesis there so he could take it off and shove it in her face. "I think I'm pretty freaking familiar with disaster." He leaned back until he felt Scott's hands against his back. Scott rubbed a knuckle back and forth across a tight muscle. Liam found a way to lower his voice. "I've already heard everything you have to say. You said me leaving Scott was the best decision of my life. Yeah. That worked out great." He lifted his crutch up and used the tip to shove the napkin holder a few inches off center.

Tucking her hair behind her ears, Mom ignored the evidence and went back to her sales pitch. "Which is why I think you should go to Nar-Anon. You'd learn so much. Sweetie, you're only going to keep hurting each other."

"I told you Scott would never—"

She cut him off. "Emotionally, I mean. Haven't you ever wondered why you find Scott so irresistible?"

Liam choked back *Have you seen his ass in tight jeans?* Scott squeezed the chair back so hard Liam felt the wood shift in the seat.

His mother sighed like she'd heard his thoughts. Her tone sharpened as she leaned forward. "You think dysfunction is love. And that's my fault, I know. But you just keep creating it because it's all you know. You chase chaos. Of course you would pick Scott over someone emotionally steady like Deon. You want the codependency of an addict relationship; you need someone to try to save."

Shock hit Liam like a sucker punch, driving the air from his lungs. As he caught his breath, he waited for the guilt worms to start squirming around, letting him know she was right. That Scott was just someone else Liam would try to fix and fail.

The worms were quiet. They already knew what Liam's brain was just catching on to.

Scott jerked his hands away like the chair had caught fire and slammed out of the house.

"At least he knows I'm right," Mom said.

"No. That's bullshit." Liam tucked his crutches under his arms. Greg stumbled out of the hall, but Liam charged by him without a word.

He wasn't running for his life or even from it. He was running to it, and it had damned well better wait for him.

SCOTT SLID into the Mustang and rested his forehead on the steering wheel. He blew out a breath and then punched the top edge of the dash.

Fuck. Right the fucking hell staring him in the face the whole time and he'd never seen it. Liam had grown up loving disaster. No wonder he'd fallen for Scott.

And the shit cherry on top of the whole shit sundae was that Marilyn Walsh was the one to open his eyes.

He jumped as something slammed into the car window. Not something, Liam. On crutches in nothing but his boxers.

Goddamned lunatic.

"Wait," Liam yelled, knocking on the window.

Scott shook his head and started the car.

Liam leaned against the car, and it wasn't as if Scott could drag the ratfucker down the street.

He rolled down the window. "What?"

Liam panted. "Hang on."

Typical Liam. He'd chased after something, and now he didn't know what to do when he got it. How had Scott missed that when it was so fucking obvious?

"Step back."

Liam's eyes widened. But it was the hurt in the droop of his mouth, the way his lips parted in a gasp like Scott had fucking stabbed him, that made Scott unbend a little.

"I can't, Liam."

"Can't what?"

Scott sighed. "I thought I could do this. Try again. But I can't. We'll just end up hurting each other again."

"What happened? I mean—I know Mom was... Mom, but—wait, let me get in."

Liam turned to limp around the back of the car. Scott put her in first and eased off the clutch. He glanced at Liam in the rearview mirror, saw he was clear, and pressed the gas.

Liam threw a crutch at the back window.

It bounced on the trunk, then kicked off the spoiler. With a lurch, Scott stalled the car. After putting it back in first and setting the parking brake, he climbed out.

"Did you just throw your crutch at my car?" Scott demanded, though he'd seen Liam do exactly that.

"What the fuck was I supposed to do, run after you?"

"Here's an idea. You could just let me go. Like I said I wanted to."

"Why?"

Scott dragged a hand through his hair. Obviously they were going to do this in the middle of the fucking street. "Because it's over. And if it wasn't over before, it sure as fuck is over after you threw something at my car." Scott patted the trunk where he figured the crutch had hit. Felt smooth, but there was no light to help him pick out a dent.

Liam snorted. "Seriously?"

Scott stared, eyes narrowed. "Don't I look serious?"

Liam took a couple of hops toward him. Scott groaned and bent down to scoop up the crutch. He carried it back to Liam but kept a couple feet between them as he handed it back.

"No," Liam said. "'Seriously' as in you, Scott McDermott, seriously believe some bullshit social worker psychobabble coming from my *mother*?"

Scott froze. Liam took advantage and swung closer.

"You think I want to be with you because you're dysfunctional? That you're some chaos that lures me in?"

Jesus, Liam was right in front of Scott now. He might as well have been stuck in fresh tar because he couldn't make his legs take any steps back.

Liam balanced on one crutch and grabbed Scott behind the neck to pull him close. Their foreheads touched. "You are the only part of my life that isn't chaos. The only part that's ever worked. No matter what I've done, no matter what shit I've pulled, you stood by me."

God, Scott wanted to believe that Liam meant it. Everything in him wanted to grab and hold on, and fuck anything that tried to stop them. He took a deep breath.

Liam swayed a little. Scott steadied him with an arm around his waist.

"Exactly like that," Liam said. "And I don't care if you never fucking say it. Because I still know it. You love me. You love me so much that I might forget how to hate myself when I can't get things right."

"Liam." Scott grabbed him then, hugged the stupid half-naked bastard. He knew what he should say. That loving Liam made him forget what hating himself felt like, but he could only hold on harder.

Liam took a big breath and sagged against him. "So. After we get out of here...."

Scott pulled away enough to look at his face, and then he remembered the game. "We'll get a place."

"And—"

"And I'm getting you your own car because you'll be lucky if I let you ride in the Batmobile after that stunt, Robin."

Liam laughed.

The sound rippled in Scott's chest like the warmth of a shot of Johnnie Walker Black and the thrill of the rumble from all three hundred and thirty-five horses under the Mustang's hood. The first sheets of rain started slamming into them then. Maybe that had just been thunder.

Liam gave him a sweet, short, ozone-sharp kiss. Scott had never loved the smell of rain more than right now, reflected from Liam's skin. He wanted to taste more of it, but they were in the middle of the street and Liam was an excited dick away from public indecency. Scott let Liam go as he pulled free.

"I swear we don't have to stay, but can we go back in for my leg now?"

Scott glanced down. "Let me make sure I've got this. You want me to not give a shit about your leg, except when you want me to give a shit about your leg."

Liam nodded. "Basically."

"And go back in the house with you when your mother just said I'm the reason you can't have nice things."

"Yes, but I'm not staying."

"And not lose my shit when everybody wants to fuck the lead singer of the best new band in Baltimore."

"Well, maybe you could stare at me the way you do when you think I don't see you." The look Liam gave him was filthy. Dangerous for a guy in his state of dress.

"And what do I get out of this, Walsh?"

"You get to say 'I hate you,' and I'll know what you mean. You get to pretend to be a miserable asshole to everyone, and I'll never admit you're actually the most loyal, decent guy they'll ever meet. Oh. And you get to fuck the incredibly sexy lead singer of the best new band in Baltimore."

"Most loyal, decent badass they'll ever meet," Scott corrected.

"Agreed. Should we add something in about regular morning blow jobs?"

"Don't push your fucking luck."

Chapter Twenty-Four

PREDAWN LIGHT reflected off the puddles in the parking lot by the time Liam clambered back out of the car at the good old Best Maryland Inn.

Scott slammed down the hood and pointed with his precious distributor cap. "Want me to grab your leg?"

Liam shook his head. "Tomorrow's good." He swung himself up onto the sidewalk lining the strip of rooms.

The clerk in the office hadn't seemed to care that Liam was paying for a room a few hours before checkout. And when Liam remembered he was scheduled to work ten to six today, he added on another night, but his brain couldn't seem to plan further than that, further than his leg, a backpack full of clothes, and his toothbrush in the back seat of Scott's car.

Mom had continued right on with her intervention bullshit when they were back inside. "You need to know you'll always have a place with me, honey."

"Wrong. I don't belong anyplace where Scott doesn't feel welcome."

Which was true, but since Scott was currently living in the storeroom of a bar, a place to live was going to be a major priority. Tomorrow.

Liam balanced his weight forward on his crutches and pulled the room key from his shorts pocket. The Best Maryland Inn went old-school, metal key hanging off a red plastic square with the room number on it.

He swung a crutch forward to keep the door from slamming shut, and Scott's hand slapped into it at the same time.

Normally there'd be a flash of resentment and disgust at himself, a defensive reflex of *I got it*. But this felt right, Scott working with him. He locked the door behind them, and it was like the beach again. They were alone together and the rest of the world could go fuck themselves.

Scott shot him one of those looks, the one he did when he was trying not to get caught but then he'd somehow end up staring. That look had been putting the cream in Liam's Twinkie since he was fifteen. Right then, he wasn't tired anymore.

Scott pinned him back against the door and dove onto his mouth like Liam was holding all the air in the room. He latched on to Scott's face, one crutch falling away, the other trapped between them. The stroke of their tongues together did what it always did to Liam. His stomach made that sweet fluttering dip and his dick urged him closer. Scott latched on to Liam's ass and got their cocks grinding together in time with their tongues.

Scott slid a hand down the back of Liam's shorts and squeezed. "You are out of your goddamned mind. You know that, right?" He breathed the words on Liam's lips. "I'm living in a fucking closet."

"Tomorrow."

"Huh?"

"Talk about it tomorrow."

"Yeah."

This time Scott's hands went down the front of Liam's baggy shorts, but as good as a little friction was, they both wanted more.

Scott hooked his fingers in the belt loops and the shorts didn't need much encouragement to go sliding off, Liam's boxers following.

Scott moved his head so his mouth was at Liam's ear. "Don't get pissed, okay?" Scott grabbed Liam's ass and lifted so that Liam had to drop his other crutch and grab Scott's shoulders. "Gonna carry you."

There wasn't a lot to be pissed about. The sooner they got to the bed, the sooner they'd be fucking. It was a little weird and pretty fucking far from graceful. Liam tried to get his leg high enough to keep it out of Scott's way and hung on. As soon as Liam's ass hit the mattress, Scott leaned back to tear open his jeans and yank his shirt over his head, eyes on Liam the whole time.

It wasn't just an expression. He felt the look on his skin like a touch. Intense. Hungry. And something he couldn't remember having seen before. Possessive.

Liam shivered as he peeled off his shirt.

Scott smiled. "Thought you liked me looking at you."

"Get the fuck on me." Liam opened his arms.

Liam wanted in Scott, or Scott in him, the brain-searing heat and sensation of penetration, but that was something else that was going to have to wait.

Scott spat in his hand and climbed on, rubbing their dicks together, increasing the friction with the grip of his hand and the thrust of his hips. And he kept right on watching Liam.

Liam arched to meet him and watched right back. Scott's motion shifted into another gear, faster and harder, and Liam ramped right up with him. He was almost there already. He clamped his hands on Scott's ass.

"Jesus." Scott shut his eyes.

"Don't."

Scott blinked and then smiled. "New kink? All right."

It was fast and hard. Liam lost control of his eyelids first. He couldn't help it. The orgasm rushed up and shoved him over the top into hot slippery waves of so goddamned good he wanted to die right there.

And when Scott's motion hitched and he jerked against Liam, he wanted to live forever as long as they got to keep doing this every day.

Scott's eyes opened again and he caught his breath. His hands were wet with sweat and jizz as he held Liam's face between them.

"This is it, got it?" Scott grunted. "This time you don't pretend to be happy and hide shit. If something's going on, just tell me. You don't have to fix it alone."

Liam was glad Scott's hands were so wet he wouldn't notice the tear that leaked out. "Okay." Then he remembered what he'd wanted to tell Scott all day.

"What?" Scott's eyes went from lid-drooping sleepy to half-lidded wary.

"So the band got some good news. The bassist from Charm City Cyanide came to our show, and now they want us to open for them a couple times this fall. Like at Sunfest in Ocean City."

"Uh-huh."

Liam licked his bottom lip. "He had some suggestions for Reeve. Like, to get us noticed."

Scott leaned on an arm as he moved some of his weight off Liam's chest. "Seems to me like a packed house means you guys got that covered."

"No, bigger." They'd gotten another good review, but Schim's wasn't Sunfest or Sky Town.

"So what are these suggestions?"

"He told Reeve opening with 'Rooster' and dedicating it to vets was cool. And then Reeve told him about my leg and they think it could be a... hook."

Scott's stillness didn't feel cold. It was how he told Liam he was listening. That he wouldn't tell Liam how he was supposed to feel about it. The problem was, he didn't know. He wore shorts out in public all the time, so doing it on stage wouldn't be a big deal. But there were all those vets who had been wounded or killed in action, not because of some stupid arrogance. He couldn't act like he'd sacrificed the same way.

So he told Scott the truth. "I don't know."

Scott settled more on his side. "Here's what I know. They need you. Not because of your leg. Because of your voice. They need you more than you need them."

Liam shook his head.

"Yeah? Then how come they weren't doing so great before you started singing with them?"

"Reeve taught me a lot. He arranges the music to fit my range."

"That says to me that he knows he's better with you. You gotta decide on this now?"

"No. I mean, Sunfest would be the first big show, and that's in three weeks."

Scott nodded, then rolled away and brought them towels to clean up with. Liam set his phone alarm to go off in two hours and slid between the sheets, half on top of Scott, their bodies fitting together as exhaustion took hold.

Scott kissed the top of Liam's head. "One thing I know. You're too much talent to be a gimmick."

SCOTT KNEW things weren't going to be easy. He just didn't know they were going to be so hard at eight o'clock in the fucking morning.

Liam was in the hotel's shower when Jamie called.

"So, we're all set on the car. We can have it towed to my place tomorrow if you bring a certified check."

Scott appreciated Jamie tracking down a car so fast and offering garage space for Scott to work on it; he just wasn't sure that's where he should be putting a thousand bucks right now.

"Things have gotten complicated," he admitted.

"I-punched-my-disabled-ex-in-the-face-in-front-of-witnesses complicated or I'm-homeless-again complicated?"

"Um." Scott knuckled sleep out of his eyes. Jesus. He hadn't even had a cigarette yet. "My-disabled-no-longer-ex-is-homeless complicated."

"Christ on a cracker, McDermott. Do you work hard at complete fuckery or does it come naturally to you? What the fuck happened?"

Scott told him.

"Ah hell."

Scott could picture Jamie rubbing the back of his neck. There was another voice in the background.

"Hang on," Jamie said. "Try not to find any more complications for a few minutes."

The shower shut off. Scott moved away from the bathroom door and sat on the bed.

"Okay, okay." Jamie spoke in the distance, then he was back on the phone. "Okay, who works where today?"

So Jamie had nice friends—and a rich-as-fuck boyfriend who wanted to help. Scott got it. But he and Liam could work this shit out on their own. "What the fuck difference does it make? Thanks for finding the car. Sorry I don't know if I still want it."

"Don't get your panties in a knot and just answer the fucking question."

"Nobody's asking you to get involved."

"Did you or did you not help me fix the truck this spring?"

Scott resisted asking for a lawyer and growled a *yes* as Liam stepped out of the bathroom with a towel around his waist.

"Well, consider that I don't want to owe you a favor forever and just tell me whether the fuck you and your no-longer-ex have to work today."

"Yeah. Liam's working at the fairgrounds until six. I'm at the bar all night."

"Now was that so hard? I'll call you later." Jamie hung up.

WITH NO band on the schedule, Sunday at Schim's was on the quiet side. A handful of regulars, old guys who went through bar nuts almost as fast as they went through beers, sat at the bar and told the same jokes.

At around four, a coed bunch of nerds got a pitcher of Imperial IPA, took it to a table, and started arguing about some movie series.

Scott kept a close eye on the clock while he washed and dried all the barware, turned all the stock, and generally enjoyed a little peace and quiet. He watched Chai cash out Morty, one of the regulars who was in almost every afternoon. Morty had to be ninety if he was a day but still managed to flirt well enough to make Chai laugh, and he moved like a dancer instead of someone with stiff old bones.

Scott hoped he and Liam still felt half that good as they got older. The thought almost made him drop the pint glass he was drying. Since when did he think that far ahead, let alone that far ahead with Liam as part of his future? He tried to picture it and came up blank. But Jamie was forty and still having a life, including fucking some rich gorgeous guy. And the dude with Eli, Quinn, he had to be in his thirties at least. They seemed to be making it work. So maybe he and Liam really would someday be old enough to change each other's diapers. He thought of Mrs. Freeman hauling up her groceries alone. And Morty. Maybe he was here so much because Mrs. Morty was long gone. Liam better not try to back out of things by dying first.

"Scott," Chai called. "Think that glass is dry now."

"Right." He hung it up in the rack and got a look at the clock. Ten of six. Shit. "Hey, mind if I run up to get Liam at the fairgrounds? He doesn't have a ride… home." Or a home, come to that, but one thing at a time, right?

"Told Reeve he did."

Scott looked to where Reeve sat on the stage edge, strumming a guitar like Liam's and taking notes with a pencil he kept sticking back in his dreads.

Chai went on, "Reeve said he was supposed to pick him up but got a text saying Li had it covered. He's supposed to be coming down to work on something. Besides you." She poked his biceps sharply. "So this just a tearing-up-the-sheets thing, or is it something serious?"

Scott folded his arms across his chest.

She rolled her eyes. "Chill. Your air of mystery is intact. I'm only wondering if I'm going to have to replace one of the best barbacks we've had."

"You're firing me?" His voice went high, and that pissed him off more. This was total bullshit. He hadn't punched anyone. Hadn't even cursed that asshole out for pissing on the floor last night.

"Slow your roll, hon. Technically you don't even work here. And don't be an idiot. The job's yours as long as you want it. I just thought maybe you were ready to go back on the books." Chai slapped his shoulder and said more quietly, "Seriously, man, got my cherry popped on that old Army cot. Can't imagine it's gotten any better to fuck on."

"Ugh." Scott looked away but caught the eye of Mrs. S., and that only made it worse. "TMI." Clearly it was way past time Scott got out of that storeroom. He stomped off to talk to Reeve.

Reeve held up a hand when he saw Scott coming and wrote a bit more in his notebook before shoving the pencil in his dreads. "What's up? Liam here?"

One thing, the only thing, Scott had asked was to not be left in the dark. "No. Why? He supposed to be?"

"Said he wanted a ride because we were going to work on a song. Then he said he had a ride. Figured it was you."

Scott grabbed for his phone and didn't find it. Not in any of his pockets. Though when he shoved his hand back in the right front, his fingers went straight through to his thigh.

Jesus. Like he needed more shit to worry about. He went back behind the bar, checked under the sink, the mats, down in the cellar. It couldn't be in the storeroom. He hadn't been in there all day. Shit. Except this morning when he grabbed a jerky stick.

His phone buzzed against the base of the paper supply shelf. As he grabbed it, he saw he had seven text messages and Liam was calling.

"Yeah."

"Finally. Thought it was supposed to be quiet today." Liam didn't even pause for breath. "Holy shit. Wait until you see Beach's car. I can't even believe I'm sitting in it."

Scott was used to some verbal vomit when Liam got excited, but this wasn't making any kind of sense.

"Who the fuck's Beach?"

"That guy, Beauchamp. The one who, uh"—Liam lowered his voice—"you know, got spanked."

A man's laugh sounded over the background noise—which was pretty definitely noise.

"Are you in a convertible?"

"It's a goddamned Ferrari Spider, custom interior," Liam shouted.

Beauchamp must have revved it because the eight cylinders purred loud enough for Scott to hear over the traffic and wind. Damn. Next thing, some guy would be tempting Liam with a fucking Bentley.

"Still nothing like a '68 Shelby Fastback," Scott insisted.

"You jealous 'cause I'm riding with another guy or 'cause I'm riding in another car?"

"Shut up and put on your seat belt."

SCOTT HEARD the Spider when it pulled into the alley and went out to meet them. Beauchamp didn't stay long, just long enough to pop the hood and let Scott drool over the engine. After a few polite words about the true American beauty of the Mustang, Beauchamp displayed one of those ankle monitors, like for people on house arrest.

"I'm afraid I can't come in. My probation requires me to stay out of bars, but I still wanted to play my part, hence the taxi service. I'm sure I'll be seeing you both around." Beauchamp slipped back into the Spider like he was greased and oiled back out of the alley.

"What the fuck is going on?" Scott wanted to know.

"You tell me. I thought Reeve was gonna pick me up, but around five thirty Beach comes strolling into the first aid station announcing, 'Your chariot awaits, my prince.'"

Scott's lip curled.

Liam nodded. "No kidding. Kishori dragged me for cheating on you already."

Obviously Jamie had been a busy little redheaded bastard, but what good a fifteen-minute drive would do beat the hell out of Scott.

"Fuck do I know. No one tells me shit."

Liam nudged him with a shoulder. "Maybe they would if you'd answer a text."

"Yeah, well, I lost my phone for a tick." Scott started to pull out his cigs, then thought of Morty and put them back. "Reeve's waiting for you."

Reeve and Liam sat on the stage edge and made chords and hums every couple of minutes, but a table of sweaty dads with hall passes was loud enough to drown out most of what was going on.

Scott had just started to relax again when Eli banged through the front door and strolled up to the bar. One of the regulars gave his skintight aqua shirt a side-eye, then shrugged and grabbed another handful of peanuts.

Eli leaned over the bar toward Chai. "Do you have any more of those delicious Moon Shots?"

"Show some ID and I'll make you one."

Eli sighed and tugged out a license. He handed it over with some cash. "Perfect. I'll take two."

Scott didn't figure Eli was here alone, and sure enough Quinn, Jamie, and Gavin rolled up in Eli's wake. Chai gave Scott a look under lowered brows, but she filled drink orders and ignored it when Jamie and Quinn shoved two tables together in the space in front of the stage.

Chai sent Scott over with the tray. He slapped down the KZ bottles in front of Gavin and Jamie, then said, "What the hell?"

Jamie shook his head. "It's the Gay Avengers assembling, kid. Get over it."

Two more guys showed up. One looked a long white robe away from playing Jesus in an Easter pageant; the other was tall and thin, with sharp features and white-blond hair.

Before Chai could even ask for ID, the blond ordered a KZ X-treme Creme and Jesus ordered a freaking orange juice. Chai stared at him for a second before yanking one of the small cans out of the fridge. She handed the tray to Scott without a word.

Which was the scariest thing yet.

Two black women came in. The taller one had her head shaved and wore a long flowing dress with big red flowers all over it. The shorter woman had a suit jacket over one arm despite the heat outside. Chai gave Scott another furrowed-brow look when she realized they were joining the table in the back. The tall woman ordered a pint of Honeydew Jalapeño, and the shorter asked for club soda with lime. She sat next to Eli.

Liam and Reeve had given up on whatever music thing they were doing. Liam looked at Scott with hands spread wide, and Scott shrugged.

As Scott brought over the new drinks, Gavin said, "Thanks for coming on short notice, everyone. Would the secretary please note that we have a quorum of steering committee members as I call the meeting to order?"

Jesus took a small notebook and pencil out of a back pocket and wrote.

Scott tucked the tray under one arm and leaned against a support post to watch. Not that he was egotistical, but obviously this show had something to do with the phone call with Jamie this morning.

"The chair recognizes Vice-Chair Ardell Green."

The shorter woman nodded, sending her shoulder-length braids swinging. She had on a tight tailored shirt that was almost a match for Eli's except hers was a deep purple.

"Even before the physical space is ready, we need to address transportation. Already we have issues with volunteers who can't always get to the shelter to help."

"Transportation and safety," Eli put in.

Gavin nodded. "Is there any disagreement with an ad hoc committee to get transportation and safety off the ground? Volunteers?"

Jesus raised his hand.

Then, looking like it would kill him, Jamie lifted his barely enough to be noticed. "I've got some ideas."

Scott didn't think he was quite as stupid as his grades in school suggested, but he still couldn't figure out what the hell Jamie was up to. Back on the day Jamie had first dragged him to meet Eli and Quinn, they'd mentioned a shelter, only Scott had been too old for it. He'd figured it for a homeless shelter. Must be a pretty specific kind, since he'd have bet a carton of Newports everyone around those tables was some flavor of queer.

Liam moved to stand next to him. "Reeve thought it was a setup to catch them in some kind of code violation, but I told him you knew most of them and they were cool."

That wasn't something Scott was willing to bet on.

Scott tuned back in to hear Jamie say, "...reimbursed for parts and have personal use of the vehicle as compensation for time."

"Do we have a motion to look for someone to fill that position?"

"Moved." That was the blond.

"Seconded," the taller woman added.

"Votes for?" Gavin looked around the table.

Everyone raised a hand.

"Opposed?"

Scott half expected Jamie to go against his own proposal.

"Motion passed."

"On to the next fundraiser."

Jamie kicked away from the table and came to stand next to Scott. "Okay. Here's the deal. Try not to argue until you think about it okay?"

"No promises," Scott said.

"So there's no place in Baltimore for homeless kids. Especially not queer ones."

Like Scott didn't know.

"Now there's going to be. Gavin put together a foundation and hauled in a bunch of us on a steering committee, but he and Ardell are really the ones who know what they're doing. They've been trying to figure out something for transportation. I found the car while I was looking for something for them."

"What car?" Liam said.

Jamie raised his brows, and Scott muttered, "Later."

"If you go for it, the foundation will put up the money for a van and parts. They'll pay the insurance and registration. You donate your time to modify it to handle some accessibility issues and to perform routine maintenance. In exchange, you can drive it when the foundation doesn't need it for the shelter."

"Liam could drive it?" Scott said.

"That was the whole fucking point, right? So you can use that cash to get out of the hole and get an apartment, and Liam has a way to get around. Gotta keep a clean license, though. Anything that makes the shelter look bad and I'll take it out of your skin."

The threat was leveled at Scott, but Liam said, "I think we can handle it."

"Good." Jamie smacked Scott on the shoulder and went back to the table.

Scott scratched behind his ear. "You just made that call without talking to me?"

"You had some other idea?"

"No. But—"

"What car?"

"You remember how I told you I wanted to get you one."

Liam nodded.

"Kind of had it all lined up all ready."

Liam put a hand on the post above Scott's shoulder. "And you're giving me bullshit about me saying we'd go for the plan without talking to you first."

Scott considered. "Pretty much."

"You are such an asshole sometimes. And for that, you totally owe me a wake-up blow job."

Chapter Twenty-Five

LIAM WAS awake way too early, considering he and Scott had only passed out in a sticky pile of satisfaction less than four hours ago. He curled himself more tightly around Scott despite the morning heat in their tiny studio apartment in Towson. Breathing in the smell from Scott's neck, Liam pressed a quick kiss on the damp skin and tried to will himself back to sleep, but a seesaw of excitement and dread kept jerking him back awake.

He blew a breath across Scott's skin, aiming for the sensitive place behind his ear. Scott's head moved a little on the pillow, but his eyelids never fluttered and his breathing remained deep and even.

Tonight was Blow the Moon's last tune-up before opening for Charm City Cyanide at Sunfest, but that wasn't what kept Liam from falling back asleep. After that weird committee meeting at Schim's, Liam had talked to Quinn for a long time. Without going into a lot of details, Liam told him that he didn't feel right about people praising his sacrifice when it had been an off-base car accident. Quinn had some pretty definite opinions about sacrifice and disabilities people never noticed, and said he didn't necessarily think it was a bad thing to draw attention to disabled vets, given what was going on at the VA. All true, but not a fucking lot of help.

Liam had been about to get up when the look in Quinn's eyes held him in the chair.

"I can't tell you what to do," Quinn had said, but the firmness in his voice made Liam think the man was used to handing out orders. "How it happened doesn't matter. It's your body. And you don't need to turn it into a message board unless that's what you want it to be."

So Liam had told Reeve that opening with "Rooster" and acknowledging vets would be fine, but whether Liam went on stage in cargo shorts or jeans would be up to how he felt on any given day. Dev had whined that whatever got people to notice them was worth it, but then Mac said, "Either it's about the music or it's not," and that was the end of it.

Today was going to be a jeans day. Liam was already nervous enough about the song that was finally ready to replace one of their covers in the second set. He scooped Scott's hand from where it rested on his ribs and brought it up for a kiss. Both Scott's thumbs were a bloody mess of peeled skin and scabs from him gnawing on his cuticles, but between the nicotine transdermal patch and some nicotine gum courtesy of Maryland's smoking-cessation program, Scott had made it five days so far, insisting his decision to quit was purely financial. Liam caught Scott pushing on the patch a lot, like that would get him an extra hit.

Liam stared hard at Scott's face and saw his lips twitch. "You're faking and I need coffee."

Scott didn't open his eyes. "And your crutches are right next to the bed. Help yourself."

Bed was a pretty generous term for the futon and frame that folded back into a couch, but since it had been free—a gift from Chai because she said it hurt her back—it was what they had. The biggest problem was that it was a lot lower to the ground than the beds Liam was used to handling. He needed to sit in their one reclaimed-from-the-sidewalk chair to don his leg.

Right now, it was easiest to roll onto the floor and push up with the help of his crutches and the chair.

Scott turned over and watched him.

Liam shook his head. "You really are a bastard, you know that."

"So my mom told me. Was this one of the times I was supposed to give a shit? You got to give me a signal."

"Like falling on my ass?" Liam made it over to the single block of what was the extent of their kitchen counter, then flipped Scott off before filling the carafe.

Liam's mom had said that while he was welcome to come home anytime, she wouldn't enable his destructive patterns. What that actually meant was Liam only got to take his clothes, and she wouldn't be buying them any housewarming presents. But as Scott waited at the end of the driveway, Greg pointed to a box on a garage shelf of "stuff I keep meaning to take to Goodwill. Maybe you could drop it somewhere for me."

It had held everything that currently made up their kitchenware: an old coffee maker, some dishes, mugs, utensils, and a big pot with a lid.

As Liam scooped coffee into the filter, he spied some brown fragments on the counter. Either the cockroaches were hopped up on mega growth steroids, or they also had a mouse problem.

He turned toward Scott with a smile. "Do you think we could get a cat?"

DESPITE THE ten-dollar cover and no extra promo from the Brooks guy or the *Charming Rag*, according to Mrs. S.'s counter, they were twenty shy of the capacity. Scott tapped out the latest number and sent it to Liam.

On the drive down to the bar, Liam had been a bundle of nerves, which didn't exactly help Scott's withdrawal headache. Apparently it was a problem if Scott talked to him and it was a problem if Scott was too quiet. Scott hoped the do-gooders tracked down a van fast, because he was looking forward to Liam being able to drive himself—at least when the band had a gig.

Despite Liam's freakout, everything seemed to be going fine as they rolled through the second set. The second set was the stuff they weren't using for the shows where they opened for CCC. It had stuff they were trying out or fine-tuning, so Scott wasn't surprised to hear Reeve do an intro mentioning a new song.

Scott had just set the tap on another Bare Ass Blonde keg when the first few notes made him jerk his head up. Liam had been playing those chords nonstop, and when Scott asked him what song they were, he'd said just something he was working on.

He. Liam. Not Reeve. Scott wished he could remember whatever title Reeve had mentioned just now.

Liam's guitar had the melody line, and even from the bar, Scott could see that Liam had closed his eyes in concentration. Then Mac came in with something rougher, pushing the rhythm faster.

Liam's voice was a soft growl. "Never been wanted, never been needed."

The hair on the back of Scott's neck stood up. He moved out from behind the bar, sliding along the edge of the crowd. His don't-fuck-with-me scowl let him weave in closer.

Liam finished the verse, and there was a pause like a sucked-in breath, only a steady ringing from Dev's cymbal filling the air. Then the chorus flooded out in a hot blast. Liam lifted his head and whisper-screamed the words right at Scott.

"You hold me, you bleed me, you scar me. You fill me, you starve me, you choke me, you are me."

They both might as well be fucking naked. No, worse. Liam's song turned Scott's skin transparent, and anyone could see everything he tried so hard not to feel. Except no one else was looking at him. Just Liam.

The bridge buckled Scott's knees, but the crowd kept him up.

"Ten thousand clicks the distance, still your teeth in my skin, your bruises on my bones and I'm right back again."

Liam had shut his eyes now, and when the chorus started, the crowd had picked it up enough to sing along.

Two hundred strangers singing the words Liam had written about him, about them. Scott wanted to charge the stage, to prove those words right now. It was a perfect form of agony. Intimate and cutting. Everything he'd never been able to say, the pieces of him that he thought were locked safely away, had been pulled out and he'd never be able to bury them again.

The song ended.

Scott's ears filled with echoes, a rush of sound in and out like he kept going underwater. His skin was soaked with sweat.

He stumbled back through the crowd, past Chai asking if he ever planned to take the empty keg back down to the cellar, through the back door into the alley. It was still hot, but a breeze dried his skin.

He dug at the nicotine patch on his arm, fumbled for the gum, and then gave up and just hunched against the wall with his hands on his thighs, remembering how to breathe.

"So you didn't like it?"

Scott turned as Liam stepped into the alley.

Like? How did *like* apply to something that perfectly described the most important thing in his life but let everyone else see it?

"It was something that just came out of me. I couldn't stop it."

"It was amazing." And that was the truth. But he didn't know when he wanted to hear it again. "Just, you know, some warning would have been good."

Liam's face had lit up with Scott's compliment, but now he frowned. "I wanted to make it, like, a present. I thought it would make you happy that I wrote you a song."

"Happy? Liam, I am happy. I was happy before you wrote me a song. And I'm happy now. I'm happy when you keep playing me the same five notes and asking me what I think. I'm happy when you fall asleep on me even though I'm already so hot I can't breathe. I'm happy when your stupid fucking sense of humor makes me laugh at 4:00 a.m. no matter what time I have to get up. Don't you know how happy being with you makes me?" Scott blinked. Fuck. Was he going to cry? Goddamned stupid song. Goddamned stupid withdrawal.

Liam grabbed his face, thumbs damned close to finding a drop that might have leaked out. "I do now." He kissed him.

Scott took a shuddering breath. "I love you."

Liam smiled. "*That* I already knew."

Author's Note

THERE WILL be more Baltimore stories. Thank you so much for reading.

K.A. MITCHELL discovered the magic of writing at an early age when she learned that a carefully crayoned note of apology sent to the kitchen in a toy truck would earn her a reprieve from banishment to her room. Her career as a spin-control artist was cut short when her family moved to a two-story house and her trucks would not roll safely down the stairs. Around the same time, she decided that Ken and G.I. Joe made a much cuter couple than Ken and Barbie and was perplexed when invitations to play Barbie dropped off. She never stopped making stuff up, though, and was thrilled to find out that people would pay her to do it. Although the men in her stories usually carry more emotional baggage than even LAX can lose in a year, she guarantees they always find their sexy way to a happy ending.

K.A. loves to hear from her readers. You can email her at ka@kamitchell. com. She is often found talking about her imaginary friends on Twitter @ka_mitchell.

Email: ka@kamitchell.com
Twitter: @ka_mitchell
Website: www.kamitchell.com
Blog: authorkamitchell.wordpress.com
Tumblr: kamitchellplotbunnyfarm.tumblr.com

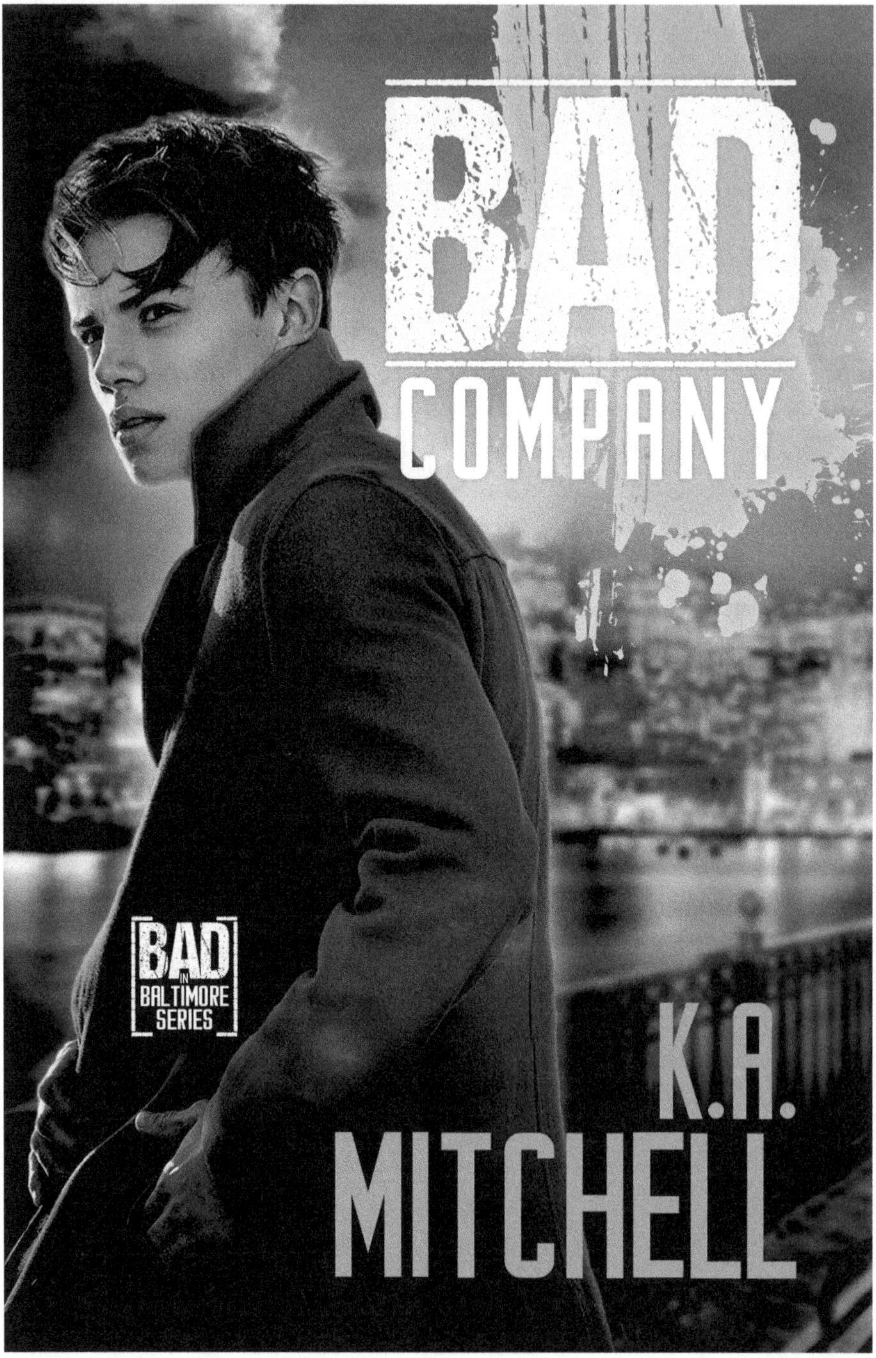
BAD
COMPANY
BAD
IN
BALTIMORE
SERIES
K.A.
MITCHELL

Bad in Baltimore: Book One

Some things are sweeter than revenge.

"I need a boyfriend."

Hearing those words from his very straight, very ex-best friend doesn't put Nate in a helpful mood. Not only did Kellan Brooks's father destroy Nate's family in his quest for power, but Kellan broke Nate's heart back in high school. Nate thought he could trust his best friend with the revelation that he might be gay, only to find out he was horribly wrong and become the laughingstock of the whole school. Kellan must be truly desperate if he's turning to Nate now.

Kellan's through letting his father run his life, and he wants to make the man pay for cutting him off. What better way to stick it to the bigot than to come out as gay himself—especially with the son of the very man his father crushed on his quest for money and power. Kellan can't blame Nate for wanting nothing to do with him, though. Kellan will have to convince him to play along, but it's even harder to convince himself that the heat between them is only an act....

www.dreamspinnerpress.com

BAD
BOYFRIEND

K.A.
MITCHELL

Bad in Baltimore: Book Two

Causing trouble has never been more fun.

Eli Wright doesn't follow anyone's rules. When he was seventeen, his parents threw him out of the house for being gay. He's been making his own way for the past five years and he's not about to change himself for anyone's expectations. For now, romance can wait. There are plenty of hot guys to keep him entertained until he finds someone special.

Quinn Maloney kept the peace and his closeted boyfriend's secrets for ten years. One morning he got a hell of a wake-up along with his coffee. Not only did the boyfriend cheat on him, but he's marrying the girl he knocked up. Inviting Quinn to the baby's baptism is the last straw. Quinn's had enough of gritting his teeth to play nice. His former boyfriend is in for a rude awakening, because Quinn's not going to sit quietly on the sidelines. In fact, he has the perfect scheme, and he just needs to convince the much younger, eyeliner-wearing guy who winks at him in a bar to help him out.

Eli's deception is a little too good, and soon he has everyone believing they're madly in love. In fact, he's almost got Quinn believing it himself....

www.dreamspinnerpress.com

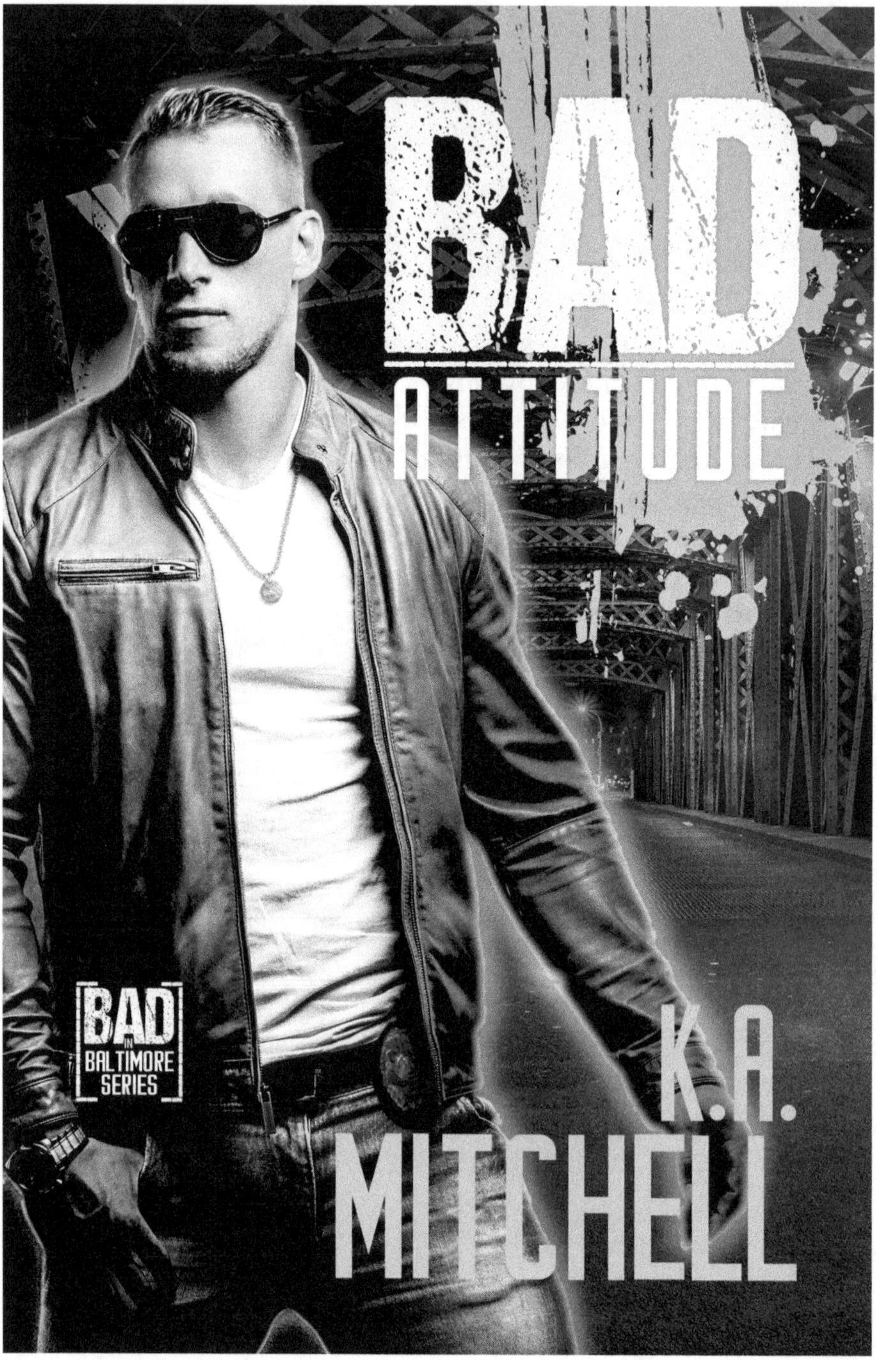
BAD
ATTITUDE
BAD
IN
BALTIMORE
SERIES
K.A.
MITCHELL

Bad in Baltimore: Book Three

Saving lives never used to be this complicated.

Gavin Montgomery does what's expected of him by his wealthy and powerful family—look good in a tuxedo and don't make waves. When a friend takes a leap off a bridge, Gavin tries to save him, only to fall in with him. At least at the bottom of the river he won't feel like such a disappointment to his family. But he's pulled from the water by a man with an iron grip, a sexy mouth, and a chip on his shoulder the size of the national deficit.

Jamie Donnigan likes his life the way it is—though he could have done without losing his father and giving up smoking. But at least he's managed to avoid his own ball and chain as he's watched all his friends pair off. When Montgomery fame turns a simple rescue into a media circus, Jamie decides if he's being punished for his good deed, he might as well treat himself to a hot and sweaty good time. It's not like the elegant and charming Gavin is going to lure Jamie away from his bachelor lifestyle. Nobody's that charming. Not even a Montgomery....

www.dreamspinnerpress.com

BAD
INFLUENCE
LOUNGE
BAR
K.A.
MITCHELL
BAD
IN
BALTIMORE
SERIES

Bad in Baltimore: Book Four

Can a future be built from pieces of a broken past?

Jordan Barnett is dead, killed as much by the rejection of his first love at his moment of greatest need as by his ultraconservative parents' effort to deprogram the gay away.

In his place is Silver, a streetwise survivor who's spent the last three years becoming untouchable... except to those willing to pay for the privilege. He's determined not to let betrayal find him again, and that means never forging bonds that can be broken.

No matter how hard he tried, Zebadiah Harris couldn't outrun his guilt over abandoning his young lover—not even by leaving the country. Now, almost the moment he sets foot back in Baltimore, he discovers Silver on a street corner in a bad part of town. His effort to make amends lands them both in jail, where Silver plans a seductive form of vengeance. But using a heart as a stepping-stone is no way to move past the one man he can't forgive, let alone forget....

www.dreamspinnerpress.com

BAD
BEHAVIOR

BAD
BALTIMORE
SERIES

K.A.
MITCHELL

Bad in Baltimore: Book Five

In a lifetime of yes, no is the sexiest word he's ever heard.

After one too many misunderstandings with the law, wealthy and spoiled David Beauchamp finds himself chained to the city by the GPS and alcohol sensor strapped to his ankle. Awaiting trial, cut off from usual forms of entertainment, he goes looking for a good time—and winds up with his hands full, in more ways than one. The situation only gets more complicated when he's summoned for a random drug test and comes face-to-face with the dominant man who took him for one hell of a ride the night before.

Probation Officer Tai Fonoti is used to handling other people's problems, but he's horrified when one of the extra clients his boss dumps on him is the sweet piece of ass he screwed the night before. It makes getting a urine sample a pretty loaded situation. Tai's unique brand of discipline has Beach craving more. But while Tai relishes laying down the law in the bedroom, the letter of the law stands between them and kinkily ever after….

www.dreamspinnerpress.com